FIGHT OF THE FALLEN

BURDEN OF THE BANISHED
BOOK TWO

ELIZABETH A. DRYSDALE

Stag
Beetle
Books

DEDICATION

To my sweet lady Morrigan.
You've sat at my feet through every book, offering silent support and warmth through many long nights. You're the best dog in the world and more than I could have wished for.

CHAPTER
ONE

Dark water ripples below me as I try to pick out my face in the water. It's hidden from me now; has been ever since I came back. The sea had always been my home, but just a few months on land changed that forever. I slam my fist against the ship rail and turn my back on the ocean.

Dad watches me with careful eyes, like I'm a spooked horse. Never in my life did I think I'd ever be able to use that term and know from experience what it means. The smell of horses and land and *life* clung to me for a long time after I made it to the boat. I thought I'd wanted to come home. It's almost all I talked about when I was on land, but when I got back... I left too much of me on land.

I pick up my rake, squeezing it hard as I gather in the trash to make sure it really hurts, really makes me feel something. I can't be like Zale: hiding in my room sending out a million letters by carrier pigeon and ignoring the fact that I failed.

This feeling is ridiculous. I made a promise to bring Zale home and I succeeded. I should feel on top of the world. But how could I when, in order to fulfill that promise, I had to leave Ry behind and forced Tristan to take on a fate he never wanted?

My heart clenches and my stomach roils with nausea. Using the rake to hold myself up, I take a few minutes to breathe. Squeezing my eyes shut, I tell myself the same thing I've said every day since I've been back: *You can't save them if you fall apart.*

The worst part is not knowing if that's even true. Sure, I can't save them if I'm a puddle of a person, but I also can't save them if there's no one left to save.

At least I know Anneliese won't do anything to Tristan right away. She needs him too much. How can she be queen without him levying her into that position? She might need Captain Wimark to keep him under her thumb, but even so, she wouldn't hurt him. Not like Ry. He has no one to make sure that he's taken care of. There's no political reason to keep him alive. Anything could happen to him.

He never should have been there in the first place.

I use the rake to pile up a big squelching mess and bring it over to Alon. Just a few months ago he would have had some hard teasing words for me, especially if he was the one left to take the mess to its final place in the hold. But today he's quiet. Everyone is quiet around me now. No one knows what to do with me. Or Zale. Especially Zale.

Sighing, I hand Alon the rake and stumble back towards the stairs. Maybe Zale has the right idea after all. What's the point of doing this work? We'll work until we die, and the Fae will never think twice about us.

"Mariel?" Dad calls, his hands open at his side as he watches me helplessly. He doesn't say it, but I can feel the words rippling off him: *stay with us.*

I shake my head and his face falls. I really am just as bad as Zale.

The darkness of the hallway swallows me up and I hesitate in it. I have nowhere to go and nothing to do, so what will a few moments in the cool darkness cost me? This is where I fit in best now anyway. Daylight is for Tristan. It's for goodbye kisses and rumbling horse rides. It's not for garbage anymore.

"Mariel?"

Dad stands on the stairs, his hand on the railing.

I peer up at him, the darkness already doing its best to swallow me up. "Yeah?"

"Come back. Come help us. There's so much to do, much more than Alon and I can manage on our own."

I don't know how they were managing before, two men on a ship meant for much more. Without Zale, and Ry, and I, it must have felt like a ghost ship. Plus, there's so much garbage around us, it feels like we're the only ones on the whole ocean taking care of it. With the way Dad's looking at me, his eyes pleading, how can I say no? No matter how much I feel like a walking hole, I must keep trying just a little bit for him.

"Sure, Dad."

A surprised smile lights his face, and he reaches out a hand for me. I brush past him even though I know it will hurt him. I can't take his hand without thinking of the many little moments that it was Tristan offering his own to me. Tristan offering to help me at great cost to himself.

What must he think of me now? Is he already on the throne with Anneliese as his wife? The thought bites into me and makes it hard to breathe. There's no use wasting energy on mourning such a thought; it's the deal I left him with.

Why didn't he try to get on the boat with me?

If we'd moved urgently enough, we could have been out on the sea by the time Joel came to make sure Tristan did his job. I highly doubt Joel would have dove in after us to force Tristan to come back. Joel was loyal to Tristan; he would have said we were beyond saving. I'm sure of it. So why didn't he come?

Was his loyalty to his father so great that he couldn't leave the land behind? I watched his father mourn their relationship, but Tristan never wanted what the King offered, so what could have changed that?

The unbidden thought rises through the depths of my thoughts: *why wasn't I enough?*

Dad hands me my rake and stays close by me with his shovel as we work through the mess on board. He doesn't ask me to talk, and I'm grateful for that. I'm not sure I could find words for him to describe what's happening inside me.

There's so much to be grateful for with my dad. He doesn't make me talk now, and he didn't make me talk then. Not when we were brought back by the fellow ship that found us paddling through the great ocean, and not when Zale refused to fall back in line, even weeks later. He took us back without yelling, without reminding us of the pain we caused him. He didn't have to; I could feel it. He clasped us in his arms so hard when we came back home that I didn't think he'd ever let us go.

But work carried on and soon enough he tried to make it seem like we'd never been gone in the first place.

The sun glares a dark red off the garbage-laden water as it descends into the horizon. Sweat drips from my temples down my cheeks and my shoulders scream as I keep raking in the garbage. Dad was right, I needed this. Hiding away from everyone only leaves me alone in my thoughts, which is the last thing I need.

Off the bow, garbage rustles in the water. We grow still, surveying the area. Through the gaps in the sludge a dark shadow moves through the water. I brace my legs, readying myself for the boat to rock. Sometimes a whale or other large sea animal will rub against us in the water, but around our ship, everything is still. Moving to the railing, I grab the rope that trails down from the sail and watch the dark shadow move through the water. It's bigger than a whale. Bigger than anything I've ever seen in the water before.

The shadow moves out from under us, traveling beneath the rotting waves. When it's completely out from underneath us, a spray of water spreads over us as though from a blow hole. Garbage shoots through the air, landing on the deck with a wet squelch.

"All right," Dad calls over the still-silent deck. "Pack it in."

I hesitate; whatever just happened out on the water wasn't right. Dad notices and gives me a small nod toward the stairs. I drop the rake with a sigh and head toward the waiting darkness. I'll do it for him. He's about the only person I would. Still, my hand grips the banister far too long as Dad and Alon pile down the stairs past me.

It'll be fine and I'll be fine. That chant is about the only thing that will get me through this twisting world where I'm beyond incapable of fixing any of the problems I helped create. Now it will have to apply to whatever was in the water with us too.

It's still strange to me how normal my room is. It doesn't bear the changes the rest of us carry now. Everything is just as it was when I left, with the hammock rocking softly as the ship shifts.

I feel like a stranger here.

Climbing into the hammock, I pull a blanket over my shoulders and close my eyes to keep from counting cracks in the wood ceiling above. My body sways to and fro, matching the movement of the waves pushing against the boat.

I still don't understand how we got here. Just months ago, I was content with my life without much thought of wanting more, and now the ship is so foreign to me that being here puts an itch under my skin.

But after all that I've lived, would I change the past if I could?

No.

It's such a selfish answer. If I were to go back three years, I would have my brother back the way he used to be, but I would never have met Tristan. I'd have Ry, but I would never know what it was like to really be on land. And that experience alone has changed everything.

I can never go back to how things were.

Days pass in the same unending tedium. Rake all day, hide all night from myself. Zale only comes out for meals and new paper supplies, avoiding my gaze every time as though all of this could possibly be my fault.

His delusion makes me want to lash out. I didn't make him leave the ship, I didn't get him involved with the rebellion, and I didn't make him into a murderer with his own nickname that drew the attention of the Fae. All of that's on him. He's such a sulky baby and won't acknowledge even once that I helped him. I saved his life, and he still wants to act like I ruined all his plans.

We meet in the hallway on the way out of breakfast and

I throw my shoulder at him. It connects with his chest and pushes his unprepared body into the wall.

"Watch it, Mariel," he hisses as he moves back to his room, paper clenched tight in his fist.

Dad comes out of the kitchen, staring after Zale. He lets go of a hard sigh. "You really should leave him alone."

"You should really make him drag his head back out of his—"

"Mariel!"

I scowl. "I wasn't going to say anything bad. And even if I did, he deserves it and so do you. How can you let him treat everyone like –" I hesitate and then say it anyway. "Like ship! Why is he exempt from the work now?"

Dad tilts his head, still looking at Zale's closed door. "He's really been through something Mariel. It's not my place to tell him how long it takes to grieve what he's lost."

"And what about what I've lost?"

He sighs. "You made different choices than him. You left with a singular purpose and were able to achieve that. Zale left with things undone."

Heat builds behind my eyes. "I left for *him*, Dad. I would never have risked my life if he hadn't left first. And it's not like I got everything I wanted. Is it so easy to forget Ry?"

He flinches. "Of course not, but Ry was his friend, too."

The singular use of 'was' makes me feel like I'm back in the last two years with all of us acting like Zale was dead. I just know Ry can't be. After all that we went through on land and all that he already survived, there's no way he's gone now.

Which is why I need to go back.

The thought has swirled around my mind many times since I've been back. I made a promise to Tristan, and I have to save both him and Ry. I can't leave them with the choices I made. They're my consequences to bear, not theirs.

I have to find a way back, but that's where my thoughts have failed me every time. I can't go back like I did before with no plan and no way to make a difference. No, this time I have to do better. But how is a human, a banished, supposed to get to land any other way? And even if I was willing to leave the same way I did before, we don't have the emergency boat anymore, and the boat that brought us back is long gone, taken by others who needed it more. I'm stranded on this ship, an island in an ocean of regret.

But there must be a way. Tristan said there was a way long ago, even if it doesn't exist now. I need to find the loopholes that must exist somewhere and use them to get back to him. To get back home.

Home.

As if such a thing even exists anymore. I don't belong here and I don't belong on land. There's no place for me now.

I shake my head at Dad and brush past him to get to work. Standing here won't solve my problems, and there's work to be done.

Dad leaves me alone for the rest of the day, not even calling me in when the rest of them retire for the evening. I sit high in the rigging, letting the rope cradle me tighter and tighter as I stare up into the night sky. Stars stand out brighter than fire in the vast expanse of darkness. A cool breeze travels across the water, bringing with it the smells of salt and adventure. But it has no claim on me anymore.

Around us floats an island of garbage, the rotting sludge slapping against the hull with dull thuds. Sometimes I can't believe that this was ever my real life. That this is what I was content to live with for the rest of time. But not anymore.

The stars mock me, flocking together in constellations that mimic Tristan's face. Even here, a world away from him, he's everywhere and in everything I do.

Does he think of me like this? Or is he already married to Anneliese and my desire to do anything at all to help him is futile and unwanted?

My chest pinches tight and I wrap my hand further into the ropes holding me up, letting the rough fibers sink deeper into my skin.

A heavy *thud* rattles the ship, knocking it aside in the water and nearly throwing me from the rigging. Digging my nails into the rope as my breath catches in my throat, I glance around for the source of the disturbance. Has the dark shadow from earlier come back to finish the job? I turn, tangling my feet into the rope just in case we're thrown off balance again, and there behind me sits another ship. Moonlight streams through the holes in its sails and it sags to the side in the water.

I've heard of abandoned ships from men working alone and passing away far from the incinerator, leaving their ships to float through the sea until they find humanity again, but I've never seen one. I scramble to release myself from the rigging to climb down, but the rope only cuts tighter into me.

A light comes up the stairs as Dad comes to check out the source of the sound. He stands on deck for only a moment before a large grin breaks out on his face.

"Delmar?"

Something shifts on the deck of the other ship, the large blackness breaking into parts to reveal a wizened old man in a large straw hat with fraying ends. He limps toward the

edge of his ship, his back a curved hump under his thread-
bare jacket.

"What are you doing here? You usually stick to the outer
edge," Dad says as he helps him cross the distance between
our ships.

"I heard the news," the old man says. "It was time to
come home."

I stay up in the rigging until Dad and Delmar disappear down the stairs, and even then, I wait until the light in the hallway fades. Tripping over the rope, I slip to the ground. Rope burn tingles in my arms, but I ignore it as I make my way to the stairs.

The low rumble of men's voices comes from the kitchen where the door is only half closed. Dad sits across from Delmar, offering him some of our meager food stores. It's the way of the banished to share, even when there's nothing left to eat.

I keep my footsteps slow and shallow, avoiding the planks I know will let out a loud squeak. I don't know what Dad would do if he found me out here, but I don't want to take the risk and find out. I press against the wall and peek through a hole from an old knot in the wood.

We don't often get a lot of visitors on the ship. Why would we? Everyone has their own work to do, and we do much of our socializing at the incinerator. But I've never seen this man before, something that seems like quite the accomplishment when there's so few of us out on the sea. Dad said he stuck to the outer edge. Is that why I've never seen him? That doesn't seem right, not when Dad seems to know him so well. Surely, I would have had to run into him during one of our incinerator trips.

"So, what brings you out, Delmar? What news could be so interesting you'd have dragged that creaking mess you call a ship all the way out here?"

Delmar rests knotted and aged hands on the kitchen table. "I heard about what happened with your son and daughter. The time has come."

Dad shakes his head, the smile slipping from his lips. "There's no reason to come for them. They're just kids, and the mess they got themselves in is all over now. You've wasted your time coming out here."

"You're kidding yourself if you think word of their little adventure hasn't spread. You're going to have trouble on your hands. Haven't you heard what your son has been up to?"

"There's no reason why this should be such an issue. As far as my son goes, all he does is sit around below deck. There's no way he's getting himself into any trouble." Dad's voice is quiet, and his gaze doesn't stray from where his hands rest in his lap.

"I've always thought you were a smart man; don't prove me wrong, now. Make no mistake, your son has been plenty busy. Haven't you noticed the extra weight in the water lately? Men have stopped working. There's talk of a revolution. And I'm sure you've noticed some movement from the depths," Delmar says.

Zale and I are in danger? Sure, I knew that was the case when we were on land, but what do we have to worry about now? We're where we belong. No one is going to come looking for us out here to deal out justice. That's what's waiting for us on land.

What does this old man know that sent him across the

ocean to come knocking on Dad's door? What is he talking about concerning Zale? I was certain the pigeons he was sending out were love letters to Azalea.

"I don't know if it's a good idea for you to stay here," Dad says. He rises to stand, his chair clattering to the ground as it catches on a knot in the wood floor.

It's a severe breach of hospitality, one Dad would never have allowed us to make. What is he so afraid of?

Delmar stands, his body barely taller than it was sitting. "You're making a mistake. I'm here to help you and you know it. Don't let your fear push those of us away who are ready to help you. The time has come for war again. Men are rising against the regulations once more. You can feel it in the water."

"Leave us."

Delmar shakes his head. "I wish you the best of luck. May you survive the coming storm."

I scuttle back, shoving myself into my room before they leave the kitchen. My breath catches in my throat as Delmar's heavy footsteps linger outside my door, but he continues in his uneven gait. Dad stays longer in the kitchen, the sound of something shattering echoing through the hallway.

I swing back and forth in my hammock while my brain continues to analyze Delmar's visit.

He knows Dad, but something in the way he looked at us says he knows all of us, but I've never seen this man before in my life? And the wars he talked about... Dad has never said anything about a time when humans didn't work together to survive against the Fae regulations. Was there another time when men were dreamers, like Zale? Did the men who came before us also dream of living on land and being free from the burden of their ancestors? It would make sense that others before us considered that life could be different. I wish we had talked about them. I wish their names and dreams hadn't been stricken from our collective memory. And I doubt the ancient old man's mind is fully intact enough to share the story faithfully.

Moving on to what he said about Zale, and the men... Have people really stopped working? It hasn't escaped my notice that there's more trash in the water lately, but I thought we'd just found a heavier patch. No one has ever stopped working that I can remember. We need the supplies it brings too much. And the creatures in the deep... That has to be what rocked our ship earlier. It makes a tingle run down my spine at how close we came to trouble.

My muscles itch to move and I throw myself from the bunk, grabbing my grey, faded jacket and making my way upstairs. A round, full moon practically kisses the ocean, pale cool light flooding the water. A breeze blows across the deck, and I rub my arms to keep warm against the bareness of the unforgiving salty air.

Clacking echoes through the chill air, and to the side of our ship, Delmar's boat is still docked. I would have thought he'd been long gone by now. He gave Dad his warning, what else is he hoping to accomplish?

My feet drag me to the railing, and I lean against the cold wood to gather my thoughts. Delmar isn't here to talk to me. He barely acknowledged we exist at all, so he'd certainly not welcome his friend's daughter sneaking aboard and snooping around. Yet, I have so many questions I want to ask him. Questions I don't know if Dad will give me the full truth about. Not that Dad can't be trusted, but I know he'll do everything he can to protect me, even if that means lying to me.

Before I can think better of it, I throw my feet over the edge of the ship and catch myself on Delmar's railing. Getting back home will be much harder, but I'll at least have some answers then. Dad can't take away what I already know.

Delmar's ship is well worn with age; the planks under my feet creak with every step. It almost seems like a miracle that it's holding itself together when it looks ready to splinter into pieces any moment.

It's beyond rude to board another's boat without their invitation, but I've stowed the part of me that adheres to those rules far in the back of my mind. If there's a storm coming, I need to be prepared. I need to know if there's a way I can use it to get what I've been waiting for: an approved way back on land. I don't know if it's even possible, but I have to know.

I inch my way down the stairs, the light still on in his cabin. Would me knocking on his door scare the poor old man to death, or will it bring my own as he retaliates before he knows who came for him? He seems like the kind that would have a gun on him, something few of us have and fewer have in working order. Still, a man alone on the sea? He needs something to guarantee his safety, and I would rather he didn't use such a weapon on me.

My toe catches the edge of a hard piece of garbage, and it clatters across the floor. I freeze in place; the moment has come and I'll find out just what kind of man Delmar is.

"Who's out there?" His voice is gruff and there's a scuffling across the floor as he comes to the door.

"I-it's me." The words barely squeak out of my suddenly constricted throat.

"It's me, eh?" The door to his cabin opens slowly, creating a triangle of orange light on the floor between us. "And just who is 'me'?"

"It's Mariel; you were just on my ship." I wince. None of this is going how I hoped it might. "I want to know what you were talking about with my dad, about the wars."

Delmar's eyes grow wide as he takes in my slight form. "You're the girl, the one who came back from the land."

"That's right." I nod.

"You're in a heap of trouble, girl."

I resist the urge to sigh. As if I don't know that. I've been in nothing but trouble since Zale left, even if I didn't know it right away.

"Can we talk?"

He raises a brow and waves me inside his cabin with a crooked hand. Life on the sea is hard for all of us, and I can't imagine what his body went through taking on the ocean all by himself.

His cabin is small and filled with the clutter of a long life. Scraps of garbage litter the floor and the smell of must fills the air. A table with a single wobbly chair is set in the middle of the room with a candle perched on top and in the corner sits a bunk with a faded red quilt tucked around the sagging mattress.

He sits on the edge of the bed, and I take the chair. My body rocks back and forth on the uneven feet paired with the movements of the ship. I hope the creatures of the deep don't show up while I'm on this rickety boat. I don't think the age-weakened wood would make it.

"You want to talk?" he asks.

"Yes, I— there's so much I need to know. What were you talking to my Dad about, about wars?" I don't dare tell him I've never heard anything about this part of our history, or really any of the banished history at all. And I'm not sure I want to know what Zale has been up to yet.

Delmar leans back, his old eyes clear as he watches me. "This should have been taught to you by your father."

My heart sinks. Of course, he's not going to help me. He's my father's friend and his loyalty will be to Dad. I rock forward in the chair, preparing to leave.

"Now, now. Sit back down, land girl." He leans forward, forearm braced against his frail thigh. "Just because your father should have told you our history doesn't mean I'll leave you hanging." He shakes his head. "I don't know what your father was thinking. Not knowing doesn't save you."

Obviously. I learned that the hard way with Zale. "Land girl?"

Delmar chuckles. "That's what they're calling you now, did you know?" He watches me shake my head. "Of course, you wouldn't. Not if your father is so insistent on keeping you away from the incinerator."

My brow furrows. I hadn't thought much about the fact that we'd stayed away from the incinerator since I got home. Dad never liked to go to the incinerator, so why would he want to hang around it now?

"What do you know of humanity's history?" he asks, watching me with his ice-blue eyes.

I bite the inside of my cheek. "Not much. We used to live on land, then the Fae rose up and kicked us off, forcing us to clean the garbage of our ancestors until the end of time."

"That's certainly a simplified version." Delmar takes off his hat, revealing a mostly bald scalp that he scratches with thickened fingernails. "That's not the whole of it though."

"What's the rest then?"

His eyes get glassy as he goes deep into remembering. "Long, long ago humans were the top of the food chain on the planet. We could do anything we wanted, there was no one who could stop us. Unfortunately, that also meant there was no one to warn us of the danger we were careening toward. We'd filled the land and the oceans with our planned obsolescent society. Plants began refusing to grow. Everything was brown, disposed of, and crumbling. Humanity was on the fast-track to destroying itself and bringing the planet down with us. I'm sure none of this is that surprising to you."

I shrug even as my chest grows tight. No, it's definitely not news. How could it be when my whole life has been spent cleaning up the mess left behind by my thoughtless ancestors?

"The Fae had lived beneath us all this time. There had been a war at the early point of our industrial awakening, and against all odds, we had won. This had left the Fae and all their creatures to live below the land, waiting for when the time was right so they could rise above again." He coughs to clear his throat. "It was when the world had turned brown that the Fae knew they could take over. The war between us lasted only hours as humans had grown fat, sluggish, and complacent in the years since they had first fought the Fae. The Fae, rather than deal with revitalizing humanity and putting them back in their rightful place, decided that a cleansing was necessary. They felt that it would benefit all to have a land cleanse, especially because it could rid the ground of the polluted taint humanity had left behind. And so, they burned it."

"Burned what?" I can barely breathe.

"The entire planet."

"What do you mean the entire planet?"

My mind spins and I have a hard time breathing.

Delmar coughs. "Just what it sounds like. They burned the planet, cleansed the whole thing. They saved what animals and such they could by taking them below ground with them, and then burned the whole thing down. How else do you think all our infrastructure was able to be so completely erased? Humans had built over everything, they had to use white hot flame to get rid of us."

"So how are there any humans left?" I tilt my head, trying to understand.

"Well, that's what the Fae hadn't accounted for. They hadn't thought that there were such great bodies of water that humanity could hide in and be safe from their ever-consuming flames. When the fire died down and they came back to land, triumphant little craps that they were, they were surprised to see boats floating just off the coast as humans crept closer to find out what was happening. The Fae had never planned for any humans to live through their extermination, and they had to figure out a way to deal with them. Lucky for the Fae, their happy little fire hadn't taken care of the waste that still littered the seas. So, they granted the remaining humans their lives if they agreed to stay on the ocean forever more, to clean and purify the seas."

My heart falls as his antiquated history lesson comes to an end. I was hoping to hear something that would help me get on land again, or at least help me understand why Dad is worried about rumors about me and Zale.

"I'm sure you're wondering what does this have to do with anything," Delmar says with a smile. I nod, trying to keep my mouth from looking so sullen. "Well, the issue with the Fae's bargain is the same issue your brother has been fighting against: none of us actually agreed to it. Over time, many humans have decided they were done paying for their ancestors' sins and took up weapons to overthrow the Fae control over them. As you can imagine this didn't go well."

No; if it had, we wouldn't be sitting on his rotting boat talking about it.

"Every so often, humans would strike down the Fae

that were tasked with bringing them supplies, and the fights always went quick and in the human's favor." He notes my raised brows. "Surprising, isn't it, that humans could be successful against the Fae after a life spent wasting away on the sea? Well, we discovered something that the Fae have been desperate to keep quiet ever since. They recruited several humans to their cause, plying them with all manner of money and supplies to keep them loyal to the Fae and to keep any other human from having contact with them."

"But you know the secret?" I can't imagine he wouldn't with this kind of buildup.

He nods. "I'm rather old for a human, wouldn't you say?"

I wouldn't say it to his face... but I tilt my head in agreement anyway.

"That's because I was one of them once. The incinerator men."

"How could you have been sent back to the ocean if you knew their greatest secret then?" I don't bother trying to keep the disbelief from my voice. I've never met anyone who worked on the incinerators before.

He waves his hand. "I told them I wanted to spend the last few years of my life enjoying the ocean again, so I was sent to the edge."

Ah. He was essentially banished from the banished. Forced to live alone even among men. That's a pretty harsh consequence to take on.

"Then what is this great secret?"

Delmar smiles. "Have you ever thought how weird it was that we've been left out here to our own devices without Fae to watch over us and ensure that we do the work they've left us here to do?"

I can't say that I've ever thought much about it. The Fae weren't really a part of my every day until I went on land.

"Well." He leans forward conspiratorially. "It's because they can't. The garbage out here is like poison to them. It kills their magic and makes them sick. Same goes with the Seafolk beneath us. They need us. Don't you understand?"

The words swirl around my brain, doing their best to force me to understand.

"Your brother has convinced the other ships to go on strike. He thinks this will bring him back into the rebellion with some power." He holds up a hand to stop me as my mouth drops open. "Yes, I know about your brother, 'the great hand,' or some such nonsense. But your brother is a fool."

He surprises a laugh from me. "On that, we agree."

"The longer this strike continues, the more you're going to see creatures of the deep. They're disturbed by the poison leaching down to them through the water. Mark my words, the Seafolk will be coming. They live in fear of the creatures just as much as you do."

"I don't fear the creatures," I say, keeping any fear from my voices.

He meets my gaze. "You will."

THREE

When I get up in the next morning, Delmar's ship is gone like he was never here. But the trash still is. Heaps of garbage pile against the side of the ship, packing us in with its thick sludge.

Dad and Alon get to work right away. The way Dad looks at the mess, his brows furrowed while his mouth forms a wet frown, I know Delmar was right. Everything has been different the last few weeks. Zale's been busy.

Before I've even decided what I'm going to say, I'm dragging myself to his room and knocking my fist against his door. I just know this can't stand. We're not ready for that shadow creature to come back and actually *notice* us this time. It's all Zale's fault.

He cracks the door open, blinking at me with sleep-weary eyes as he pushes his hair back from his face. "What do you want?"

"I think you know." I push the door forward, almost catching it on the side of his face before he can move out of the way.

The musty smell of unwashed boy fills the room like a heavy fog. The blankets are tossed off his hammock and his bunk is filled with rolls of paper, some with writing and others still blank in their rolls.

"You've been awfully busy in here, haven't you?" I demand.

He grabs his arm and looks at me with sullen eyes. "What does it matter what I do? You brought me back like you wanted. What I do now is up to me."

"Not if you're inciting a strike," I hiss. "What were you thinking?"

His eyes go wide before he can make his face smooth and uncaring again. "We're just lowly humans, what does it matter if we clear the trash or not?"

I grab him by his tunic, wresting his face closer to mine so that he must stand hunched over. "Delmar was right; you are a stupid boy. Have you any idea the consequences of all your little letters?"

"A stupid boy? I'm your older brother. You don't get to treat me like this. I considered that some people might go hungry, but I thought that would be worth it if we're able to earn our freedom."

I thrust him away from me. "I can't even stand to look at you. Children going hungry should have been enough for you to put your quill down."

"You don't get to decide what's best for everyone, Mariel. Some people agree that the risk is worth it." He straightens out his collar with a scowl. "Just because you brought me home didn't mean I was going to fall in line. I have a mission to fulfill."

"Oh yes, how could I forget, you're 'the hand,'" I mock.

"You know nothing. I spent years on land. You were there for only a month. What do you know of what I had to go through in the name of the banished?"

"In the name of the banished, huh? Is that why you took

off without telling us and then treated me like garbage even though I was risking my life to find you?"

"I never asked you to come after me." He folds his arms over his chest, straightening out his spine.

"Are you dense?" My voice raises in pitch. "We're family! And I made a promise that I would protect you. Did you really think you could disappear, and I wouldn't come after you if I even found the barest hint of you?"

"I never asked you to do that, Mariel, and I'm tired of you holding it over my head as though I'm entirely beholden to you now. I won't apologize for starting the strike. It's about time we did something instead of collectively sitting around and doing exactly what's been asked of us. This is what I need to do. I can't stay here. I need to get home." He points his finger at me. "Don't get in my way."

"Don't do this," I plead. "I've already lost Ry, I can't lose you too."

He hesitates for only a second then leaves the room and slams the door closed behind him.

I hunch my shoulders and throw a punch at the wall as anger builds in my chest. He may not like it, but I have to keep protecting him. It's obvious he doesn't know what's best for any of us, let alone himself. I'm going to have to take care of this. I need to take care of both of us. It's the only way I can fix my mistakes.

Knowing what I know now, it's time to write letters of my own. I grab a stack of papers out of Dad's office and get to work pleading the banished to stop the strike. I know it's not enough to tell them we'll find another way. We've been banished far too long for anyone to take a suggestion like that seriously. So instead, I do what I have to do: I tell them there are beasts below who've grown restless with the trash sinking into their domain. I can only hope others have seen evidence of their movements like I have.

Then it's a simple matter of getting to Zale's birds before he can and sending them on their way. Easy.

But as the weeks pass, it's hard and harder to ignore the continual onslaught of trash coming our way. Zale's strike stunt is paying off.

Dad stands at the railing, staring out at the garbage with his hat pulled low over his face. I lean next to him, my forearms resting on the sun-warmed wood of the ship. The rake is loose in his arms, the pile of trash on the ship barely making a dent in the mess surrounding us.

"I've never seen it this bad before." I keep my voice low so Alon can't hear me across the deck where he struggles alone with the shovel.

Dad shakes his head. "It's not normal."

"Do you think we should... maybe we should head to the incinerator and find out what's going on?" It's a risk. Just mentioning the incinerator can make Dad reject any idea attached to it. But it would be the best way to get my point across. My letters aren't nearly as effective as Zale's.

Dad looks away from me as his knuckles go white around the rake. "You know how I feel about going there."

"How else will we get answers?" I conveniently fail to mention that he could send a letter just as easily as any of the rest of us.

"Why are you so sure we need any?"

I wrap my hand around his arm, resting my head against his shoulder like I did when I was a little girl. I can feel the tension rippling through his muscles as he stands on edge. How could he think I wouldn't notice that?

"Something's wrong. We both know it."

Just yesterday we had another incident with the dark shadow in the water. It rocked the boat hard enough that I could have reached out and touched the water if I wanted to. And if I wasn't hanging onto the edge of the boat for dear life.

Dad glances at me and the edges of his frown soften. "I suppose we're close to full anyway."

I give his arm a squeeze. That's as good of a win as I can expect from him.

He calls to Alon to get us moving and I can feel the atmosphere of the ship change. It was tight before, but now it's thick with anticipation. We all know that whatever we learn at the incinerator could change us forever.

ZALE SURFACES during our trip in. We scowl at each other, but the moment is brief before he looks with eager excitement at the water parting in front of us. His hair blows in the breeze, making him look years younger. Almost like he was before all of this happened. Does he realize that we've somehow become enemies?

I can't help but be excited, too. We may be going back because of problems, but I still like seeing other humans. It feels like it's been far too long since I was surrounded by my own people.

The thick layer of garbage follows us the whole way to the incinerator. It sits heavy in the currents that brought it here, sinking with the memories of people long gone. The smell gets worse too. The incinerator tends to release heat into the water and with all the trash left behind, there's a stench of rot sitting in the air.

We don't pass any other ships. We're like ghosts passing through the water.

"It's not right," Alon says. He steps up beside me, his gaze traveling over the heavy sludge.

"Have you ever seen it like this?" I ask.

My older brother sighs. "Never."

I peer around Alon to look at Zale, a big grin spread across his face. How could I be related to someone so stupid?

"Did you notice that creature last night?" I ask Alon.

He shifts on his feet. "It was closer than it's been before."

"Did you get a good look at it?" I've still only seen it as a shadow.

He shudders. "More than I ever wanted to. I've known there were worst creatures in the water, but to actually see one... I don't know that I'll ever rest easy on the water again."

"I might have a solution for that, brother." Zale claps a hand on Alon's back.

"And just what might that be?"

Zale gestures to the mess around us with an open hand. "See all this? This was my work. The Fae will take us seriously or they won't get our work. We might get to move back to land and then you'll rest better than you ever have."

"This was you?" Alon wrenches himself away from Zale's reach. "How could you do that? What were you thinking?"

Zale flinches. "I'm thinking about all of us. I'm not nearly as narrow-minded as you assume. I'm making real change. Azalea and I came up with this plan if I ever had to go home, and look! It's working! All they needed was direction and my letters gave it to them. Just a few months without work and the currents have done the rest."

I shake my head but don't intervene, moving away from the two of them. I've gotten what I wanted. We're almost to the incinerator and then I'll be able to fix this. I'll get everyone to go back to normal and not provoke the oceans any more than they already have.I haven't let myself think what might happen if I can't. If Alon said those creatures are getting closer... how long will it take for them to make a move against us? I've seen how big they can be. It wouldn't take much for it to knock us under the water forever.

With what Delmar said though, I should probably be more worried about where we're going. Dad must not think the incinerator men are much of a threat though if he's willing to take us into the belly of the beast. Maybe it's just that it's too late to worry about things like that.

WHEN WE REACH THE INCINERATOR, we find the boats that were missing on the open ocean. This is our usual meeting spot, but today the ocean is so full of boats that it looks like land of our own creation. Everywhere I look is just more and more wood with barely any chance for water in between.

The noise of so many humans pressed together is nearly deafening. It's raucous and messy. People swing from the masts and hang over the railings. It's worse than when we usually sit here waiting for our turn to burn. There's no purpose in any of the ships I can see. Men need purpose or they find trouble.

My fingers close into fists that are meant for Zale and his stupid plans. I bring them against the railing of the ship instead. Taking a deep breath of the stagnant air, I decide to find Dad before I do anything too rash.

He's holed himself up in his office, his body slumped into the wooden chair behind his desk. The room is dark without a single candle lit. I stop in the doorway, feet refusing to go any further.

"We're here, did you know?" My voice is weak, and I want to slap myself. If I can manage taking on the Fae, what makes me so scared of my own dad?

He groans and sets an empty bottle on the table. "I know."

"Well... what would you like us to do now?" The anger that built up in my chest dissipates in the wake of seeing Dad like this.

"Did we find out why the work isn't being done?" his voice comes out like a whisper.

I shake my head, loose hair coming down around my face. Dad's got enough on his plate without knowing all the trouble Zale's been up to. "We haven't talked to anyone yet, but these ships look like they're sitting light in the water. There are too many of them and no way everyone is here for the incinerator."

Dad sighs. "Then Delmar was right." He rests his head in his hands. "I'm sorry I failed you, Mariel."

I come to my knees beside him, taking his hands in mine so he's forced to look at me with his red rimmed eyes. "You never failed me. You've done nothing wrong."

He rips his hands out of mine, our blisters catching on each other. "I have done nothing but fail you. I should have told you what happened to Zale. If you had known, then maybe we could have avoided this whole mess and the danger that you're both in."

"You... you knew about Zale?"

He laughs but there's no humor in it. "What was I supposed to think when my dreamer of a son that talked about land to anyone who would take the time to listen went missing, along with our emergency boat? I knew it wasn't the storm that had taken them both."

A deep ache builds in my chest. "You knew that whole time? I was devastated, I needed you, I—"

"I wanted to keep your feet on the deck where they belong, and not go chasing after your brother and his misguided notions! Fat lot of good that did me." He rubs his face with his large palm. "I wanted to do what was best for you and all I did was make it worse."

I pull myself to standing, every muscle in my body tight and hot. "Regardless of your intentions, this is what we've been left to deal with. I need to take care of the mess your son created for us."

Dad looks at me blearily. "What has Zale done now?"

"Clean yourself up and you might find out."

My boots click across the wood floor. I can't even look at him again before I slam the door.

A MAN WITH A WIDE, black hat stands on our deck when I come out from the darkness. He gives me a grin that reveals too many missing teeth. He leans on a narrow cane, one leg missing past the knee.

"Good to see you'll be joining us, Mariel."

I look for my brothers, but the deck is empty of any reinforcements. Straightening my spine, I tuck my hand behind my back and curl my fingers into a fist.

"Is there something I can help you with?"

He laughs, the sound like the waves crashing on the shore as he leans harder on his cane. "I don't think we need to dance around this, land girl. I know what you and your brother have been up to, and I've come to take you to the meeting. Do you not see the army that's gathered for you?"

I resist the urge to look at the boats so tightly packed around us that the air is filled with the clacking of wood knocking against wood. I breathe heavily through my nose to try and expel the wave of emotion ready to knock me down. So, this is why everyone is here. It's another of Zale's misguided attempts to save us. "This is not my army. If you have an issue, then you'll need to take it up with my brother. I'm here to stop this madness."

He shakes his head, his hat falling forward and blocking the sun from his face. "Why stop such a glorious protest? This is our moment to change everything. Never before have we been able to organize ourselves so well. We owe it all to your brother. Now, he's already left, will you not join us at the incinerator to talk over the terms?"

Warning bells go off in my head. I take a step back from him, hoping against hope that Dad will be right behind me on the stairs.

"This isn't my fight. I see no need to go to the incinerator. My issue is with the people."

His smile widens, the dark holes in his mouth feeling like a trap. "The time is past for your coyness. Now, come."

He holds a hand out for me, the length of his pinky finger missing with a scabbed-over nub as the only reminder it was once there.

I tighten my fist until my nails bite into my skin to ground myself. I took on the Fae, I don't need to be afraid of this simple human they sent to gather me.

I laugh, the sound loud and brash. He flinches but doesn't take his hand back.

"It's cute that you think you can control me." My voice takes on the syrupy nature I learned from my time with Anneliese. "But if you know my story, then you know that mere men have no control over me. And I see no one stronger here."

He frowns. "We are your elders. You will do as we say."

I open my mouth, something snappy on my tongue, but

the sound of splintering wood breaks my concentration. The boat beside us rocks in the water, and the man hanging in the rigging shouts at us, but his words are lost as a tentacle longer than the ship slaps across the deck.

My hand reaches for the harpoon we keep beside the helm. The peg-legged man follows after me, his good foot slipping in the spray from the monster. The harpoon is warm in my hands as I point it at the tentacle making short work of the mast. The thick wood groans, cracking before I can fire. It comes down on the ship beside me with the weight of the monster behind it, breaking through to the ocean beneath. I make eye contact with the only man I can see on board. His face is red, and I can see him mouthing something before he's pulled under.

CHAPTER

FOUR

The ships are in chaos. Everywhere men are shouting, wood is breaking, and a hole sits in the water beside us where the ship went down. I hold the harpoon tightly, looking everywhere for a sign of the monster. Men gather on the ships around us, everyone staring down into the black depths. My breath stills in my throat.

The water ripples, moving away from our ships. I follow it along the edge of the ship until it leaves the wide berth of ships. The harpoon hangs limp in my arms as the creature moves farther and farther away.

Slowly, my body comes back to life. Feeling builds in my fingers and toes. That could have been us. It was right next to us. What made it choose that boat and not ours?

Zale comes onto the deck, his eyes narrowed as he watches the men get back to their own ships. I meet his gaze and raise my brow. How can he not think that what he's been up to has had no effect now? He shakes his head, forehead wrinkling. His hand is loose where he rests it on the rail.

Anger comes back in full force and I can't stay on this

ship with him for another second. I grab a rope hanging from the rigging and use it to swing onto the ship next to us. There's no time for manners or waiting to be invited.

This ship is empty, but that's okay. I'm looking for bigger fish than just one at a time. Somewhere in this ocean is a congregation of these men who are just as dense as Zale with no forward thinking at all.

My jaw clenches tightly together as I travel from ship to ship, getting closer and closer to the incinerator. I probably should have waited for Dad to do this, to find answers for all of us, but how could I when I've already tried the slower way? I sent letters like Zale, and it hasn't made a difference. It's time for action, and not the way they've been doing it.

In the inner ring of ships, I finally find the men. Everyone sits gathered around one man standing on the deck of a ship patched together with wood that still gleams with a young brown sheen.

My feet thump against the deck as I land, drawing their attention.

The man in the middle gives me a side smile, his skin dark and weathered by so many years on the sea. "Glad to see you could join us."

I brace a hand on my hip to hide its shaking. These men shouldn't scare me more than the Fae. I shouldn't be afraid of them and yet here I am.

"You've been causing quite a lot of trouble," I say. I try to put as much authority in my voice as possible to sound less like a little girl. "You should all get back to work and stop listening to my brother's idiotic letters."

He barks out a laugh and the men around him echo. They look at me with dark eyes, pinning me in place. "That's an accusation there. And what do you have to back it up? Because so far, we're enjoying our little vacation here."

"You just saw what happened! " I point back at where the lost boat once sat. "Monsters are rising out of the deep! If we continue like this, it won't take long until there's none of us left. We can't just sit here."

The man waves away my worries with a large hand. "The Fae won't let it come to that. They need us."

I have to bite my tongue to keep from shouting the truth of it to him and how the truth means no delegation will be coming.

"They don't need us; not like you want them to. They'll let those creatures take us down before they even think about changing the terms of our existence."

He shakes his head. "I don't think so."

"And while you sit here thinking, people are going to die. People have already been dying. It's not worth it."

"Not worth it?!" he shouts, taking a few heavy steps in my direction. "We've all be touched by death's hand out here. We're dying younger than we used to. We've lost children to this sea because there weren't enough eyes to keep them safe! This is not the life we were meant for. This is not how families should be raised. We have to change this now. It cannot continue like this any longer."

The men around him shout their agreement, rising to their feet to surround him.

"They— they can't help you like that. The Fae won't come here."

He rubs his chin with a scared finger. "Maybe they won't, but others are coming."

"Others?"

"The Seafolk are coming. Received a message from them just this morning."

Ship.

My face goes numb. *The Seafolk are coming?* I mean, I guess it makes sense. If the monsters are bothering us, they'll bother those below as well. I can't remember a time when they actually deigned to work with us. We mean as little to them as we do to the Fae. They're different sides of the same coin.

I cross my arms over my chest. "Then I'll wait and have a word with them as well."

"You think they want to talk to you, little girl? You're supposed to be on our side. You've seen the land; you know what we should have. Your brother understands this. What's wrong with you?"

I screw my jaw closed so I don't gape at him like a goldfish. "It's precisely because of the time I spent on land that I feel this way. I *will* speak my piece to them."

He shakes his head and laughs. "Whatever you need. Maybe this will help you finally come around."

There's no way. Still, I give him a tight nod and settle against the edge of the ship to wait.

Two HOURS in and the sound of Zale's followers and their brash laughter has me wanting to tear my ears off. They sit huddled together discussing all the ways that they're going to bring the Fae to their knees. But they just don't understand, and I don't know how to explain it to them.

They barely spare me any attention, instead sitting completely enraptured as their leader explains Zale's plan. The man in question though has yet to show up. I want to pretend it's because the ship going down changed his opinion, but that feels like too much to hope for.

Sun beats down on my exposed neck and my shoulders as it moves across the sky. I hold my position and wait, gaze circulating from the men to the water beside me. Just when my legs have begun to cramp, Zale climbs aboard.

The men roar out to him, his own personal fan club. He steps towards them with his arms outstretched. The taste of vomit burns at the back of my throat. Does he really think he's some kind of savior to these men?

He sees me standing off to the side and his eyes go wide. "Mariel?"

It's hard to even see him, swallowed up as he is by his adoring fans. The man in the hat who had their attention before shifts to watch Zale and me. He steps closer, hand clenching like he wants to pull me away. I back away, letting my frustration take over.

"This needs to stop, Zale." I couldn't convince him before, but I have to try again. "People are getting hurt."

He shakes his head, slinging his arm around a man half his height. A letter sticks out of his pocket, Azalea's name across the back of it.

"It's for the greater good Mariel. Plus, there's no way we can stop this now that the Seafolk are sending a delegation." He turns to the men, raising his fist in the air. "I told you we could make a difference!"

Tears burn in my eyes, and I blink them away, not letting my vision get too bleary. He's let me down ever since I first left the ship to search for him; I shouldn't be surprised by his actions. Yet here I stand watching my brother-turned-stranger be welcomed by these men like some kind of rebel leader. I shouldn't be surprised that I don't know who he is anymore—he may as well have changed his name while he was off inciting a revolution. The mark of our family no longer lives in him. *How can he do this to us?* I don't want a revolution; I don't want a war; all I want is my brother back.

He tucks the letter deeper into his pocket with a gentle pat, watching me with dark eyes. "Mariel, are you sure you don't want to go home? I can take care of this," he whispers.

Shaking my head, I settle back into the shadows. Zale frowns and moves back into the crowd.

As the sun settles deep beneath the sea, movement ripples the water below me. I reach for my harpoon, cursing when I remember leaving it on our ship. Fins breach the water, and the tension runs out of my shoulders, but I keep them just as tight.

The sea froths with foam around the delegation. Five of them come to the surface, with scaly skin that would catch the light of the sun if it was still overhead. They each have long hair framing the pale green skin of their faces. A woman with pearls strewn through her navy-blue hair and clothing made of sharkskin leads the way. The men lower ropes to the water to hoist the Seafolk up and onto the deck of the ship.

It's a pretty daring move when the long powerful curl of their tail fins are revealed. Instead of feet, they have sleek tails that unfurl across the deck. There's no denying the strength and sheer power that each of them must hold. To invite them on our deck is vulnerable on our part. We don't know them, they've never wanted to work with us before. To have them here on our boat... I don't think we've earned that honor.

"Welcome," Zale calls, a hand braced against his hip. He gives them a practically jaunty smile. "We're so glad you could come."

The woman frowns, revealing pointed teeth that come to dagger-like points. "The feeling is not mutual, human. I am Isla of the Seafolk. Have you any idea the chaos you have caused?"

The smile slips off his face, and for a second the boy underneath is revealed before he recovers. "Sometimes chaos is necessary if it gets our point across."

"And what point is that?" her voice is harsh like the calling of gulls.

"That the Fae can no longer use us as they have."

Isla laughs. "Poor, sad human. Don't you realize? The Fae are not who you should be afraid of. We are the ones who have come to enforce the contract."

"A contract we never signed."

"Be that as it may. It cannot continue thus. The monsters of the deep are stirring."

Zale waves a hand at her, a small smile inching its way back onto his face. "We aren't afraid of those creatures. This is all temporary after all. It is our hope to soon be off the water all together."

"It cannot be. You are the only ones who can clear the debris. It is the steady sinking of it that has woken the monsters. If you do not act now, you will not make it to land and your kind will be eliminated, and ours with it."

"So you're saying you need us."

Isla picks at her sharkskin top where it ends just above her tail. "You gravely misunderstand your importance."

"You've just said yourself that without us you will die." He places his fist back on his hip and straightens his shoulders.

This could not be going better for me. If I'm lucky I won't have to say anything at all. The leader of the Seafolk will say it for me, putting Zale and his men in their places.

She straightens up, her strong tail scraping against the deck as she pushes herself to Zale's height.

"You." She points a finger at him, and he goes pale. "You have no idea the powers that you are messing with. Your place has been determined long before your birth. We are all part of the wheel that continues life. Each contribution is needed. How dare you ask for more while not doing your most basic of tasks?"

"Th—" he coughs. "This is the only way to make our voices heard."

Isla shakes her head, shells woven into the bottom of her hair clacking together. "This way will only end in blood."

"Then what do you suggest?"

"A meeting must be called. If you are so disgruntled with your place, we will have to discuss it. But you cannot continue this way. If you will agree to continue your work on the ocean, we will discuss your sentence."

Zale lights up. "You may hate our methods, but it got your attention." He looks back at the men, shoulders shaking with his swagger. "You hear that, men? We're going to get our meeting after all."

Isla moves so fast that I don't see her until she has her hands around Zale's throat. "I will not tolerate your insolence, human."

Behind him the men shuffle back, falling over each other to get away from the Seafolk. She tightens her grip, trickles of blood seeping from between her fingers where her rough skin has made its mark.

"Now," Isla whispers. "You will act respectfully, or I will destroy you as an example."

He sputters, but words fail to materialize. Finally, he nods, careful so his chin doesn't hit the exposed skin of her arm.

She releases him and he falls back on the deck with a thud.

"Now that we understand each other. We have a meeting set up with the Fae already. We thought it might come to this and planned accordingly. As such, you may choose who among the humans to send as your delegation."

Zale moves towards the men. They speak in hushed

tones, all the toughness in Zale eliminated as blood continues to trickle down his neck.

My steps are heavy against the deck as I approach them. They won't ruin this for us.

"You can't send Zale," I call to them, careful to stay far enough away that I can't be easily silenced. "He will only continue to make the same mistakes he started last time. Send me. I know the Fae and can find a compromise without sacrificing respect."

Zale chuckles, the sound low and growing as the man in the hat joins him. The crowd joins in, the deep rasp of men's laughs echoing around me. My cheeks heat as I do my best to stand my ground.

"We'll not be sending some girl who didn't believe in our cause in the first place," the hatted man says and the group around him snickers.

"You've misunderstood. It's not that I don't believe in your cause, it's that I thought your strike was the wrong way to go." I point at the Seafolk who sit silently watching us. "What I said has been no different than them."

Zale shakes his head. "This isn't your cause, Mariel. You made that clear. You should just go home. This isn't your fight. Go home where it's safe."

"Just because I disagree with what you're doing doesn't mean this isn't my cause."

My hands tighten into fists. This is just as much my fight as it is his. How can he not see that? I left behind just as much as he did, even if I wasn't there as long. Does he think I've so easily forgotten about Tristan? About Ry?

I take a step closer, finger ready to poke Zale right in his self-righteous chest.

"We have a proposition for you," the Seafolk woman rasps.

The men quiet down, shifting on their feet to get just

that little bit farther away from her. Her gaze is on me, on my suspended finger.

I let my arm fall back to my side. "I thought you already told us your proposition."

"That was for the men. We have something different in mind for you." She smiles, her sharp teeth making the words feel like a promise. "Come. Let them make their choice, you and I will talk."

My feet don't want to move any closer to her; everything in her words feels like a trap. Zale watches me with lowered brows as I work my way closer to Isla. He takes a step closer as though to stop me and I shake my head. I'm touched by what looks like brotherly concern, but I don't need him to protect me. He frowns as he watches us, but gives me space.

I stop at a good distance where it feels like it would take a little effort for her to reach me. "How can I help you?"

She leans back on her tail, coming down closer to my size. "We have called the meeting with the Fae, but there is a problem with our delegation."

"Sorry, I'm trying to deal with my own problems. I don't know if you noticed, but there's issue with our delegation as well," I ramble, my gaze straying to where the men still talk. There might be a chance if I can wrap this up.

Isla reaches out a long finger and it takes all my willpower to not move out of her reach as she runs it down my cheek. Her skin is cold and rough like the fish we eat from the deep. A shudder runs down my body and I have to steel myself.

"A little bit of quiet would do you well," she says with a close-lipped smile. "I am offering you the solution you are looking for."

"You're going to send me for the humans? If that was

your plan you should have said that, and not let them think they had control over—"

Her finger presses against my lips, the scent of salt and kelp becoming overwhelming.

"Not for the humans. Did you not see how very hard it is for us to come on land? There is no way we can travel far enough inland for the meeting with the Fae King. We would not survive being out of the sea that long. Even now, our time is running out."

Isla points at her companion. His skin has taken on a grey pallor under its green tint, and he sits lower than the rest of them. The muscles in his neck are tight as though it's taking everything in him just to be here.

"I didn't realize—"

"Yes, yes. And why should you? We have kept our people apart from you for as long as you have been relegated to the sea with us. It has been for your safety as much as ours, but the ocean is shifting, and that time is over.

"We need someone to plead our case to the King, someone who has an interest in maintaining the peace between us. Would you be willing to do that?"

"Would I..." My mind goes blank, swirling around as I try to understand what she's saying. There's so much to unpack there. Why would we all need to be protected from each other? Couldn't we have been allies from the beginning?

I shake my head, hair flying around my face. This isn't where I should get hung up. She—they want me. They're picking a human to go in their place, and they think that human should be me.

"Why?" I can't find any other words. Crossing my arms over my chest, I hope I can at least feign some sort of confidence.

She slides closer, scales rasping on the wood of the

deck. "We know of your travels on land. We heard you want to return and seek peace between your people and them. This has not been the case for other humans."

We glance at the crowd surrounding my brother. He grins at them, his face maniacal in the fading light.

"I don't know anything about your people. I wouldn't know how to advocate for you." I must tear this down before hope grows too bright in my chest.

"That is easily remedied. Our goals are not so different from yours. We need the truce between us to be back in place. There is no time to even pretend to ask for more. Every minute we spend talking is another chance for more creatures to stir from the deep. Our people have already faced far more damage from them in the last few weeks. It must stop."

"Isn't there anyone else you could send? Someone who understands your cause better?"

Isla tilts her head, watching me closely. "You want to go more than anything, and yet you still ask if you can be replaced. Interesting. As for others, there are many who answer us, some who can even spend time on land, but they do not have the mental fortitude for the games that are ahead. However, that does not mean that we will not use all in our power to achieve the balance. The Fae would do well to remember that."

Thinking of the Fae spending any time fearing the sea forces a laugh out of me. She raises her deep blue brow for me to explain and my cheeks feel hotter than ever.

"Sorry, it's just that I don't think the Fae think of *anyone* being a threat to them. They seem confident that they're the top of the food chain here."

"That may be so." She places a fist under her chin. "And now is the time to challenge that thought."

"How do you intend to do that? You've already said you can't go on land."

There's just no way the Fae will find the Seafolk threatening. How could they when the Fae don't go into the sea? This woman might be just as crazy as Zale.

"My brothers and I may not be able to cross onto land, but there are many under our control who can. What do you think the King would think about selkies coming to sit at his table?"

I wince. I've never seen the seals myself, but I've heard stories of sailors who had the misfortune of bringing one on board. It always ends in blood.

"So, you want me to go on land and threaten the King for you using selkies?" It still doesn't seem like enough.

She tilts her head. "Something like that."

Isla's plan is crazy, but what other option do I have? Zale and his crew won't let me be part of their delegation and I must get back on land. It's the only way I can fix all the messes I've left behind and the new ones I'm sure Zale will create.

"All right. I'll go for you."

It doesn't take long for the men to choose Zale to go on their behalf. It's enough to make me want to vomit. They still believe he has their best interest at heart. Why can't they see the trouble he's caused them?

The Seafolk outfit me in their colors of bright blue. The outfit is in two pieces and feels like it was designed for one of them with the scratchy texture of the material like it came from the ocean floor. The top is lighter blue and covers my arms and comes down my torso in a ruffled point, with the darker blue skirt reaching to the floor. I may look dignified, but if there's a fight, I'm in big trouble.

"May you find peace for us," the Seafolk leader says with a smile, her hand on my cheek.

I give her a tight nod, ignoring the sick feeling that settles into my stomach. If this goes poorly... I'm sure she'll come back for me. Her touch feels like it's left the residue of magic behind. If I want to survive this, I'll have to find solutions that meet her wishes.

"These are the missives we received from the King." She hands over a packet that looks like paper but feels like wax.

"If they don't believe you are our representative, just show them these."

The top paper has a large, looping scrawl across it with the King's signature at the bottom. There are several more in his same hand, but as I flip through there's one that stands out, the writing on it tight and delicate.

My breath catches in my throat as I pull it out, my gaze going directly to the bottom. *Princess Anneliese* mars the page, a confirmation of everything I've been worried about.

With my heart in my stomach, I scan the page, wondering what she could have to say that's so important she'd get her own missive.

To my dear Seafolk,

I am so pleased to hear that you will be meeting with us. This association feels long overdue, and I am glad that we will be able to know each other and our wishes better for the first time. There is no reason for us to live in fear of each other when we are capable of being such rational creatures.

However, as your future queen, it seemed important that I write to you myself. My wishes may not always be in line with the King's, and I wished for us to understand each other for when the day comes that I take the throne.

I wish you all every happiness. May this be enough to keep us on the same side, for that is what I truly desire. This is something the humans could never understand, despite so many terrible accidents.

Yours in Peace,

Princess Anneliese

I crumple the page in my fist, wishing I could toss it over the side of the ship. Making a deal with the King feels even more important now. Anneliese thinks to threaten us before we can even begin talks? She's dreaming. I would be more than willing to give her a few consequences.

A messenger was sent to tell Dad we were going. His step across the deck to us is hesitant. I feel like my heart is breaking just as much as his to be leaving again. It's wrong to do this to him again.

His touch is soft as he takes me in his arms, so full of forgiveness and understanding. I don't deserve him.

"Be safe. Come back to me." His voice is gruff as I tuck my head into his neck.

"I'll do my best."

He clears his throat as I pull away. Zale nods to him and claps him on his shoulder. I pinch my lips. Our dad deserves more than that.

We climb into an emergency boat and memories of the first time I left come flashing back. Ry's face, his easy smile, the way he was so ready to do anything for me. Biting my lip, I stare out over the water to keep from crying. I can't cry now. I'm going to save him. Everything's going to be okay.

It *has to* be.

Two of the male Seafolk take the rope tied to the front of the boat. They'll make sure we get to the right place on land, and quickly. I'm grateful because I'm not sure I can take days at sea with my brother, or the eventual stumbling around on land looking for the right Fae either.

I keep my gaze on the long swishing tails as we cut through the water at a rapid clip. I don't look back at the boat where my father waits, and I don't look at the brother I gave up everything for.

I have to keep my focus ahead now.

THE SEAFOLK MAKE it seem like our boats were docked just off the coast with how quickly they move us. The sea sprays up on our faces, and if I were alone, I might stand at the front with arms outspread so that I could pretend I was a bird. But there's no way I'll do that in front of Zale, not when it would look too much like the games we played as children. I don't want to breed that familiarity in him again.

We're taken to the same beach we left from, the one that only takes a day's walk to reach the castle again. It makes sense, but I can't help but look around with a tight chest for any sign of Tristan. This is where we said goodbye. This is where I left him to his fate.

"We will wait here with you," one of the Seafolk says, his voice like the whisper of a wave.

"Thank you for your assistance." I give him a nod and take his hand as he offers to help me from the boat and into the shallow water.

I wait for his cold hand to tighten around mine and drag me under, but he only makes sure that I make it to shore. His sculpted chest reflects the sunlight back to me in a shimmer as he waits in the deeper water beside the boat. Zale stumbles out of the boat without assistance and drags it further onto shore. His jaw is tight, his face grim as he stares at the path that will take us back to the castle.

I have no idea what he's thinking, and I wish I could ask him. Is he thinking of Azalea? It sends a shiver down my spine to think of the ring perched on her stupid finger and the letter tucked in his pocket. His connection to them is going to bring us nothing but trouble, I can feel it. How could the men not feel the same thing when they spoke to him? What magic does Zale have over the banished?

My shoes slip on the rocky shore. I kept the same boots I got from the rebellion when I got home. They're the nicest ones I've ever had, even if they do make me a bit of a hypocrite.

The trees around the beach rustle in a soft wind, their

leaves green and bright in the afternoon sun. The path to the castle stretches into the woods with bright white stones. It's the path to my destiny and it's hard not to go running up it right away.

Lifting my skirt in tight fists, I try to keep my balance as I make my way off the beach. Tense as I am, I make no attempt to relax or calm myself. When the Fae find us, I want to look strong. I want to stare into Anneliese's eyes and let her see that her plans are about to fall.

"So." Zale kicks at the pebbles under his feet. "When we get to the meeting, you need to let me do all the talking. I know what I'm doing."

I give him a side glare. "I don't think that's something you get to determine, especially considering that we're delegates for different groups."

He's already proven himself incapable of working with me or listening to me. I tried. I tried talking to him and he wouldn't have it. We're on opposite sides of this now and I have to do what's going to be best for everyone, even him.

"Don't be like that, Mariel. I'm still your big brother. I'm only trying to help you."

"You're only trying to help yourself," I grumble.

He grabs my arm. "Is that really what you think?"

"How could I not?" I wrench away from him and his face drops. "You've just been holed up making trouble. You didn't even pretend that you were back with the family."

"How could I when my family was still on land?" His voice is loud despite our audience. "I have to do what I promised Azalea. I can't leave her here on her own."

"But what about us?" My throat goes thick and it's hard to swallow. "What about me and Dad and Alon? Do we mean nothing to you?"

He clenches his fists. "I'm doing this for you, too. We all deserve more than we've been given."

The heavy thundering of hooves travels down the hard-packed dirt road and leaves my response burning in my mouth. My heart beats heavy in my chest and I do my best to tilt my head up in a haughty way like I've seen Anneliese do. Beside me, Zale goes tense.

I have every right to be here. I have every right to be here. If only those thoughts could penetrate through the thick fog telling me to get back on the boat and get out of here.

The horses come around the bend and slide to a stop. Their riders wear the same silver armor I've seen on Tristan. My tongue grows thick in my mouth as we wait for them to do something. If things were different, maybe I could reach out for Zale, but there's no way I want to be holding my estranged brother's hand when we meet the Fae.

Captain Wimark leads the party, and stares down at us with a frown, the sharp angles of his face beautiful in the sunlight filtering through the trees. Instantly my body grows tense. This is the only person who might know what happened to Ry. "Are you the delegation?"

Even with the new clothes from the Seafolk, it's still not enough for me to look like I belong here. Or anywhere.

I open my mouth to speak, pausing to work around the tight ache growing in my chest.

"Yes, we're here on behalf of the banished. I was told you were expecting us," Zale says with an easy grin.

I give him an outright glare. If he thinks he can mush me under his wing when I've been very clear that isn't going to happen, he's going to find himself in a world of hurt. At some point, he's going to have to realize that I'm not the same sister he left behind. He can't treat me like her anymore.

Captain Wimark sneers at us. "We were told to meet

you at the water, my *apologies* for being late. Now, if you would like to—"

"Actually." My voice shakes a little and I clear my throat before continuing so the Seafolk man can here me. "I'm here on behalf of the Seafolk."

Zale frowns at me and shakes his head like I'm somehow ruining things. The only thing I could possibly ruin is his little power trip that I didn't agree to go on.

A rider comes up behind Captain Wimark, and my throat tightens as I take in Anneliese and her soft pink dress. She smiles at me like I'm a baby.

"She speaks for us," the Seafolk man says from his place in the water.

Anneliese frowns, a perfect wrinkle forming in her forehead as she clenches the reigns tighter.

Captain Wimark looks at him and back at me, his jaw tightening as he glances over my clothing. "I see… well, the same applies to you. If you would?"

He gestures to the man behind him who approaches with two horses trailing behind them. My heart leaps in my chest as he looks up at me and recognition runs through my body.

Tristan.

After so long it's almost too much to see him face to face. His tightly cropped hair shines in the sunlight and his wide shoulders are proud as he strides over. My hands shake as he gives me a smile and offers the reigns. Am I going to be expected to ride alone? I've never done that before. I've always ridden with him.

I glance back at the Seafolk man who gives me a curt nod and disappears into the water, then I turn to Zale. His fingers curl into fists even as he keeps an easy smile on his face. Is this some kind of test? How could they possibly think we'd be able to ride horses? They know we come from the sea. There's no hiding it this time.

Tristan hands me the reigns of a beautiful white horse and a tingle runs through me as our hands touch. He doesn't give me another glance though before he remounts his own grey mare, his armor jangling. I stare at the leather reigns in my hand for a moment, not sure what I should do and wishing Tristan would come back and help me. If he's going to act like doesn't know me, it must be for a reason. Out of the corner of my eye, I see Zale in a similar position. His smile turns to a grimace as he swings himself onto the beast, landing with a thump on the saddle.

I guess that's what I'm going to have to do, too. I stick my right foot into the stirrup and stare up at the side of the large animal. Zale is taller than me, so it makes sense that he would find a way on. I'm reduced to a slight hopping on my left foot just to keep my right one in place.

"Is there a problem?" Captain Wimark asks. His tone reminds me so much of Anneliese's. So much syrup and not enough substance.

Grinding my teeth, I grab the reigns more firmly and jump up. Using the reigns to help me, I swing into place. I hit the saddle hard, pain radiating up from my center as I swallow my groan.

"No problem; shall we?" I use the same tone even as my body aches to make its pain known.

He gives me a nod and stares at me for a moment. I wait for him to tell me I've done it wrong, to point out something so common knowledge that I've missed for everyone to laugh at. Instead he simply turns around and heads back toward the castle, Tristan and Anneliese trailing behind him. I'm not sure how delegations are met, but I'm sure they're not dismissed as easily as we are.

They might invite us out of the sea, but they have no intention of letting us get too comfortable here.

~

I'M SAVED from having to look too stupid on the ride back by having a horse who knows where she wants to go. I lean forward slightly, and she's more than happy to follow the others. I sit back in my saddle, trying to look natural, but honestly, all I want is Tristan.

I stare at his back and wish he could look back at me. I want to stare into his eyes and show the apology written in mine. I want him to know it was never my intention to leave him with Anneliese. *Does he know how much that decision has kept me up at night?*

I can only imagine him ignoring me has everything to do with Anneliese as she rides beside him. I want to force her to see me as a player, but that's especially hard when she rides like an angel and I'm sure I look like I don't know what I'm doing.

Captain Wimark picks up his pace and my horse follows, forcing me out of my thoughts. My body jostles along the broad back of my ride and clenching my thighs together does nothing to make me feel stable. Beside me, Zale grimaces but doesn't look entirely out of place. Maybe learning how to ride was something the rebellion helped him with. Would that be considered a necessary skill for blending in? Probably. And as I can't help but remember, the rebellion cared little for my blending skills. I'm so lucky all their 'help' didn't kill me.

I hold tight to the reigns and lean close to the horse's neck as though that could save me. All I have to do is make it to the castle. Then the real work begins.

My gaze stays pinned to the long white mane in front of

57

me. I have to block everything else out in order to stay upright. Time passes and my eyes grow weary, but I keep going until finally, my horse slows down.

I clear my throat, wiping away the traces of stress that would be very apparent in my voice. My body is unsalvageable It's wound so tight that I'm not sure how I'm going to get down.

"Welcome, welcome," a deep voice calls across the cobbled courtyard. "I'm so glad you could make it."

My neck is slow to turn, but I turn it anyway to see the King standing in the doorway. His light grey robes look almost silver, matching the circlet gracing his brow.

"It is my sincerest desire that we'll be able to come to terms that all of us can feel good about while you're here. In the meantime, come, eat, and relax for you are my guests and under my protection." He gives us a bright smile.

I'm not sure what my face is doing, but I doubt it looks as diplomatic as it should be. Beside me, Zale's scowl is still firmly in place. I'm sure we're making quite the impression.

"Can I help you?" Tristan stands beside the horse, watching me with a furrowed brow.

I give him a tight nod with a matching smile, hoping I appear aloof and not incompetent. He reaches out a strong hand and helps me clamber down, my skirt catching briefly on the saddle and showing a whole length of my thigh. He turns away, but a flash of red crests his cheeks as I hit the ground.

Zale doesn't wait for assistance, swinging off the horse as easily as he swung on. Silently, we all follow the King into the castle. Captain Wimark, Anneliese, and Tristan form a blockade behind us in case we felt like changing our minds. Chills run down my spine as I pass through the castle's solid stone walls.

"It will be so wonderful when we can put all this

unpleasantness behind us," the King says as he marches through the wide hallway. I wonder if he knows that I could lead him to the dining hall just as easily as he can. "The stirring of the Seafolk has already caused much distress to our people living close to the waterways."

Did they do that on purpose? Make a little commotion so the Fae can feel just as uncomfortable as the rest of us? I hope so and it isn't just a sign of all creatures becoming out of control.

"I'm not sure that negotiations will go as smoothly as you'd hope." Zale's voice is clear and rough.

The King's shoulders stiffen but he continues on, keeping his voice as jovial as it was before Zale's interruption. "We shall see. It is my sincerest wish that we'll be able to find a solution that accommodates everyone."

The heavy rumble of voices echoes through the hallway as we get closer to the dining hall. I've never been inside when it's full, fear never would have let me before and threatens to keep me from doing it now. I'm so painfully, obviously human now. There's no hiding, no pretending. It's so vulnerable. I miss my fake ears. Things were so much easier when I wasn't expected to be myself.

The King seats us on either side of him at the head table, with Anneliese and Captain Wimark seated farther down. The wood of the table is thicker than my arm. Plates of roasted meat and potatoes sit on silver platters before us. Saliva thickens in my mouth. No matter how much time I spent on the ship, I could never forget just how much better the food is on land. Even Zale's eyes gleam as a servant loads up our plates.

Before us, the long tables are full of rapacious men. They're loud as they yell to each other and louder as they slurp up their meal. I flinch back from the noise as it assaults me. If not for the meal in front of me, I'd run into the hallway and never come back. Instead, I use the meat slopping in its own juices as a buffer between us as I shove it into my mouth. I want to keep my gaze down, but it switches between my plate and the men spread out before me. Could one of them be Ry? It's a stupid hope, but one I can't help having anyway.

"We have so much to talk about," the King says between mouthfuls of bread. "I have seldom had the opportunity to talk to humans. You tend to keep to yourselves out there on the sea."

I have to grind my teeth together not to snap at him. Does he really understand so little? This man who was so kind to Tristan and so worried about his future has never once thought about the banished and what we go through. The meat turns sour in my stomach.

"It will be a historic moment, the meeting of the three of us. It should have happened a long time ago." He uses his bread to sop up the juices left on his plate.

"Yes," Zale says carefully. "I don't believe humans have ever been invited on land during my lifetime."

The King frowns and puts down the bread. "I suppose that is true. Hence why we need to rectify this now."

"Are you really interested in changing things then?" I can't help the eagerness that bubbles in my voice. It takes everything in me not to look for Tristan in the room to share this with him.

"I am not sure how much can be changed, but I do believe we should find a better way forward. Your happiness is something I wish to achieve."

I stare back at my plate. I'm not sure how much of this is real, and how much is just political talk. I want to believe him. It would make things so much easier if this were real. I would be able to do what I promised the Seafolk and it wouldn't even be hard. I can't even remember the last time things came together so well.

Zale leans forward and gives the King a hard stare. "You must realize that our happiness will never be achieved without serious changes in our living arrangements."

The King raises a brow at him. "Is that so?"

"Yes. It must make some sort of logical sense that not all humans would enjoy living all their lives on a ship or even on the water at all. Plus, have you ever seen the kind of work we're expected to do all our lives? It breaks us down far before our time."

I want to leap across the table and stop Zale before he can say anything else, but the King is nodding, his eyes pensive.

"It is true I have never been to see the humans on the water. It is not something that is easy for me." He puts his fork down. "It is a good thing that you have come. More of us need to hear what is happening to all our people."

My fingernails dig into the wood of the table as my heart lurches. My gaze finally finds Tristan farther down the table. I grin at him, and he smiles back at me.

"Perhaps these talks won't go so poorly after all," I say to the King.

He gives me a smile and takes another bite. "That has been my hop—" a gurgle rises from his throat, his eyes going wide.

"Your highness?" My voice is too thin in the loud room.

My chair clatters to the floor as the King slumps over, his face landing in his plate. I grab him by the shoulder and push him back against his seat. His face gets a purple hue as his eyes gaze forward unseeing.

"Help!" I shout, voice taking a hysterical edge. "Somebody help him!"

A servant rushes up, brushing me aside as she pulls the King out of his seat. She presses on his pulse points and wraps her arms around his chest squeezing to help clear the airway.

Her movements attract the attention of the men in the room, and everyone goes quiet, watching her work. The King's face darkens, his eyes going glassy. She places him back in his seat, her arms shaking.

She looks at the men with her hands out. "The King is dead."

CHAPTER

SIX

The room erupts in noise as the men rise to their feet and charge to the head table. I stare at the King, his circlet resting on the floor. His hands are half curled, hanging limply at his side.

"Mariel." Zale takes my arm and pulls me away from the King's body as the men get closer to us. "We need to get out of here."

My mouth opens and closes but nothing comes out.

"Mariel, if we don't get out of here, we're going to be next."

But I can't move. I can't connect the King I met months ago to the still body sitting in the chair beside me. It can't be.

Where's Tristan?

My gaze moves over the men who surge like an angry ocean, looking for the one person who can help me. But the faces all blur together and I can't see him anymore.

Zale tugs on me, pulling me away from the table. My legs tangle in my knocked-over chair and Zale curses under his breath as he pulls me free. He pushes me forward, but my stiff legs can't do it. I stumble in my skirts, landing on the cold stone floor.

And then it's too late.

Men vault over the head table, jostling their king. They grab at us with fingers still greasy from their meal. Zale gives me a panicked glance and grabs the letter out of his tunic pocket.

"Make sure she gets this," he says before he turns to fight, swinging his arms and yelling, but it's no use.

There's too many of them. They pull my hair as they pin my arms behind my back. It's so loud in here that I don't know how they manage to be coordinated at all. But there must have been plans for what to do if the king is murdered in front of you, because they all move as one.

Zale's letter crinkles in my fist as I twist around to find someone to help us.

Where is Tristan?

Surely if he's in the castle he'll have heard the commotion and come running by now. Could he be that securely wrapped up in Anneliese's spell by now? The day that he had vacant eyes and was completely under her control flashes through my mind, but I can't worry about that now. Either he can help me, or he can't, but I can't save him. Not with the cold metal chains someone pulls out to wrap around my wrists.

Zale struggles in front of me, muscles bulging as he fights off the Fae. He has to know it's a lost cause. There's too many of them. My shoulders sag and he shakes his head at me, roaring out his frustration. Men crowd around him, blocking my view as I'm tugged against the wall by my own captors.

I was so scared before. Too scared to come back until I felt like it was safe. I waited all this time. I was so stupid. It was never going to be safe, not really. No matter what happened, I was always going to be human and they were always going to be Fae.

Zale screams and then the sound is cut off. Not just his but everyone's. The room goes silent, save for the sound of my beating heart and the scuffling of feet as the men pull away from Zale.

His body slumps against me, knocking onto the floor. His arms are still wrenched behind him, his feet stretched out like he's sleeping.

I wrap my arms around him, crushing the letter into his back as I twist to hold him closer to me.

Redness weeps from his chest, soaking into his tunic and spilling onto the floor. A table knife stands erect in his breast. His body is so still. So, so still.

Screaming erupts in the room, loud, hysterical, and gut-wrenching. My skirt soaks up the warm blood, and I press my hands into my eyes as hot tears fall. My chains jangle, but I'm not pulled back to my feet. I take a deep breath and the noise stops. It's me. That sound came out of *me*.

"Mariel."

I flinch away from my name. When the last person who used it...

"Mariel." Tristan moves into my line of sight, face red as he breathes heavily. He is gentle as he moves Zale from my lap and blocks him from my view. "Let's get you out of here."

Why didn't I listen to Zale when he said that? I should have left with him when he said to. I should have gotten away from the body the men were surging for. This is all my fault.

Tears drip down my face, down my nose, and I lose control of my body. I slump over and he catches me, lifting me like I weigh nothing.

"We will find the man responsible," Tristan calls out to

the men who are still now that their blood lust is sated. "These humans were under the protection of the King. They came as delegates. His death cannot go unpunished."

He backs out of the door, but all I can see is the limp foot of my brother laying on the crimson tiles.

~

"I AM sorry I could not get to you faster. As soon as I saw what happened..." Tristan's voice chokes as he moves us through the halls. "All I have thought about for months was seeing you again. If Anneliese had not been there on the beach... but I guess none of that matters now." His arms tighten around me as though he can retroactively protect me from the pain now coursing through my chest.

It was never supposed to happen like this. Zale was supposed to annoy me and make all the wrong choices and I was supposed to fix them. I was supposed to fix *him*. We were supposed to go home at the end of this with him smiling at me like he used to. With him looking at me like he was still my brother.

Now he'll never smile again.

My body lets out a low moan and I tighten into a ball against Tristan's chest. I cradle his letter to my chest. One of his last thoughts was making sure Azalea got his last declaration of love. How could my brother that was so full of life and dreams and love be gone? How will I ever look my father in the face again? I should have left when he told me to. I should have moved. Why couldn't I move? It's all a blur that begins with the King turning purple and ends with my brother's life turning red.

Tristan kicks open a heavy wooden door, revealing a room set up similarly to his own. A fire blazes in a corner fireplace, thick red rugs line the floor, and a dark four-poster takes command of the rest of the room.

He lays me on the bed, and I sink into its soft plush like a body falling back into the sea. What will happen to Zale now? He'll never get to go home, to have the service the banished give each other as we return to the water for the last time.

"Nothing is going to happen to you," Tristan says, brushing my hair back from my forehead with his fingertips. "You have my word. I suppose you might even have my word as King, if you would like."

"K-king?"

The King is dead. I saw his purple face, his bulging eyes. He can't help me any more than he could help my brother.

"Do you not remember your own deal?" His smile is a tight grimace as he sits on the bed next to me. "I have been forced into taking my father's offer. I have become his heir apparent."

My brain is a swirling mush, but it snags on a thought before it can get away. "Does the prince know that?"

Tristan frowns. "He will soon."

CHAPTER
SEVEN

Tristan leaves me to rest, something I'm not sure I can ever really do again. How can I lay here in comfort when I know about the mess waiting just outside the door? The mess I'm wholly responsible for. I get out of bed to put Zale's letter in the desk, it's damp with sweat and tears but I'm grateful there are no touches of red on its envelope. I bury my face into my pillow and cry, and only when I've run out of tears does sleep come.

When I wake, it's to a new world. I groan and shove my face deeper into the pillow. I'm not sure I'm ready to face the realities of a new day. My first without Zale in a long line of what will quickly become my normal. There is still work to do.

Anneliese said there would be consequences. She warned me and I still didn't understand. I never thought that meant that she would take down my brother before we even started. Not that she herself touched him, but his death still bears her fingerprints.

I slink further into the heavy blanket Tristan put over me.

Tristan.

Is he really married to that snake? Did she get every-thing she wanted right away? Was there never a way for me to save him from my deal? My chest tightens and my eyes burn. Every life I touch is filled with pain.

I never should have come back here.

What was I thinking? What could *I* possibly do? *Ship, ship, ship.*

The door cracks open and I lift my head to watch Tristan slink inside. His clothes are disheveled, and his shoulders are tighter than they were before. I didn't realize that could even be possible. What could hit him worse than his father dying?

"Were you able to rest?"

I nod and sit up in the bed, rubbing my palms against my face to get rid of the evidence of my tears.

"Good, good." He collapses into a chair set beside the fire. "I am glad to hear it."

I wait for him to explain himself, but the only sound in the room is the crackling of the still burning flames.

"What's going on out there?"

He runs a hand down his face. When he turns to me, there is no hint of a smile, nothing but a heavy tiredness. "It's a mess, as I am sure you can imagine. Preparations are being made for the funeral of the King. I am doing my best to oversee it, but the Prince is returning."

The King's legitimate son. "Is that a bad thing?"

How could it be when the King already made Tristan his heir?

"It has led to some contention of the King's wishes. You see I was never technically made the crown prince. It was discussed but never written. That has created a loophole for anyone wishing to press it."

"But I thought the Prince was a loser." The words slip out of my mouth, but I don't apologize for them, not when they earn me a wry smile from Tristan. "Why would anyone prefer him to you?"

"The Prince has his own... talents. Plus, he has earned the respect of many with the time he has spent at the front."

I lean forward. "You mean your country is in negotiations with more than just us?"

"We are besieged on all sides," he says with a sigh.

Tough break.

"So, what does this mean?" I'm glad that's the question that comes out instead of the one I so desperately want to ask: will this break my deal with Anneliese?

"It means that if there is not outright violence like we experienced yesterday, then there will be subtle political violence instead until the majority are happy with the results."

The blanket crinkles in my hands. "And you think they won't want you? You really think they'll want the Prince instead?"

He glances at me with bleary eyes. "Many have already voiced that thought. It is my assumption that some are hoping to gain favor with my brother by usurping me. What they do not realize is that he has no idea what's going on to even give them favors."

"Did the King never tell him his plan?"

Tristan shakes his head. "He was planning on doing it in person. He thought it would go over better." He lets out a dry laugh. "It was never going to go over better. I think he simply wished to avoid it all together. And now I'm left to pick up the pieces."

"But you're not alone." I sit up straighter in the bed as though that will make me look more powerful. "You have me on your side."

He gives me a side grin that is devoid of humor. "One human will not be enough this time."

"Maybe not, but I'm not just one human this time. I represent the Seafolk." *And maybe all the humans now, too.* I have no idea how that will work. We were supposed to have protection. This never should have been an issue.

I swallow down the growing lump in my throat. "Wh—what will happen with my brother?"

"His body has been removed from the hall." Tristan's brows knit together. "I suppose when things calm down you will be asked what you would like to have done with him."

"He'll have to be sent to my father."

It may mean that I can never go home again, but my father will give Zale the proper rights. It's the least I can do for him now.

"I am sure that can be arranged."

I hope so. The odds don't feel as great now that I know their secret. Which Fae will brave the water full of poisonous material to return the body of a human?

Knocking pounds on the door and Tristan sighs. He stands and it takes him a minute to straighten out and bring himself back to nobility.

When he opens the door, it's with the posture of a King.

The man on the other side gives him a crisp bow. "They are asking for you, Your Highness."

The muscle in the back of Tristan's neck twitches. "But of course. I was just making sure our Seafolk delegate would still be able to perform her duties after the incredibly distasteful scene in the hall."

"Yes, I am sure her presence will also be needed." The Fae's face pales.

I wonder if he was in the room with us too when my brother died. Was it his hand that held the blade? My face feels too tight, my body too wound. I need to do something.

Tristan dismisses the messenger and turns back to me. He keeps his shoulders straight, but his face relaxes enough to show me the exhaustion already laying underneath.

"You will come with me, right?"

I slide out of the bed, my bare feet freezing as they hit the stone floor. "It's my job."

He nods. In this I understand him. We're both here to take care of business we have no interest in, at least right now. But I have to finish what we started, and I need to find a way to bring peace between all of us.

For Zale.

My top is wrinkled, and my skirt is spattered around the hem with my brother's blood. It's hard not to touch the stains to see if they're still warm, warm with the life my brother was so full of. This is all so wrong. This isn't how this was supposed to happen.

I follow Tristan through the hallways, half-wishing he would take my hand. I want to know he still cares about me, but I also need him like an anchor before my thoughts wash me away. It doesn't matter though because he doesn't so much as twitch to take my hand. I have no one to blame but myself. He's probably already married to Anneliese, and I've been too much of a chicken to even ask him about it.

He opens a heavy wooden door, revealing a room already filled with people. They gather around a large table, the wood burned in a pattern that twists around the edges. Tristan pulls out a high-backed chair for me before sitting in the only other chair open, at the head. Hopefully, that means something and isn't just a coincidence.

My gaze travels around the table as the hum of talk ceases, stopping as I come to the woman sitting directly across from me: Anneliese.

Of course, she would be here. This is a political meeting and she's proven she wants her part of it, but my heart shrinks in my chest and the pressing urge to run away grows just looking at her in her midnight black dress. She watches me with a small smile, leaning forward like she just found something interesting.

"Thank you for coming on such short notice. These are not the kind of circumstances we ever like to meet in, and I appreciate your willingness to find solutions to this matter as soon as possible," Tristan says, hands flat on the arms of his chair.

"You speak as though something small has happened instead of the assassination of our king," says a Fae man with long blond hair. "Why has there been no retribution for his killer?"

The crowd around the table rumbles their agreement. Tristan holds a hand up and the murmurs cease, although the looks of displeasure remain.

"Enough action has already been taken for the moment and an innocent man has died—"

"How innocent could he be? Everything was fine before the humans were invited into our hall," the blond Fae continues, his face turning red as he moves to stand. "We never should have let them think for a moment they were equals. Look at the disaster that invitation has brought us."

Anneliese's smile stretches across her face as she watches me. Her slender fingers press together under her chin as she tilts her face to the side.

Tristan's voice is level. "We cannot be positive the actions that occurred today were enacted by the humans, however, we do know that a human under our protection was murdered. This cannot stand. We will find my father's killer, but we must also face the consequences of our barbaric actions as well." Tristan stays in his seat, not rising to the other Fae's level. Tense as he is, he keeps his shoulders loose to hide the stress.

"Will the human's murder take precedence over the King's?" Anneliese asks Tristan, her voice like syrup.

"Of course not," Tristan snaps, the cracks already showing as the temperature in the room seems to rise. "I am simply pointing out that killing the human was not the right course of action and there will be consequences for it."

I do my best to keep my back straight even as the Fae around me shift in their displeasure. I shouldn't be here. This isn't a meeting for peace, this is a witch hunt for the King's killer.

"There is another small matter to attend to as well," Anneliese says. She keeps her attention on the other men gathered at the table, meeting the gazes of each one individually. "And that is the issue of who will be king now?"

Tristan's head jerks to her, his eyes widening. How can she even be fishing for protests of Tristan's place as king when that was part of the deal?

"We must consider the fact that Tristan was never officially made the heir. With the Prince coming home, it is something that must be discussed." She taps a finger against her jaw as though deep in thought.

"She's correct," a dark-haired Fae says from the other end of the table. "Our true successor is not here."

Now Tristan stands. "You all sat in this very room as my father declared that I would be king. Will you really go back on that decision now?"

"Maybe he never made it official because it was not his true wish. He already had a legitimate son, why change his mind for you?" The words come from someone on my side of the table, and I watch Tristan try to hide his flinch.

"We should perhaps wait until the Prince returns and all potential candidates have gathered," Anneliese suggests.

Tristan swallows and sits back down, trying to maintain control. "If that is your wish then we can do that, but I believe you will all remember my father's wishes where the inheritance was concerned. My brother's presence will not change that."

I don't like the look on Anneliese's face as she leans back in her chair. Her smile is too smug, her shoulders too relaxed. She keeps her gaze focused on Tristan like a spider who's already caught something in her web.

"That would appease everyone I think," the blond says while other men around the table nod. "It is a much better plan to see all the late King's candidates in one spot. That way we can ascertain what the King wanted and make the best choice for the kingdom from there."

Various voices around the table agree and burning builds in my chest. How can they do this to Tristan after everything he's gone through? He may not want to be king, but I can see how much he doesn't want his brother to take up that mantle either. I want to grab the blond by his long, beautiful hair and yank him around a bit until he comes to his senses. Instead, I keep my hands demurely in my lap and try not to ruin my skirt any further than it already is.

"In the meantime," Tristan raises his voice as does his best to continue. "I will resume my post as heir apparent and continue managing the day-to-day activities. This will be especially important as we continue to assess the threat that our neighbor, Naicroft poses. It remains to be seen just how much damage the Prince has done during his time there. If that pleases the room?"

I don't know how he keeps the snark out of his voice.

There's no way I could say something like that and not have people know exactly how I feel.

"Yes." The blond smiles. "Prove yourself to us, *Prince*."

Before Tristan can respond, the men stand and file out of the room. Tristan watches them, wrinkles forming at the sides of his eyes as each one leaves. Anneliese sits beside him, her pretty pink grin stretching wide.

She places her hand on his forearm. "Do not trouble yourself too much, my dear. These things have a way of working themselves out."

He nods, jaw tight, and she leaves the room, her skirts swishing behind her on the stone floor.

The heat from the room evaporates as he falls back in his seat. His shoulders slump as he watches me with defeated eyes.

"I'm guessing that wasn't how that was supposed to go." I try to chuckle, but the stone look on his face stops me.

"No, it was not." He kneads his forehead with a tired hand. "I expected so many more men to be there. Usually, when the King dies, all his potential successors come snapping at the heels of the heir."

"Wasn't it a relief then that they weren't here?"

Tristan sighs. "Perhaps."

I press my hand against the cool wood of the table. "What do we do now?"

"We wait for my brother."

EIGHT

Tristan does his best to keep things going, despite Anneliese being there at every turn to give him one of her pretty little smiles and tell him how he's tried his best. I know she doesn't think he'll find any comfort in that and is just digging the knife in further, but I don't understand what her angle is. She already has Tristan, and he's primed to take the throne, what more could she want? Why the push to wait for this Prince that everyone has said has no business being king? It just doesn't add up.

Tristan asks me if I want to say goodbye to Zale before they send his body back to my father, and the very idea makes an icy trail shudder down my spine. I don't know if I can see him like that, cold and devoid of life. How can I face him when I know things were never made right between us? I never understood who he became, just like he never understood me and now that chance is lost to us forever.

In the end, I bow my head and give it a shake and he moves forward with taking Zale home. I'm a coward. I failed him and I can't even face him. It's the least I should be able to do at this point and instead, I leave that entirely up to my father.

Tristan just gives me a tight smile and moves forward like he understands. But how could he? How could he when he's about to face his own brother?

Tristan settles into the throne, but his shoulders never relax, as though even they know this might not be permanent. I stand beside him, unsure of my place but unwilling to leave him. There's not much I can do, but I can at least offer my silent support.

"How long has it been?" I ask when the room is empty besides us. I keep my voice low, so it doesn't echo through the high ceilings. "Since you've seen your brother?"

He stares ahead, eyes vacant. "Years at least. I have done my best to ensure that we are not in the same place."

"Do you not like him?"

"It is not about liking him and all about the respect I tried to give my father. How could I constantly throw in his face the choices he made that threatened the throne when there was a son ready for that mantle? I could not do it. I loved him too much."

I lean against the throne, not caring if it isn't decent. "But not your brother?"

"My brother..." Tristan grimaces. "Things have never been well between my brother and me. In large part due to his mother, I suppose. She never liked that the King so obviously preferred me. I do not blame her for that. I took away her position. She was supposed to create the heir, and I was supposed to disappear."

"But you were just a kid."

Tristan turns to look at me, his blue eyes like ice. "That has never mattered in this court."

I shake my head. The Fae prance around like they're so much better than us, but we don't punish children for their parents. People make mistakes, but that doesn't mean that a child is any less deserving of love.

"Is that why you stayed away so much?"

He nods. "It was what was best for all of us, until you meddled in it."

We still haven't talked about what I did that day. I've been too afraid to bring it up, and I know he's too angry to talk about it. I changed his whole life. I muddled the lines that he spent his whole life making sure were clear. It wasn't fair and I know that. All I wanted was to save his life, but I had no idea the history I was messing with. Maybe it was wrong, but I don't regret it. Not when it saved his life. I have no idea how to tell him that.

"I'm sorry." It's too little and too weak, but I try it anyway.

Tristan gives me the barest of smiles. "I know. How could you understand our politics when we did our best to make sure humans were as far away from it as possible? I cannot hold you accountable for that."

But that doesn't mean he forgives me.

A sharp pain goes through my chest and my fingers tighten around the wood vine carvings in the throne. No amount of squeezing will take my pain and guilt away.

I stare at the side of his face, at the sharpness of his jaw where it wasn't before. He doesn't look at me even though he must feel my gaze. The time apart, the time when he's had to deal with Anneliese and his position as future king, it's been too much.

My eyes burn and I look away from him, shifting my gaze to the floor. I'll make it up to him. I've been wanting to do that since I made the deal. I can still fix this.

The doors at the end of the throne room bang open. A Fae in a dust-covered traveling tunic makes his way through the room with heavy feet. When he reaches the throne, he barely spares me a glance before going down on one knee for Tristan.

"Your Majesty," he says, face towards the floor. I try not to notice how the title makes Tristan flinch. "We have news from Naicroft."

"Is it news of my brother?" Tristan asks.

The man looks up at him with a start. "The Prince was informed of the King's death and left to join you at the castle immediately. He should have made it here before I did."

Tristan frowns and the man shrinks back, shoulders shaking. What does he think Tristan will do to him? Throw him in the dungeons because he doesn't know the where-abouts of the Prince? It's ridiculous. However, Tristan's hands are clenched around the arm of the throne so tightly that I can see every vein in them.

"Then continue, what is your message?"

The man straightens up only a little, so that he still looks like a cowering mess on the floor. "Our line has been breached, Naicroft's army will soon be upon us. We did not have enough men to stop them, and without the Prince there was no one to bolster us."

My skin turns icy. We're facing an invasion on land, and Tristan doesn't know it yet, but more is to come from the sea. I haven't gotten to do my job yet as a delegate to even let him know. This whole thing has turned into such a mess. What will Tristan do when he realizes he has a war on two fronts?

"And you ran here instead of continuing to push them back?" There's a fire behind Tristan's question.

"I—I— we thought it was important for you to know. To protect the people."

"It would have been much better if there was nothing to protect them from."

I reach over and put my hand on Tristan's arm. He stiffens under my touch, but I keep it there. "There is something I wish to tell you, regarding my position as delegate of the Seafolk."

The Fae on the floor looks at me for the first time, his eyes wide. I do my best not to squirm under his gaze as it travels over me as though looking for proof of what makes me worthy of such a position.

Tristan speaks out of the side of his mouth. "That is a conversation that should be had at a better time."

"Unfortunately." I push on even as he pulls his arm away from me. "What I have to say is just as important as what he has already told you."

"Mariel, you will wait your turn," he says through gritted teeth. The heat of anger spreads over him and I take a step back.

My moment for telling him my information was when I first got here. Instead, I let myself get distracted. There was just too much going on. I didn't know I would get here, and the King would die. Or that the King's death would bring my brother's.

My face heats up and a tear slips down my cheek. Without bothering to say goodbye or ask permission, I turn on my heel and charge from the room. I pass the man on the floor and almost knock him over. But just because he's a sniveling coward doesn't mean I should punish him for it. No, I have work to do.

Whether Tristan likes it or not.

DESPITE MY BIG talk to myself, I hide in the room provided to me for the rest of the afternoon. My heart aches on too many sides, and I'm too bolstered up by the anger that

Tristan should have to treat me with the respect afforded to my position, while at the same time not at all respecting his. I know he doesn't want to be king.

A soft knock comes from the door, and I lift my tear-stained cheeks from the pillow long enough to invite them in. I'm expecting Tristan, not the young girl who comes instead.

"Pardon miss, your presence has been requested at a meeting." She gives me the shallowest curtsy before sliding out of the room and closing the door behind her.

I stumble from the bed and use the drinking water set out to pat down my face. Finger combing my hair, I try to make myself look respectable and not like I've been hiding for hours.

Will Tristan be at the meeting? Of course he will. Who has an important meeting without the King? Unless it's been called by the men who would prefer to see another man on the throne.

I gnaw at my lip as I leave the room. In so many ways I feel the same as when I came here the first time: completely out of my element with no real way to help anyone. I had thought when I came back things would be different. I had hoped when I came back things would be different with Tristan.

It's possible my hopes keep turning me into a fool.

The girl waited outside the room for me and now leads me through the halls at a rapid clip that only youth is capable of. I arrive in front of the door breathing heavily and knowing that my attempts to look more put together have been for nothing. I take a deep breath and open the door.

The inside of the room is dark, but I square my shoulders and head inside anyway. I don't know what their meetings entail, maybe there are things they would rather talk about in the dark.

"Mariel, how kind of you to join me." Anneliese's voice fills the room as the door closes behind me. "There is much I have been waiting to discuss."

"We have no business together anymore."

Anneliese laughs. "You poor girl. We will always have business together. You cannot shake me off so easily. You came to me, and I took you in. You have debts."

"I consider our debts to be paid considering your attempts on my life." I keep my voice hard, the emotions of the day giving me an edge that I didn't have the last time we saw each other.

"Sad, naive girl, you really think you can brush me aside so easily?" She steps out of the darkness, making a soft tutting sound. "This isn't one of your silly games."

I sigh. "What more could you possibly want from me? You got what you wanted. You have your crown, you have Tristan. There's nothing left I could give you."

Maybe I should be afraid of her. She's hurt me before. But I'm too tired.

"I warned you that there would be consequences to coming here."

"Well, not *me*. You told the Seafolk." Pointing it out is probably pointless, but the letter was never supposed to even come to me. The warning didn't even apply to me.

Her smile turns cruel, and she takes a predatory step closer to me. With a hand like a claw, she reaches out and grabs me by the chin.

"I think you know that those threats always included you." She wrenches my face closer to hers, her nails cutting into my jaw. "And I think I made it clear before that you were never to come back."

I try to shake my head or speak, but nothing comes out but a dribble of spit as she tightens her grip.

"It is too bad you were so willing to let your brother take your consequences. He had so much potential that has been lost."

She releases her hold on me and I stumble back, hitting the door. "You didn't have anything to do with Zale. He was just—"

"In the wrong place at the wrong time?" She laughs, all the gentleness gone from her voice. "As if I could not arrange for an accident to happen to him?"

"You couldn't have known what was going to happen. You couldn't have made him—"

"Could I not?" She uses one hand to daintily pick at her fingernails. "Let me assure you, my men are everywhere. I can easily arrange something. You are not safe from me, no matter where you go."

My mind travels back to my father and brother at sea. I never told them to be careful or to watch for anything. Fae are bringing Zale's body back right now, are one of them her men?

I open my mouth to speak, to say something, to plead for their safety, but she presses a finger against my lips.

"Think about what I said before you try to cross me. You are the stranger here, and no one will mourn you."

She taps my cheek with her open hand and brushes past me. She leaves the door open behind her, a bright triangle of light flooding the small room.

I press my hand against my cheek where she hit it, the skin still feeling cold to the touch. I slam the door after her, but the hallway is already empty.

What was her angle in threatening me; in implying that she killed my brother? I'm torn between anger and fear, the hot and cold racing under my skin. I hadn't even had a chance to do anything yet. My presence couldn't have threatened her than much, could it? I hadn't had an opportunity to make a difference yet. I haven't mentioned anything about the banished or about what the Seafolk sent me here to say. She had no reason, but when has she ever needed a reason?

Anneliese is never going to be my ally. I know that. Something about that thought makes me hold my head a little taller. She wants me to be afraid of her, and maybe I should be, but I won't. Not anymore. She doesn't get to just threaten my family. I won't be afraid of her anymore. Let her be afraid of me.

CHAPTER

NINE

I scurry through the halls, hoping to find a real meeting or Tristan. The Fae I pass in the hallway don't give me a second glance, but their disinterest only makes me straighten my posture further. It doesn't matter how they feel about me. I was invited here, and I have a purpose their disdain can't stop.

The throne room sits empty when I pass it. Tristan's proud yet tired form doesn't grace the throne. Despite this, I drift into the room, running my hand along the cold wood. I wanted to save Tristan from this fate when I was still on the ships. I thought I could rescue him from the corner I had pinned him into, but that just isn't possible. The wheels have been turning here without me and now I will have to fight to keep him in this gilded prison. He may not like it, but his being king is what will be best for everyone. I can feel it. Tristan is a good man, and the position should go to a good man.

"Can I help you with something?"

I glance up from the chair at Tristan moving across the floor toward me. Despite everything, seeing him makes me smile. He doesn't return the gesture.

As he gets closer to me, he feels less like Tristan, though he still looks so much like him. His gait is wrong, the way his slim shoulders sit on his narrow frame, and even the length of his hair isn't right. Where the Tristan I know keeps his hair tighter to his head like he's ready for battle, man has allowed it to grow longer, the light brown waves cresting the tops of his shoulders. The overall look makes him seem more like a prince than a captain.

A prince. Ship.

"Back from your time at the front?" I venture. I have no idea how to talk to this man, the disappointment of his father and the potential pawn of so many on the council.

He smiles now, the edges of his full lips cruel. "It would seem so. That is the nature of one's father dying."

"I'm so sorry for your loss."

I move away from the throne as he gets closer. His lithe body moves like a jungle cat, all slim and dangerous muscles casually flexing as he places his hand on the arm of the throne.

"Yes. It is unfortunate I could not be here when it happened. My father had other plans for me that detained me from being by his side and almost cost me my life." His hand curls into a fist. "It is good to be back though. Hopefully we will be able to put all this contention to bed soon."

He glances at me, and I can't hide the flinch that ripples across my body.

"You are the delegate for the humans?" he asks, gaze flickering over the slight curve of my ear.

"The delegate for the humans was murdered." The word is salty on my tongue. "I am here on behalf of the Seafolk."

His grin turns feral. "Interesting. And what role do the Seafolk hope to have in this new world?"

"That is something best left to be discussed at our

formal meetings." There's no way I'm going to gossip with the Prince about why I'm here. I won't give him that acknowledgment. He's not going to be king.

He tilts his head and steps closer to me. "If I want to discuss it here, then that is what we will do. Your people do not require a cabinet meeting to be told no."

My jaw slams together, heat building up through my face. I need to get out of here before I say the wrong thing and ruin everything for Tristan. Where is Tristan? Why is he never around when I need him?

"Good day to you," I barely manage to spit out before turning to leave the room.

He grabs my arm and yanks me back. "Hold on there."

"You will release me."

"I will do what I please." He sits on the throne and drags me towards his lap. "And you will listen. Do not presume to be an equal with us. If it were possible for you to join our ranks, don't you think it would have happened already?"

I yank on my arm, but he doesn't let go. His touch makes me feel sick. I wish I could go back to just being curious about who the Prince was. This man... how could he come from the same genes as Tristan? How could he come from the gentle King who sat at the table missing his son? I pull harder, ready to kick him in the leg if he doesn't let go. Just before I fight, I hear the door opening behind me. He hears it as well, and looks toward it, releasing me.

"Brother?" he calls.

I hit the floor, sprawling across it. Tristan stops by my feet, helping me up with an easy hand.

"I see you have returned." Tristan keeps his voice curt. "There is much that needs to be discussed."

The Prince runs his hand over the arm of the throne. "I think there is less to talk about than you believe. There has been much trouble at the castle in my absence."

"Much less than you would think. It has been calm here without your talent for stirring up political messes."

The Prince laughs. "You wound me, brother. I have never stirred up anything that was not already trouble."

Tristan grabs my arm, leading me from the room. "Be that as it may, there is much to discuss now that you are home." He pauses to survey the Prince as he sits on the throne with his feet out in front of him. "Do not get too comfortable."

My heartbeat travels up my throat as Tristan pulls me closer to the door. It slams open before we can reach it. Members of the cabinet file into the room, their heads held high as they find the Prince on the throne.

Tristan tugs me to the side of the room, avoiding the growing crowd. His hand is warm in mine, and he gives it a tight squeeze.

"What were you thinking?" he hisses in my ear. "You cannot be alone with that man."

"I didn't mean to. I was looking for you." I choose not to tell him about my encounter with Anneliese. There's no reason. I can handle that woman on my own.

I hope.

He shakes his head. "It is dangerous for you to be out alone. There is too much unrest right now. Anyone could decide it is not the right time for concessions."

"Is that what I represent?"

He gives me a sidelong glance as he turns his back on the Prince. "That is not all you represent. Will you let me worry about you a little bit?"

It's not like I have any choice in the matter. Even so, the idea that he's worried about me makes my chest grow warm.

"Tristan, I need to talk to you—"

"Not here." His voice grows hard as he guides me into

the crowd by the small of my back, his gaze never leaving the Prince.

He doesn't understand. There's so much I need to say. There's so much between he and I that still doesn't feel right and so much I haven't done as a delegate.

Tristan stands opposite the Prince, hands clutched tight. The Fae file in around us, forming a half circle on either side as their gazes flit back and forth between Tristan and the Prince. Anneliese doesn't hesitate as she makes her way to the throne.

He runs a hand through his dark hair, then slowly relaxes his body. The Prince grins from his place on the throne, looking down on us like he's already the confirmed leader. Cold sweat trickles down my back. If Tristan doesn't become king, then what is going to happen to the banished?

Anneliese stands behind the Prince, her hand resting on the arm of the throne. Her gaze narrows as she looks between Tristan and the Prince. What did she think? These are the men who could be king. She's just as much a pawn as I am. Although, by the look on her face, it seems she thinks these men are the real pawns.

A dark shadow darkens the doorway for a moment and my stomach drops out of me all together. Captain Wimark. My nails dig into my leg as I watch him without looking directly at him as he joins the other members of the cabinet. Of everyone in this room, he would know where Ry is. That is one promise I can still make good on.

"Welcome everyone," Tristan says as silence fills the cavern of the room. Unsurprisingly the blond that was so vocal before has found a place closer to the Prince. Our list of allies feels thin.

"There is much to discuss since I have been gone." The Prince rises to stand, looking for all like the true leader. "It is my wish that we can manage the issue of who the next king will be swiftly so that we may move into more pressing topics, like the fight coming from our border."

Would this be the right time to bring up the Seafolk? I glance at Tristan, his jaw clenched tight. No. It needs to wait.

"Yes, the issue of who the heir apparent is should be resolved swiftly," Tristan agrees. "As all of you here know, it was my father's wish these last few months for me to take that position. You all heard him say so in our last few meetings."

The blond shakes his head. "And yet he never made it official. Where was it written down that anything should change from the Prince?"

"Is that really necessary when you can all act as witnesses?"

The Prince laughs. "I am not sure you can count the ramblings of an old man as truth. Especially if he did not remember to go through the proper channels to make sure everything was prepared. Unfortunately for you, dear brother, his declarations towards the end of his life probably have more to do with a desire to make things right with a bastard son, than a true desire for you to be king."

The room fills with low murmuring. Anneliese practically glows as the tension rises. The torchlight flickers in the dark room as Tristan stands to match the Prince.

"There is much you do not know about the King. You have been gone well over a year and—"

"You cannot use that as a reasoning point with me. After all, you were gone just as many years. Wasn't it you who never desired to come to the castle again? No wonder the King was willing to make concessions for you. All he wanted was to see you." The Prince points out with a wicked grin.

Anneliese looks up at him, her lips twisting. I still don't understand her game. She's engaged to Tristan, why try to shift that now? She could have everything she wants if she backs the right man. Not that I want her to win, but there has to be something going on that I don't know about.

The growing tension is broken temporarily by servants bringing in trays of meats and cheeses and place them on small tables between us. My stomach threatens to growl so I grab some and shove it in my mouth as quickly as I can. The salty flavor bursts across my tongue as I swallow down the thinly sliced meat. I feel like a mouse in a trap. I want to get out of here, but I know that the only reason I'm here is because of these awful meetings.

The man standing across from me looks at the Prince and then at Tristan. "It has been my understanding that the King wanted Tristan to become king for many years. He was only able to make the changes he was working on before he died because Tristan finally agreed to them."

"Is that so, brother?" The Prince leans on the throne, palms flat on the dark wood. "Something made you change your mind?"

Anneliese watches me, her cruel smile the only evidence that she knows just as well as I do what finally made him change his mind.

"I realized that I needed to grow up and do what was asked of me and what was best for our country." Tristan keeps his voice hard and unrelenting.

"Perhaps," a woman in the middle of the group says, her long purple sleeves trailing over the table as she grabs a piece of meat. "It might be necessary to have a trial."

"You want a judge to decide?" Anneliese asks.

"No, no." The woman waves away Anneliese's question as though it were a fly. "Each man needs to take the helm for a while to give us the opportunity to see how they might govern, and then we can decide as a counsel."

It's not the worst idea I've heard, but from the frowns on the Prince's and Tristan's faces, I know I'm the only one who doesn't think it's a terrible idea.

"I do not believe we have time to dither back and forth in this matter. War is coming," the Prince says.

"Your bride negotiations went that poorly?" Tristan asks with a sly grin.

The Prince's hands curl into fists. "It would seem that our desire to find peace at our border has backfired."

I guess Anneliese's ladies were right when they said he would be unsuccessful. It's almost enough to feel bad for him. Almost.

"Am I correct in assuming then that the issues we are having and the war that is coming has everything to do with your attempts at peace?" Tristan asks, his voice smooth as a smile takes over his face.

"To say that would be an oversimplification. However, the nature of our border is now in question, regardless of why it became that way."

"I think the question of why it became that way is more than relevant." Tristan's face remains even. "It brings into question your ability to rule at all if you cannot manage simple border disputes."

Murmuring travels down the table. Maybe Tristan isn't as eager to play nice about his position as I thought. Regardless of how he feels about being king, he's not going to let his brother take it away from him.

Anneliese's grip on the throne tightens, her knuckles white.

"Perhaps..." The Prince's lips curl into a bitter smile. "The issue of these complicated politics may just be too much for a bastard to understand."

All talking comes to a standstill. I have to remind myself to breathe. My neck cracks as I turn my head to stare at Tristan.

His face is hard for a moment and then he begins to laugh, the low sound coming deep from his chest. "Oh poor, poor William. Are you so afraid that you have to resort to petty name-calling?"

"It is not name calling." The Prince puffs his chest out a little. "It is the truth. It is the reason the crown was always denied you. I see no reason why that should change now."

"You may not, but our father did. I know it is hard for you to understand, but everyone in this room can attest to the fact that it was his desire."

I stare down the table, watching the council's faces. The blond looks guilty as he looks away, but others look bored as they watch the two men verbally duel.

"It's true," the woman next to Tristan says. "We all stood in this very room when the King declared his intentions. Regardless of whether it was made known in writing, we know that is what he wanted. I believe we owe it to the late King to see his words honored. Let Tristan take the crown."

The Prince's face turns red as others murmur their agreement. "We have to follow the law," he shouts, spit hanging from his bottom lip and marring his otherwise perfect face. "And the law says the heir must be in writing."

"Be that as it may, I believe the council is ready for a vote." Tristan gestures to the woman beside him. She stands as he sits, the Prince still huffing at the other end of the table.

"All those in favor of allowing Tristan the right to act as king, say 'aye.'"

A chorus of ayes travel around the room. Anneliese stays suspiciously quiet.

"Any opposed say 'nay.'"

The Prince is loud with his nay, the blond doing the same, as though their volume can change the fact that they're outnumbered.

"The ayes have it." The woman turns to Tristan, her sleeves running across the table. "Tristan, you are our interim king. Do not disappoint us or your father's legacy, and we will see you crowned."

Tristan gives her a short bow and the members of the council stand to slowly filter out of the room. I flinch as Captain Wimark passes me, but he doesn't even glance my way. The room is nearly empty when Anneliese leaves. She runs her hand down Tristan's arm before she goes, giving him a long look.

"I would not get too comfortable if I were you," she warns with me a smile before flitting through the door.

"I thought this would make her happy. Isn't it exactly what she required of us before?" I ask Tristan in a low voice.

He shakes his head. "Much has transpired since you were here last."

The Prince stops before Tristan on his way out, his eyes hard as he stares at his brother. "I would echo Anneliese's thoughts, but I find it would be unnecessary. I think you and I both know you are unfit for the role, and it will soon pass to me, as it should."

"We shall see." Tristan motions with his hand toward the door, and the Prince scoffs as he stomps from the room. Anneliese gives Tristan a quick glance before hurrying out behind him.

And then it is just us.

"We will have to have a formal council soon. The one we were meant to have when you came here. Do you think you will be able to act as the human's representative as well?"

I chew my lip to keep the memories of my brother from overwhelming me. "Yes."

He nods, his gaze on the table before us. "Good. Don't worry, Mariel. This will all be figured out soon."

I want to agree with him, but I saw the look in Anneliese's eyes. There's something more going on here and I intend to find out what it is.

TEN

Tristan told me not to go off alone, but I can't wait for him to have time to come along. With the official role of the king being placed on his shoulders, his time is no longer his own. He leaves me in my room to wait for him, but I have no intention of doing so.

Anneliese is up to something, and if history is to be an indicator, she can't be left alone with her schemes. She's not just a pretty courtier looking to get ahead. There's something else there. Otherwise, why would she have dropped Tristan so quickly?

I tiptoe through the hallways, my boots softening the sound of my steps. I pass a few servants in the halls, but the darkness between torches helps me hide my heritage from any casual onlooker.

Tristan worries too much, and he has since the moment we met. Why else would he personally have brought a scrawny nothing human all the way to the capital for a trial he never intended to go through with? He's watched over me from the beginning, and I know for that I owe him my life. There's a burning in my heart though that would give him so much more. I have to tamp those feelings down though. The time isn't right. I don't need to distract him with my feelings.

I won't lie, I want him to look at me like he did when he first saw me on the beach.

My feet carry me to Anneliese's rooms, the memory of my time there all too fresh. I'm glad I'm not here under the guise of being one of her ladies anymore, but I would have liked to be on the inside of her circle to find out her schemes.

Her door is closed, and I can barely hear the tinkling of voices inside. What would she do if I snuck inside? Not that there could be any sneaking. The second I opened that door, all eyes would be on me. Regardless, I can't just stand outside her door if I want to figure out what's behind her threats.

I'm still deliberating when the Prince comes around the corner. He hesitates when he sees me, feet stumbling before he can maintain his composure.

"And to what do I owe the pleasure of running into my brother's little human pet?" His smile is cruel as though that will cover up his previous hesitation.

"I'm not here for you." I keep my voice harsh even though I have no idea what I'll say if he asks what I *am* here for.

He moves faster than I can see, standing in the hall one second and in my face the next. He places a hand on the wall beside my face and leans in as he studies me.

"For too long my brother has been a thorn in my side. What would he do if I took away his little pet, *hmmm?*"

I bare my teeth at him as though we are animals in a standoff, and he chuckles. It's a dark sound that makes me wriggle away from the brace of his arms.

Behind him, the door to Anneliese's room opens and I

freeze. There's nowhere for me to hide, trapped as I am with the Prince.

She runs her hand down his arm and cloudiness pierces his eyes. "Have you come to see me, William?"

He shudders as he nods.

"Perfect. Come inside and leave this…" Her lips curl as she studies me. "Trash behind."

"Of course."

He steps away from me, his eyes unseeing as he moves into her room. Anneliese gives me a nasty smile and closes the door behind them.

I should run away before she can come out again. I got lucky this time that someone she was more interested in was there to take the attention from me. That won't happen again.

Instead, I find myself creeping even closer.

His eyes had the same look as Tristan's when he was under her spell. If Anneliese asked him to do something crazy that resulted in his death, would the Prince even know? He would have no way to resist. I was able to break the control she had on Tristan, but I'm *not* doing that for the Prince.

Despite the danger of being caught, I move to the door and press my face against the cool stone floor so that my ear lines up with the crack. It's a ludicrous position to put myself in, and there's no good way to get away if I'm caught, but I need to know what's happening in that room.

The voices are muffled, even at this angle. The door is just too thick. Still, Anneliese speaks with enough authority that her words break through.

"Sweet William, it has been too long since you last visited."

There's a soft mumble I assume is the Prince but I can't tell what he's saying.

She laughs, shrill and harsh. "Call me Anneliese. There is no need to say 'cousin.' For we are not *truly* cousins. Not in any way that matters. And lingering on those words would only create awkwardness between us. That just will not do when I have the desire to bring us even closer."

Cousin?

Tristan never said he was related to Anneliese. It would make sense that she would have a close relationship with someone in power to get permanent rooms in the castle.

Still, she wanted to marry her cousin? Humans may have few options, but we still wouldn't do *that*.

"Dear, dear William, I am doing my best to make you King. After all, you are the rightful leader. It does not matter what Tristan says. He is nothing. He has always been nothing. The fact that he thinks he could take over now is laughable. He only attempts it because the King is not here to set him right. I will help you with him, William. I will help you receive that which is owed to you."

The heavy tread of footsteps comes closer to the door, and I scramble back on all fours, tripping in my skirt. My body feels tight as I push myself to my feet and practically run down the hallway.

I run to find Tristan, his voice coming from the throne room. My face is red and blotchy and I'm completely out of breath as I stand panting before him.

"Mariel? What happened to you? You were supposed to stay in your room." His voice grows harder as he speaks.

"I wasn't going to wait around for danger to find me. I can help you, and I knew just where to look."

Tristan raises his brows. "You went after Anneliese?"

I nod and he frowns.

"That is precisely what I did not want you to do." He collapses onto the throne, face in his hands. "How am I supposed to keep you safe when you refuse to listen?"

Falling to my knees beside him, I take his hand in mine. "I'm not trying to make things harder for you, Tristan. All I want to do is help you."

He looks down at me with a sad smile. "I know. But you have no idea how hard it is to have my heart walking around here. Everyone knows it. It makes me more vulnerable and places you in danger. I wanted to see you more than anything, but I did not ask you to be part of the delegation out of fear. And now that fear is walking around and getting tangled with Anneliese."

I brace a hand against my hip. "I'm not tangled with Anneliese, but something is going on between her and your brother."

It feels weird to call the Prince his brother. I want him to be our enemy and nothing more.

He sighs and moves to speak as the door on the other end of the room slams open. He grabs my hand and shifts to his feet, studying the young messenger boy running across the room.

"Your Highness." He dips onto one knee, not daring to meet Tristan's gaze. "I have come to report trouble. A mass of kelpies is moving across the land, killing any they come across."

I flinch. The time to talk to Tristan about the Seafolk's plight is long past. Is this them taking matters into their own hands, or further evidence that trouble is brewing in the water?

"Tristan?" I squeeze his hand. Tingles run down my arm from our contact as his callouses rub against mine.

"Just a minute, Mariel." He turns his attention to the boy. "How far away are they?"

"They have reached the field outside the castle."

Tristan swears under his breath. "Thank you."

Dismissed, the boy runs from the room, leaving the door open behind him.

"Tristan, I—"

"Mariel, it will have to wait until later. I have to find a way to subdue the kelpies without angering the Seafolk." He stands, pacing in front of the throne.

Anger blooms in my chest. I grab his arm, holding him in place with a firm hand. "I am the Seafolk's delegate. You *will* listen to me."

His eyes widen as he stares at me as though seeing me for the first time. "What is it you have to say, Mariel?"

"I needed to talk to you when I first got here, but everything went so wrong right away." I hold on to my anger so that there's no room for pain. "There's trouble at sea—"

"Yes, yes, I know. That is the whole reason why we were interested in having a meeting in the first place."

I squeeze his arm. "I need you to not interrupt me. I know that you know there is trouble with the humans and that they're striking. But did you know that that has woken beasts from down below?"

His forehead wrinkles and he sits heavy on the throne. "Beasts?"

"Yes. They're destroying our ships and attacking the Seafolk. Their belief is that the strike has caused this. We have to appease the humans and get them working again before trouble comes, because it won't just be us who suffers."

Tristan shakes his head. "Trouble is already here. Are you implying that the Seafolk have no control over their people?"

"Would you stay in the water if you knew it could kill you? Even if you'd been ordered to?"

He frowns as he thinks it over, his self-preservation warring with his soldier background. He runs a hand over his face and tips his head back against the wood.

"Are you saying that in order to get the kelpies under control, and avoid similar problems, we need to fix the issue with the humans?"

"Exactly."

He blows out a long breath. "The council will not be happy with that."

I couldn't care less what the council thinks. I mean, I guess I should, since I'm almost a part of it, but the last thing I want to do is sit in that stuffy room again listening to those privileged fools tell me that they refuse to change things for us. That's not an answer I can bring home. The humans and the Seafolk won't accept it.

"I thought when you were king that things would be different." I keep my voice quiet.

Tristan gives me a side smile. "Maybe there would have been a better chance of that if I were the real and true king."

"But the council agreed it should be you."

"Not completely." He sighs. "They are waiting for me to make a mistake. I think they know my brother would be terrible on the throne, but it is easier for them to accept him than it is for them to accept me. It does not help that I have lost my men."

Of course. Anneliese left him with no allies when she turned his men against him. He's completely at the mercy of the council.

"If I start acting in ways they do not agree with, the council can change their minds and place William on the throne. It is their ultimate trump card with me. Honestly, it's probably one of the only reasons why they were so eager to put me on the throne." He looks down at his hands. "Tristan, the puppet king."

"That's not true. It only feels true. Plus, after your coronation, that's the end, right? Then you can do whatever you want, and they can't just take you off the throne to punish you."

"Perhaps, but I do not believe William and Anneliese will let it get that far."

I want to reach for his hand, but my body stays frozen, too afraid of the answer to the question I finally dare to ask. "What happened with you and Anneliese?"

"Me and Anneliese," he says with a grimace. "Something I never wanted to hear."

I step closer to him, encouraged by his reaction. "So, what happened?"

"We were engaged, just as you agreed." His gaze turns far away. "For a little while she was content. She signed 'princess' to everything despite the fact that I had not been instated as a prince and we were not married. It was not as terrible as I thought it would be. She had little use for me and seemed to only want the power to boss people around."

"Something she was already doing," I mutter under my breath.

Tristan looks up at me and smiles, reaching for my hand. I gladly take his, comforted by the warm of him surrounding my hand.

"I think my father knew what was happening. For all that he wanted me home, that did not make him a fool. I believe that it was because of this that he did not officially change the documents and make me his legal heir."

I squeeze his hand. "I really am sorry about what happened to him. He seemed like a nice man."

"He was." Tristan leans his head into my hand. "He was a better father than I deserved. He found a way for me to be at the castle with him and I refused it. I thought I knew better. How many years could we have had together?"

"You had no idea that you wouldn't have more time together. You can't beat yourself up over that."

His eyes are red as he looks at me. "Can I not, though? He was the king. His life was always in danger. I knew that. There had been attempts before. I just believed he was invincible. I suppose most boys think that of their fathers."

He's not wrong. I've never thought there would be a storm that could take down Dad. He's always been an unmovable force in my life. The only time he even remotely came close to falling apart was when we lost Zale, and even then, he was strong.

The childish part of me is glad I won't have to face him when they bring Zale home.

"You'll have to find a way to forgive yourself. I don't think your father would want you to suffer like this, and I don't think you'll be able to be a good king if you let this hover over you."

"Perhaps." He pats my hand as he stands. "But for now, there's work to do."

CHAPTER

ELEVEN

Worry gnaws at my gut as I follow Tristan from the room. He can't continue like this, it's just not sustainable. Not that I'm a great example of being able to recover and let things go.

The sound of Tristan's boots echoes through the hallway as he brings us back to the council room. My heart hammers in my chest. Will they take Tristan seriously now that there's a real threat? I mean I don't know much about kelpies, but I imagine they pose a genuine problem if a messenger was sent to warn the King.

Tristan falters as we round the corner and I almost slam into his back.

Two Fae men stand before the door, their silver armor glinting in the firelight. Their hands clutch the handles of their swords as we come closer.

"What are you doing here?" Tristan puffs his chest up, looking more like the captain he was when we first met.

"I have been asked to keep the council members uninterrupted during their meeting," the one to the left of the door says, his mouth twitching into a frown.

"Then you will let us in. I am acting as king and am

therefore a member of the council," Tristan says, a muscle twitching in his jaw.

"I am afraid that is impossible. The King is currently inside working."

I shift around Tristan to stand beside him. "What do you mean? The council just decided to honor the late King's wishes."

The man rolls his shoulders back. "There must have been a misunderstanding. For now, you will have to leave."

"I will not leave. You must realize how ridiculous this is." Tristan moves a step forward, arms uncrossing as he clenches his hands into fists. "I am the acting King, and I was your captain even before. It is my right to be in that room."

"I only take orders from the King now," the man says. "You will have to leave."

I take a step in front of Tristan, hoping that will deflect some of the anger building in the room like a thick fog. "If something has changed, then Tristan should have the right to confront the King about it. Right?"

Confusion moves through the guard's eyes. "That was not my order."

"Surely you could share your orders with Tristan as your captain even if you don't see him as your king."

I'm not sure how true that is. There's not much I do know about Tristan and his time in the army. He thought the men under him were loyal before and that all came tumbling down around us.

"I do not owe him anything," the guard spits. "He chose humans over us. What makes him think he could possibly be our king with such a betrayal?"

Tristan moves forward, his breath hot against the back of my neck. "I never chose the humans over you. That was never what this was about."

"You put us all at risk to save that one." The guard nods at me. "You should have remembered your duty for us."

"That—she is different."

I glance back at Tristan, a stupid grin threatening to grow across my face. This is definitely not the time. But after the last few days of being together, it feels good to hear.

"You chose her over us. You saved that rebellion scum," the guard points out.

"It was never to just 'save' him. It was always to get him and Mariel back on the boat." Tristan slowly moves me aside so that he can stand directly in front of the guards. "Zale was nothing in this."

The guard on the right shakes his head. "He was not nothing. He was the rebellion's *hand*. How many of our people did he slaughter, and you were ready to let him go without so much as a warning."

"I never forced any of you to help me in this. My father understood that we needed to work with the humans. The deal with Zale was part of that."

"That is the problem though, is it not? You may not have forced anyone, but it was still a betrayal of our King. All your men have been sent to the front to deal with what they did under your instruction. Consider this the consequences of your actions." The guard moves away from Tristan, dismissing him as he takes up his residence in the doorway.

Tristan grabs me by the arm, his grip uncomfortably tight as he leads me back down the hall. His footsteps are even heavier as though he can pool all his anger out into the floor.

He passes the room I've been assigned and takes me back to his little room. The tightness in my chest eases to be back in the familiar space. A fire crackles away behind the grate and a blanket has been left on the chair.

"So that's what this has all been about," Tristan huffs. "Rather than talk to me about what happened, the men were all too happy to take up with Anneliese instead."

"I thought they understood what we were doing." Why is Joel upset? He knew what he was doing when he agreed to help Tristan. Sure, there's no love lost between Zale and the Fae, but that's to be expected. He was never in it to help Zale. It was always to help Tristan.

"As did I." Tristan slumps into the chair, resting his boots before the fire. "Apparently we were both wrong."

I shake my head. Something about this still doesn't add up. How could Anneliese have gotten her hands on the men so quickly? There was barely any time to explain grabbing Zale before they were turning on him. There has to be something else.

"Are they really going to keep you out of the council?" Without Tristan, there's no way I'll be able to share what's happening on the ocean. They're fools to do this now, but then maybe they don't know about the kelpies.

"It would seem so."

"You can't let them get away with it." I move to stand in front of Tristan, and he gives me a wry grin.

"Are you my little defender then?" he teases.

My shoulders deflate a little. "I would be if I had to. But there's no way I fought so hard to get here just to give up now. We can't let the Prince become King."

"It would not be right for the country. Not with the way things are. And we have no idea what happened to dissolve the marriage contract he was working on that has somehow led to war." Tristan rubs his temples. "Tact has never been William's strong suit."

I pace in front of the fire, fist pressed to my chin. *There has to be something we can do. There has to be a way to fix this.*

"They're looking for a human delegate again, aren't they?" I ask as an idea blooms in the back of my mind.

Tristan nods. "That is what they last said."

"Well, I doubt they'd be willing to use me. I have to focus on protecting the Seafolk's interests. So, we need to find another human."

"Right." Tristan doesn't look at me. He clearly isn't following along.

"So, if we find a human we can work with, that gives us an in with the council. Right?"

He lets his arm fall hard on the armrest of the chair. "Mariel, we don't have time to run back to the ship to find another human. As it is, the council could have already done that, or even decided they have no desire to work with the humans at all. William has no fondness for humans."

"We don't have to go all the way to the ship to find a human. I could find you one on the street."

Tristan laughs. "In case you did not know, humans still are not allowed to wander the land."

"But that hasn't stopped the rebellion."

His eyes light up as he glances at me, finally understanding. "You want to team up with the rebellion?"

I slide onto the armrest of his chair and throw my arms around his neck. "I'm just saying. If we want back in, that's a pretty good way to do it. Don't you think?"

"Yes." He puts his arm around my waist. "Yes, I do."

It feels weird to be back on the streets again, especially with Tristan beside me. He borrowed some clothing from the laundry and now we're walking through the market in bright colored clothing that's just a little bit less nice than what we'd usually wear. Zale's letter is tucked into my skirt pocket. The press of memories threatens to weigh me down, but I keep my head held high.

The air is full of the smells of people and roasting meat. The bright-colored awnings above the stands full of wares brings a cheeriness to the street that the people's faces don't emulate.

"They will have heard of the King's death by now," Tristan whispers in my ear, pulling me close as a cart goes by.

"And that would make them this upset?"

He snakes his arm around my waist as he leads us further into the market. "The death of the King throws everyone's lives in jeopardy. Especially with my brother being the one most likely to take the throne."

A woman knocks into my shoulder as she goes by, her arms full of baskets. She gives me a dark look and continues on her way without saying anything.

I was afraid the last time I was here, and for good reason. I was still avoiding being caught while looking for my brother. Even though Tristan is with me this time, and I'm in no danger of being caught, I feel more at risk than I did before. The people have turned. If the Prince could walk among them, would he still be so eager to become king?

It takes a minute to get my bearings enough to lead Tristan toward the last place I remember being with the rebellion. They made sure I wouldn't be able to find their hideout, but I know they have people here watching the market. And I know they'll recognize me.

I stop in the alley where the tunnel is that I climbed through before. That seems like a lifetime ago now. Everything has changed since then. Most of all me.

"So, what do we do now?" Tristan asks as he leans against the wall. I know he's trying to appear casual, but with every muscle in his body tight, there's no way he's getting away with it.

"We wait."

I can't imagine it will take long. The rebellion won't like us hanging out on their doorstep.

Sure enough, a little boy approaches us from the mouth of the alley, his hands in his trouser pockets as he watches us with a tight smile.

"We need to see Azalea," I tell him. I try to match the confident posture I've seen Tristan use before, but I'm not sure it works as the boy barks out a laugh.

"You think you can just waltz in? If the boss wants to see you, she'll see you. Otherwise, you'll have to wait."

"We already were waiting," Tristan grumbles to me under his breath.

I take a step toward the boy and watch a nerve twitch over his eye. "You will take me to her. I promise you she wants to see me."

"Why would she want to see you after what you did to Zale?"

Tristan's eyes widen and I take a step toward the boy. "If she wants to find out what happened to Zale, she'd best talk to me. I have something for her from Zale."

He bounces on the balls of his feet, looking from me to Tristan. "And what do you think you're doing out here?"

"Trying to save the country," Tristan says honestly.

The boy laughs. "You big Fae and all your plans. Have you finally realized how necessary humans are to all your little games?"

"I have, but I guarantee those on the council still have not. That is why we're here." Tristan holds his hands out to his sides to appear less threatening. "I need to talk to your leader. I believe it's time we worked together."

The boy grins. "All right then, let's get you to Azalea."

The trip back through the tunnel is both easier and harder than the first time. Being able to see is a huge bonus, but what I can see doesn't make me feel better. As we crawl through buildings, bricks and metal sheets hang precariously above us. One wrong move from me and it looks like the whole thing might come down. Claustrophobia builds in my chest, and I have to focus on Tristan's legs in front of me to keep me going.

When we get to the end of the tunnel, and into a room where we can finally stand, the sounds of men in the room next to us as me crouching in a more defensible position. They sound much happier than the Fae we passed on the street, but I'm not completely comfortable with the idea of what could have made them so chipper. It's probably not anything that would make me feel safe.

"Come on," the boy says, pushing me forward. "You want to talk to Azalea, you're going to have to go in there."

Tristan gives him a tight nod. I want to grab his arm and lean on his strength as we head into the heart of the rebellion, but that would appear weak. I've already been weak for the rebellion. Those days are over. Instead, I straighten my spine and paint my face with a tight smile.

The door hits the wall with a loud bang as the boy shoves it open. The rumble of voices goes silent as Tristan and I stride into the room.

"Welcome Captain," Azalea says. She sits at her desk, watching us with red-rimmed eyes. "I never thought to see you here."

"Likewise," he says.

Men press back against the walls of the small room as they take in Tristan and I. Light filters in from the gaps in the roof and a few candles set up in holders along the wall. The remnants of a meal sit half eaten on the desk as though we just interrupted a meeting.

"And what brings you to our humble abode? Looking to get your hands on more humans? I heard you had replaced your men with our little spy." She gives him a hard smile without sparing me the slightest glance.

"Are we really going to waste each other's time with meaningless goading?" Tristan asks, the room going still.

Azalea stands, her clothes hanging on her slight frame. "Are you really going to come into my home and disrespect me?"

"It is not my intent to disrespect you. However, time is of the essence, and I am hoping to find a way for us to cooperate."

She pulls a dagger from her side strap and spins it on the desk. "You're hoping to work with us?"

"I believe it would be in both of our best interest to find common ground." Tristan keeps his voice light as though talking to a spooked animal.

Azalea slams the dagger into the desk, leaving it sticking straight up as she stalks toward us. "Now you want to find 'common ground'? Do you have any idea how long we've been working for change? Do you know how many p-people we've lost to the cause?" Her voice catches and I know she's thinking about Zale. The silver ring is still on her finger, and she lifts a hand to cover it when she sees me looking. "You're too late."

"I am only too late if you wish for their sacrifices to mean nothing."

My reflection dances back at me from off her dagger and I don't even recognize myself anymore. The soft lines the ocean used to show me have all been replaced with hard edges. I don't know which is more likely to have caused them: my time on land or losing Zale.

I jump as Azalea slams her hand down on the desk. "You know nothing of sacrifice."

"I know far more than you think. But this is not a comparison. I did not come here to be shamed or to shame you. I came here because I was hoping that we could work together. I was hoping that with your help we could create a better world." Tristan steps forward, holding out his hand to her. "Will you help me?"

I wait for her to laugh, to spit in his face, to do anything that I'm used to this hard woman doing. I have to say something before she can shoot us down.

"Zale gave me this to give you, before he..." I choke on the words that refuse to come out. Pulling the letter out of my pocket, I try not to wince at how crumpled up it is. It's nothing like I remember it being when I first saw it in Zale's pocket.

She paces behind the desk and wrenches her dagger free. I slide the letter across the marred wood surface, and she takes it with shaking fingers.

I never opened it after he gave it to me, so I have no idea what to expect from him, or from her. She slits the letter open with her dagger, her gaze roaming over the paper as they fill with the shadow of tears.

"What would you require of us and what would our reward be?" she asks, putting the letter in her desk and spinning the dagger between her fingers. She doesn't look at us, her gaze on the floor.

"I need someone to act as the human delegate. As I am sure you know, we lost the human delegate we came with at the same time as the King," Tristan says as Azalea winces. "Our mission will be the same as it always was. We are hoping to find peace between our people and a better balance. Things cannot continue as they have, and when I am King I refuse to look at humanity as my enemy. That idea is antiquated and not worth perpetuating."

"But you're not King, are you?" Azalea gives him a hard smile.

I don't know how many spies they have, but their network is *good*. If only they had let me be more involved with it the last time I was here. Maybe things would have gone better for Zale and me.

"I was appointed such until this afternoon," Tristan says. His fists clench and unclench, and I know he still hasn't come to terms with all the changes.

She leans against the desk. "But you are not such now."

"No," he agrees. "That is why I need your help. With the human delegate and the Seafolk delegate on our side, you will be able to act as my eyes and ears until we can set things right."

"And you really think a couple of humans will really be able to change things?" she asks. "Because we have been working to better the lives of humans for years with precious little to show for it."

"That was before you had my help."

It's hard not to admire Tristan's confidence. He stands there, shoulders wide in the den of the people who have been his enemies for years and barely bats an eye. Not only that, but he comes to offer them a deal without so much as pretending it's better for them than it is for him. Tristan may not have been raised to be the king, but I can see why his father wanted it for him so badly. He's a man who knows people and isn't afraid to take risks.

"Plus." I can't forget the news we just learned. "With the banished striking there's been issues on the seas with the beasts from below. Some of them are making their way on land. We don't have much time if we want to stop this progression without further loss of life."

"Okay." Azalea comes around from the desk, dagger still in her hand. "Let's finish this. For Zale."

CHAPTER

TWELVE

I expect there to be a lot of planning with the rebellion, but Tristan doesn't waste time with that. Instead, he asks Azalea to appoint a delegate that he can take back to the castle with us. It wouldn't surprise me if she picked herself, although there is much for her to do for her own people, but instead she gives me a sly smile and heads out through a side door.

"I don't like the way she looked at me," I whisper to Tristan as the men around the room finally start talking again. The show is officially over.

He grabs my hand and gives it a squeeze. "We are working together now. It would be in her best interest not to harm you."

"There's a lot of ways to cause harm that won't stop the cause."

Tristan shrugs and the door opens again. Azalea marches through, her body lighter than it's been the whole time we've been here.

"For our delegate, we offer you a little surprise." She waves her hand forward and a dark-skinned man steps into the room.

My breath catches in my chest and time stops. It's *Ry*. It's been a long time and though the last time I saw him was brutal, but I would still recognize him anywhere.

He's been outfitted in the rebellion's clothes, all traces of the sea left far behind, and it looks like he's been well-fed. The fullness he was lacking before has been replaced and his skin gleams with a healthy glow.

It's him. It's really him.

A whimper presses out from between my clenched lips and Ry glances at me with his dark eyes. "I—I…"

"I know," he says.

He takes a step forward and wraps his arms around me, holding me tight against his chest. Despite all the changes, he still smells like home. I nestle into him and take a deep breath, filling my lungs with the touches of salt, sea, and wood.

"We found him on one of our missions and decided we couldn't leave a fellow human behind," Azalea says with a shrug like saving my best friend was nothing to her.

Maybe it was. I don't know this woman well enough and it's not like I've ever seen her during normal circumstances. I wonder what she was like when she was happy. When she had my brother with her, at her side. Would her smile have been genuine and without the touch of malice I've been privy to?

"You have chosen him as your delegate?" Tristan asks. If he understands what this means to me, he's keeping it tight against his chest.

Azalea nods. "We've been waiting for a mission for him to come through. Plus, I think this will work out nicely. Ry and Mariel have worked together before so they should be good at finding solutions together now."

Tristan's jaw twitches and he jerks his head in agreement. Ry releases me and I take a step back from him, feeling guilty. The three of us working together will be about as cohesive as when it was us and Zale. I don't know if it's just that Tristan has a hard time working with those of us from the sea, or if he genuinely just doesn't care for the network of family I have.

"Is he ready to go then?" Tristan asks, voice sharper than it's been.

"He's been ready for weeks. It's been rough to have him rotting around here with nothing to do. Your little proposition came at just the right time. Plus..." She sits in her chair and eyes us with a wide smile that shows far too many teeth. "Ry is from the sea, so he understands the plight better than most. He knows what we have to fight for. He knows we won't hide in the shadows anymore."

Ry's body is tight as he watches her. His gaze holds more affection than I was expecting and it's like I'm looking at a stranger. The rebellion isn't a means to an end for him. This is real. The land has taken everyone I love from me. Is it already taking him too?

Not that I need him to look at *me* like that. I have Tristan. What he and I have is different from Ry and me. Even though there was that time when he wanted more... it's ridiculous and I'm sure he doesn't even think about it anymore. That's part of our past and it would be silly of me to drag it back up to the surface.

I just don't understand how he can want to be part of the rebellion. It's like Zale all over again. He's going to end up breaking me too.

"If that's what you wish." Tristan nods, his jaw clenched as he looks at Ry.

I try to see the situation from Tristan's perspective; I know we're in for trouble. Ry isn't polished in any way. He never was, but after everything that's happened to him on land, he definitely isn't now. They've dressed him and cleaned him, but there's a ripple of tension running through him that doesn't look like it's going away any time soon. He's a bomb that could go off at any time and ruin the negotiations Tristan is hoping for. Even with all that, he's the only option the rebellion is giving us and he's the one I want to be by my side. It's the best way I can protect him. That's all I want. I just need to keep him safe.

"Excellent," Azalea says, clapping her hands together. "I hope that this venture together is successful."

"I will do my best to ensure that it is, and to ensure his safety while he's with us." Tristan gives Ry a sidelong glance and I have to bite my lip to keep from beaming at him. He's going to help me fulfill my promise and I'll be able to keep the two people I'm most concerned about close to me.

"I would expect nothing less of you, Captain."

Ry turns and starts back towards the door without waiting for a more formal dismissal, glancing back at me once to make sure I'm following him. Tristan looks at me as if to ask if it's normal behavior for him and I can only shrug. I don't know what's normal for Ry anymore. The Ry I knew on the ship wouldn't have left without us, but how many times has he felt like I've abandoned him here? Maybe his problems lie solely with the Fae and that's why he looked at me and not at Tristan.

Or maybe he *does* remember that time before.

A twinge starts in my chest. There are going to be some hard conversations we need to have, and I'm afraid. I'm afraid of looking him in the eye and telling him that I've failed him. It's one thing for both of us to know it, and it's another to say it out loud. And there's so many kinds of failure to choose from when it comes to him.

I shuffle behind Ry, crawling back through the tunnel that will lead us home. Tristan follows, apparently trusting

Ry enough that he doesn't feel the need to protect me from him. That feels like a good start. I'm not sure that any other member of the rebellion would have been given that trust.

It's hard not to study Ry too closely as we move through the tunnel. Breaks in the ceiling let in just enough light to illuminate the rough walls and the dirty floors, and Ry's quickly moving form. He looks so much more like he did when we were home that it's a little jarring, especially after the last time we saw each other. What did Captain Wimark do to him when I was gone? How did the rebellion get its hands on him? It seems like every time I turn around the rebellion is involved in something it shouldn't be, but I'm grateful to them. I'm so incredibly grateful that they found him, and they cared for him. Tears well up in my eyes as I consciously realize for the first time that I always assumed I would be finding his body after all this time.

Ry leads us to the street, his gaze shifting around the alley as though expecting to find someone lurking in the shadows. When he finds no one, he gives Tristan a nod.

Tristan shakes his head and double-checks for himself. Ry grinds his teeth and doesn't move when Tristan comes up beside him, trying to see the clear path. They struggle in the shadows until both can see and decide it's okay to continue.

Tristan takes over bringing us back to the castle, and Ry moves back to walk with me. We fall into an easy pace together and my cheeks burn as I can feel him studying me. Has he wondered about me too? All this time I've thought he would be angry to see me after what he's been through, but he hasn't shown that at all.

Tristan leads us through the hallways and sets Ry up in a room next to mine. The furnishings are plain, but the bed is soft and a fire in the great brings warmth to the stone walls.

"I thought you two might be more comfortable this way. Having another human around and all," Tristan explains as Ry stands frozen in the space.

Everything Tristan has done since Ry was revealed has made me just want to squeeze him. He's being so thoughtful and kind. This room had to have been prepared before we left. Tristan had always planned for us to stay close to each other. He wanted to bring comfort to whatever human ended up on our team.

"When will the meeting be?" Ry asks, his voice rough from disuse.

It's the first time I've seen him open his mouth, and even while talking he keeps it as closed as possible. Still, I can see that he's had some magic done on him because there are no obvious gaps from the teeth he was missing when I saw him last.

"I need to alert the council to your presence," Tristan says. Is he not going to tell Ry we've basically been kicked out of the council? "If you would excuse me."

He gives me a long look before bending into a curt bow and leaving the room, closing the door softly behind him.

It's the first time Ry and I have been alone since that first night on land. My palms feel clammy as I press them into the folds of my skirt. We stare at each other, neither one of us sure what to do. I know what I'd *like* to do. I'd like to hug him tight and tell him I'm sorry with my face pressed to his chest so he can't see it. So he can't see how the guilt has been eating at me for months.

I wonder if I look as different to him as I do to myself. Land has changed us both and I'm still trying to decide if there's any part of it that's made us better.

"So..." I trail off, not sure what I even want to say.

"You look well," Ry says, his dark eyes surveying me in a way that makes me want to run away.

"I just got back." I'm not sure why that's the first thing I want to blurt out, as though it will absolve me of my sins, but that's what happens.

Ry nods, his dark curls barely moving. "I know."

"You know?"

"It is in the rebellion's best interest to keep tabs on you," he says with a shrug.

A cold rush travels down my spine. "The rebellion's been *watching* me?"

"It's possible you could become a threat to their interests."

"And what would they do if I was? Find a way to kill me?" I try to laugh as though the idea is ludicrous, but Ry's face doesn't change, so I know the idea is one that has been discussed.

I shift on my feet, trying to work out the discomfort running through my body. "I'm so sorry for what happened to you. I hope you know it was never my intention to leave you behind. I've thought of you constantly."

He clenches his jaw and I move my gaze to the floor. I can't look at him when he tells me I ruined him. It's his right to say it, so I won't stop him, but I know I'm not strong enough to look him in the eye when he does it.

"Ry, I'm so—"

"Don't say it." His voice is gruff. "Don't say anything else."

"But I want to—"

"I don't want you to. Saying it won't change anything. It won't help, not really."

A lump grows tight in my throat and my eyes burn. I give him a nod, the motion feeling like it wants to kill me. I want to run away. I want to find Tristan and bury my head in his chest. I want to be as far away from Ry as possible. Could I retreat to my room without causing any further damage between us? He probably wouldn't even care.

"I retrieved this for you, from the rebellion. I saw it amongst the discarded things and figured you'd want it back." He shifts as he pulls out a charred piece of wood. "I'm not sure what happened to it. I guess this could have been after we were separated."

My hands tremble as I take the wood from him. The tears I was trying so hard to hold in flood down my cheeks as I hold Zale's sunburst in my hand. Ry's right, something happened to it after I left when the rebellion promised to take care of it and return it to me. It leaves ashy prints behind on my fingers as I touch the charred wood. I really shouldn't be surprised, it's one of the smallest promises to me that they broke.

Still, to hold something of Zale's in my hand. To feel the wood that he spent forever smoothing out. The color has changed from the fire, turning his careful creation black and fragile. The once strong wooden lines becoming thin and brittle. Even so, it's like having a piece of Zale returned to me.

When I look up at Ry, I can't even see him anymore through the blurry haze of my tears. He's just a dark shadow, just like the rest of my past and even more of my future.

"Thank you." The words are weak and quiet, but I know he hears them. I know they pierce him right in the heart the way his gift did to me.

He moves to touch me before pinning his arms to his sides. "What happened to him?" Ry asks, his voice equally as quiet.

I run my fingers over the sun burst, my fingers turning black from the ashes. "I don't know. Everything was fine, and then the King was dead, and he was telling me to run, but I didn't. I didn't and they killed him."

It feels like my heart is cracking in two to say the words out loud. I've known it for days, but I've been able to push it away. I've been able to hide from the truth. But I can't do that with Ry.

Ry's lips thin as his frown deepens. "The Fae killed him, and you still think we can work with them."

"Tristan is different." I know how pathetic those words sound. "And I'm not sure we have a choice. If we don't work with him, there'll be no way to help our people."

"The rebellion thinks—"

"The rebellion doesn't know what I know. Have you even heard what's happening out on the sea?" My hands want to clench, and I have to be careful not to break my last piece of Zale in my moment of anger.

Ry waves away my question. "What's happening on the sea is the same thing that's always happening. We live, we suffer, we do the Fae's bidding."

"Zale changed that. He convinced everyone to strike."

Ry's face brightens, his lips almost curving into a grin. "Good for him."

"No, you don't understand." How could so much change between us? Ry was never all about the human's plight like Zale was. Has spending so much time with the rebellion changed that? Frustration makes me want to pull my hair out. "Because of the strike bad things are happening."

"Bad things?" Ry's voice is bland.

"Yes." A frustrated groan squeaks past my lips. "With so much garbage sinking, it's hurting the Seafolk—"

"Who cares about them? It's not like they've ever been any help."

"Maybe not." I can give him that concession. After all, we've shared the ocean with them for lifetimes and rarely do we even *see* them, let alone get any kind of meaningful aid. "But they came to us because the beasts of the deep are waking. The pollution is drawing them back out. Our people are dying, Ry. I saw this, this *thing* with long tentacles take down a whole ship. And not only that, but the lesser beasts are coming onto land. It won't be long before everyone is suffering. We have to stop it."

"You're so naive, Mariel. You have to realize they're all just using you," Ry says, his voice growing softer as he touches my arm. "You can't give them that kind of power over you."

I can't take anymore. Stomping to the door, I look back at Ry once before leaving. "I'm trying to help you understand what's going on. If you want to be too stupid, or too brainwashed to realize that we have a place in this world that's important, then good luck to you."

I slam the door behind me and use the heel of my hand to wipe away my tears before going to find Tristan.

"Mariel?"

I'm glad it doesn't take long to find him and completely collapse into his surprised arms. He grips me tight as weak, dry whimpers ripple through my chest.

I don't know how this all went so wrong. I've lost Zale forever, and even though Ry is here, he still feels a million miles away. This isn't the friend who came with me. The realization that Ry has become as much a stranger as Zale makes my chest ache.

When I feel like I can breathe again, I step out of his arms and take a deep breath. "Were you able to get Ry and I involved in the next meeting?"

Tristan's looks of concern immediately darken. "William doesn't care for it, but there is nothing he can do. It was the last act of my father, and they want to honor him, even if they refuse to stand up for his wishes concerning who should be king."

"Still, that's a good start, right?" I need some sort of good news. I can't keep going into so much bleakness.

He nods, frown still permeating his face. "Yes. It is a

start, but we need more. I need to find a way to be allowed in myself."

"Remember when you wanted nothing to do with the throne?" I try to tease him and bring back some sort of smile. I know *I* would feel much better if he could smile at me.

"That was before my father died. That was before I felt forced into it. There is no way out for me anymore. I could never in good conscience leave my brother to handle the war I am positive he created with his foolishness."

"You really think his quest for a bride is why the border is having problems?"

"I do not think it, I know it." Tristan finally gives me a smile but there's little humor in it. "My brother has always had a blustering nature that many find distasteful."

Many do, but not Anneliese. The thought just brings more questions.

"Do you think whatever deal he has with Anneliese will smooth a lot of that over?" I ask. He has to see it, right?

Tristan shakes his head. "She will do her best, but they would be foolish to let her. No matter what she does with him, they must know that he is a mess."

"Could he be under her spell?" I can't help but remember how it was when she was able to snag Tristan. It was scary to look into his eyes and not see him staring back at me.

"That kind of magic has no sustainability. She wouldn't be able to keep control over him for long enough. Plus, using magic takes a physical toll on us. Anneliese may be willing to use hers to further her agenda, but she would not want it to show. She is far too vain for that."

Tristan glances around the empty hallway and grabs my arm. "If you want to continue this conversation, we need to move. We're too exposed here."

I don't fully understand him. All I want is to expose Anneliese for the sneaky little spider she is. I hope someone was around to hear my accusations.

Still, I don't complain as Tristan guides me through the castle. His grip on me is warm and more comforting than I'd like to admit.

We've come a long way together. It's still strange to think that just a few months ago I considered him my enemy and was afraid he'd turn me in. Now we're working together and have teamed up with the rebellion to keep the Fae in line. It's unbelievable. It's like I'm living in a fever dream, but the pressure of Tristan's hand on my arm is all too real.

He stops at a long tapestry hanging on the wall, its fringe touching the floor in a soft sweep. He brushes it aside and pulls me after him. I'm about to tease him about his inappropriate place for us to hide, leaning in closer for a kiss, but then I see the tiny door set in the wall behind it. My stomach sinks. It's okay. Who needs affection when there's work to be done? He takes me through the secret passageway, the sound of our steps hidden by the thick stone walls. It's so dark I can't make out his back as he travels in front of me, but he walks with such sureness that I know I won't be left behind.

"I used to play in these tunnels when I was a boy," he whispers. "My father made sure I knew about them so I would have a place to escape if the worst happened."

"What could have been so bad to thrust a boy into super scary tunnels?" I try to keep a laugh in my voice so that he doesn't know just how terrifying being back here would be if he lost his grip on me.

"The same thing that kept me away for so many years. Some courtiers would be all too happy to eliminate threats to the throne."

"But you never wanted it," I point out.

Tristan laughs. "That never mattered. Nor did the fact that I was just a boy. It was when there was an attempt to poison me that my mother decided we had to leave. She had done her best to protect me by refusing any title that my father tried to throw at us. She knew that that would only encourage them and make the courtiers think that I would be coming back for real power, so she always said no."

"What happened to your mother?" In all our time together, he's never said much about her, even though it's obvious he admires her.

His footsteps still, leaving us motionless in the dark tunnel. In the silence, all I can hear is the heavy beat of my heart as it quickens its activity.

"She died," he finally says. "It was not easy for her to live away from court or away from my father. She withered away for a long time until she died."

"Tristan, I'm so sorr—"

"Stop." Tristan's sigh is ragged. "I have heard so many apologies for her."

I reach up and squeeze his hand. If he won't let me say the words out loud, I can find another way to give him my sympathies. I know what it's like to lose someone. I feel like all I've done for months is grieve.

He places his large hand on top of mine, then moves to envelop me in his arms. His strong body and the smell of the outdoors still clinging to his tunic help transport me away from the stale air of the tunnel. I press my face into his shoulder as he clings tighter to me. His muscles are taut, completely wound up with the memories of his mother and his time here with her.

We hold each other tighter and tighter, our bodies

searching for ways to lose the emotions coursing between us.

"Mariel, I—"

"Shhh," I stop him. I don't need his apologies for showing me this weakness. This is between he and I and the cold stone walls. There's no need to feel embarrassed here where I can't even see his face.

His chest shudders and he lowers his head to be next to mine. We stay locked in our embrace for what feels like hours but is probably only a few minutes. The fight and the stress of the last few days passes between us, leaving me feeling limp.

I've used so much anger and fear to keep me upright and moving, can I work as well when I've laid that aside? I want to leave it all in this dark hallway and never come back. But am I strong enough to be able to fight on my own? Is just Mariel enough?

Tristan gives me one last hard squeeze and releases me, the cold tunnel air blasting against my face without his warmth to block it.

"We really have no time for this," he says. "Though I wish this was what I could fill all my days with."

His fingers are gentle as he takes my hand and leads me through the tunnel once more. It feels like something has settled between us, but I don't have the words for what that might be. All I know is that I trust him. Despite everything I've always trusted him. No matter what happens next, Tristan will know what to do to fix it and I'll be right beside him.

TRISTAN'S TUNNEL ends and he pushes aside another tapestry to reveal his room. I had never spent much time looking at the art he collected, but there behind the knight and his lady is the entrance to the secret tunnel.

I stand in the middle of the room, processing, as Tristan builds up the fire in the grate. He glances up at me and my confusion must show on my face because he lets out a sharp laugh.

"The King thought it would be prudent for me to have an emergency exit from my room should the courtiers get any wild ideas," he explains.

"Have you ever had to use it?" I run my hand over the thick material of the door as it swings back into place.

He runs a hand through his hair and gives me a sheepish grin. "Never for what my father wanted me to. I suppose the other Fae thought it would be hard to sneak in and out of my room unnoticed. However, I did use it a number of times to get up to mischief."

The idea of a young Tristan sneaking around the castle makes me smile. Stepping closer to him, I rest my hand on his shoulder as he watches the fire he's made leap up in jagged spikes of flame.

"This will not be easy," he says in a whisper as the humor drains from his face.

"Maybe not, but I'm ready to work."

I'm tired of waiting for Anneliese and the Prince to make their moves and leave us scrambling. We've let her get away with too much. What would she have done if I'd rejected her terms that day in the dungeon? She never would have had the means to become part of the council. So much of what's happening now is my fault. With Zale gone, it all rests on me now. It doesn't matter what he did when he's not here to take responsibility for any of it.

"What do you propose we do?" Tristan rests his hand on mine, drawing small circles with his thumb.

Delight builds in my chest at the contact and the trust.

I'm just a banished and he knows that, but he believes in me. He brushes a strand of hair behind my ear, his attention making my face grow warm.

"We need to find out what Anneliese is up to. Something isn't sitting right with me that she's abandoned you so quickly."

Tristan laughs. "Especially when William will not even consider making her his bride. Did you know they're cousins?"

"Cousins?" My stomach threatens to turn. "But that would mean you and her—"

"Not at all." He pulls me forward to sit on the rug beside him. "You see, William and I have different mothers, hence all the issues we have discussed. Anneliese is his cousin on his *mother*'s side. Anneliese is nothing to me. It is why she entertained the idea of a marriage between us in the first place."

I bite my lip as frustration ripples through me. "It doesn't make any sense then that she would abandon you for him. With her support, it wouldn't have been hard to keep you on the throne when the Prince returned."

"You're probably right, but Anneliese has always had a method, even if you cannot see it yet."

Leaning my head onto his shoulder, I breathe his scent in and try to make sense of it all. Tristan is right, there's probably some deeper plot going on that I don't realize yet.

"How did she get Captain Wimark onto the council?" I hated seeing his darkly smug face at that table. That man alone is responsible for almost every trouble I've had. Without him, I never would have known Zale was even on land to come and mess everything up in the first place.

Tristan sighs. "Not long after our arrangement became mildly public, if not official, there happened to be a vacancy on the council for the military board member. She was quick to suggest his name and there are many who think his exploits have been excellent, regardless of if they are ethical."

I'll just *bet* there was a vacancy. Is that what Anneliese promised him to get him to work for her?

"Anneliese has been busy since I've been gone," I comment dryly.

"Do not underestimate her. Anneliese is always plotting, even if it looks like she is sitting back and being a lady."

He's right. Even when I did have access to her room, she was always busy with something. Her ladies knew that too and talked about her interests. I didn't care much about any of it until she'd turned her attention to me. A shiver runs down my spine at the idea of how close I came to death at her hands.

"Do you think she killed the King?" It's a valid question considering her connection to everything.

Tristan shakes his head, his legs shifting underneath me. "She would never go that far. She's cunning, not stupid."

I frown at how quickly he brushes away my idea, but who am I to disagree? He knows this woman far better than I do. Although maybe that's to his detriment. He knows she's a snake but hasn't had experience with her bite like I do. He can't have if he's so naïve to her desire for power.

"Then what do we do now?"

Tristan smiles and wraps an arm around my shoulder. His gaze dips to my lips.

I can't help it, I giggle. He's beautiful and beyond amazing, and he still wants to spend time with *me*. He enjoys these moments with me just as much as I do with him, even when I know we have better things we should be doing.

Still, I don't stop him as he leans closer to me, his breath grazing my cheek as he presses his lips to my skin.

"Do you have any idea how much I missed you?" he asks, voice so quiet that the crackling of the fire almost makes it impossible to hear.

"You can't have missed me that much. All I do is make trouble for you."

He presses a kiss against my neck and shivers pool in my stomach. "That may be the case, but a quiet life is nothing without you in it. Plus," he points out, "you left me with Anneliese, so things were troublesome even without you here."

The mention of her name has me scrambling to get up, but Tristan holds me firmly in place. His hand trails down my spine and lands on the small of my back as he pulls me closer to his firm chest.

"I'm so sorry for doing that to you. I thought about it constantly while we were apart. I was so worried that---"

He shakes his head and laughs. "You never had to worry about me. I can more than take care of myself where Anneliese is concerned. Plus, she has nothing on you."

My reflection in his eyes is small as I turn to look at him. My gaze travels across his face, cataloging his scars. There's still so much about this man that I don't know. In many ways we still feel like the strangers we were when we first met in the forest. There are still so many things happening that terrify me. But there are no lies between us anymore. We're in this together. The goals have changed, but our link has stayed the same.

He moves slowly, giving me every opportunity to pull away before he gently presses his lips to mine. I couldn't leave even if I wanted to, which I don't. He's the only person I have left here. Except Ry. A pang of pain shoots through my stomach. Things may be different, but he's still here.

I wrap my arms around his shoulders and deepen the kiss, letting the pressure build between us as I leave thoughts of Ry behind. This is how it should be. No fear of the next step, no fight, just this feeling of *living*.

A hard knock on the door forces us apart. Tristan gives me an apologetic smile before helping me off his lap and striding to the door. His shoulders are tight again, the pressures of what his father wanted for him coming back in full force.

"My—Your—" the Fae at the door stumbles over his words, he, like us, has no idea what title Tristan carries anymore.

"Carry on," Tristan says with a wave of the hand, his voice tired.

"You asked me to let you know when the council was meeting again, sir."

"And?"

He wrings his tunic in his hands, face strained as he forces the words out. "Well, sir, they are meeting now."

"Did they ask for the human or sea delegate?" Tristan asks.

"No, sir."

"Will you please escort them for me?" Tristan's voice becomes too sweet as he hides the anger I know is building in his chest. "The sea delegate is right here, and you know where the human delegate is staying."

The man gives a quick nod, his eyes growing wide as they take me in. I do my best to save him from himself and put my hand on his arm to guide him from the room.

"I'll expect a report later," Tristan tells me. His face is firm, but he gives me a small wink before he closes the door.

CHAPTER

FOURTEEN

Loud rhythmic thumping echoes down the hall from Ry's room. My feet threaten to slow, the memory of our last conversation is all too recent, but I straighten my back and continue. The Fae takes a deep breath before knocking on the door and the thumping stops immediately.

Ry cracks the door open just enough to see his eyes in the dark room. "Yes?"

"I am to take you to the council meeting," the man squeaks.

Whatever he thought about me, he obviously thinks Ry is way scarier. From how he was talking before, the man might be right. I'm not sure what Ry would do if he were left alone with a Fae.

"Perfect," Ry says as he swings the door open, his teeth gleaming in the torchlight. He puts a small ball in his pants pocket, and I realize the source of the noise. At least he's keeping himself occupied, I just hope he didn't scuff up the walls with his rubber ball.

We hustle after the little man, his speed increasing now

that he has all his cargo. I didn't talk with Tristan about what I should say to the council. I guess that's assuming they let me in and say anything at all. Should I tell them about the sea's plight? That's my job here. That's why the Seafolk picked me. But should it be something that we can leverage? I should have asked Tristan before I left.

We reach the council room doors, Captain Wimark still posted outside them, his face bored as he watches us.

"I have the other delegates," the man squeaks before running back the way we came.

Captain Wimark watches him go with hunger in his eyes. Is he remembering how he tortured Ry the last time they were together?

"Aren't you going to let us in?" I ask him, keeping all the authority I can muster in my voice.

His gaze drifts back to us and a lazy smile takes up residence on his face. "I was not told the delegates were invited to this particular meeting."

"There are things of great importance I'm supposed to share. Are you really going to bar the door to me?" My shoulders grow tight as I pull them back even farther and give Captain Wimark a bored expression even as my heart threatens to leap from my chest.

"Are you really that interested in entering a room where you're not wanted?"

"Are *you* really interested in standing out in the hallway all night to wait for a man who isn't coming?"

Captain Wimark scowls. "To protect the council is a great honor."

"But not one usually bestowed on council members themselves," I point out.

He scowls and taps a finger against his cheek. "I am tasked with making sure a certain false King is not allowed entrance. They said nothing of a bunch of humans."

Of course, they didn't. What threat are we without Tristan to back us up?

Captain Wimark gives us a grin that makes goosebumps prickle along my arms as he opens the door. The room inside is dark with no windows, only a line of torches to offer light to the group gathered around the table.

If this were just a few months ago, I would have taken Ry's hand for strength before going in. Even now I wish I could just for solidarity, but I don't recognize the Ry I'm with anymore. I don't need anyone else's strength but my own.

We stride into the room, looking like we're supposed to be there. Anneliese sits beside the Prince at the head of the table and gives us a thoughtful look as we find empty seats.

"So glad you could make it," she says with a wicked smile.

I don't know why she bothers, everyone in this room should be familiar enough with her to know she's lying. Maybe she just likes playing the lady even if she's really a spider.

The Prince doesn't look at us at all. Instead, he motions for the man who was speaking when we came in to continue.

"With the kelpies coming on land, our farms are most affected. Without Fae willing to work them, there will be no crops to harvest this fall," says the Fae seated towards the middle in a bright purple tunic. "You must realize how serious this threat is."

"I *must* not do anything," the Prince spits, his face turning a mottled red as he stares at the man. "However, I do agree that this is a grave problem."

My heart beats harder against my chest. This is my opening. This is why I'm here. Do I need to raise my hand? Can I just start talking? My chair scrapes along the floor as I contemplate standing, drawing attention toward me.

"Yes?" the Prince asks me with a sneer.

"Well, you see—"

"Actually, I do not see."

Flustered, I feel my face turning red. "This is why the Seafolk sent me. There have been issues with the human's production of late and it is waking the beasts below. They have quickly become a threat to the Seafolk and will soon become yours, too."

"Is that so." The Prince turns to look at Ry who doesn't budge under his toxic gaze. "And what do the humans have to say for themselves?"

I expect Ry to clear his throat or do anything that implies he's uncomfortable, but he stays settled back in his chair, watching them with a small smile. "The humans have decided they no longer agree to the terms created for them centuries ago. They're not willing to work until those terms are revisited."

The Prince snarls, his lips pulling up to reveal his pointed canines. "Do the humans really think themselves so important that they can strike, and we will be forced to come running?"

"Well, actually..." My voice stays calm even as my heart pounds against my chest. "That is part of the reason that I'm here. The Seafolk have been directly affected. With the added garbage sinking lower to pollute their water, they're suffering physically. Not only that, but it's awakened the beasts of the deep. It's their stirrings that have caused the issue with the kelpies."

A woman towards the end of the table leans forward. "That would make sense. We have never had a problem with the sea creatures before. Our deal with the Seafolk has been enough to keep them all in check."

There's a slow rumbling of assent and the urge to grin grows across my face even as I keep it carefully blank.

"This is ridiculous." Anneliese's voice rings out across the room and the noise settles. "The humans have no control over any of this. Their pathetic actions could never affect *us*!"

The grumbling begins anew. Of course, it would. Anneliese is placating them. They all want to feel like they live on the top of the food chain, even if it's all a lie. Zale may have been wrong about how he went about it, but he was right that our actions matter.

The Prince scowls as he glances at Anneliese. Has she been causing more trouble for him? I still can't fathom that she would think that he would consider her as a potential bride when they're cousins. It's unfathomable, and that's coming from one of the banished. It's not like we have a big dating pool.

"Regardless, we have no time for these squabbles." The Prince smiles at the table. "The issue with the kelpies will sort itself out. What will not be so easily taken care of is the small matter of the army marching across our border from Naicroft. Those Fae are a much more serious issue than some little sea problem."

"If you don't sort things with the humans, there will be more than kelpies coming for you," I warn. "The kelpies are only the beginning. The Seafolk have little control over their people when they're constantly fearing for their lives."

"We care little for the Seafolk's problems. What could their *sea beasts* do to us?"

Several people chuckle at the Prince's words. After all, when he phrases it like that, what do they have to fear? They don't live on the sea. It isn't absurd that they would think themselves safe here.

I grab at the necklace the Seafolk gave me to remind

myself of my promise before I try again. "You've already seen how there are many creatures of the sea that are not confined by the shore's limits. Do you really want to take the chance that they will stay in tainted water without the promise of change? I don't see that going well for you."

The Prince scowls at me and I lean back in my seat. I've done what I promised I would do. If they don't want to listen, then that's their choice. I can't force them to agree with me. I can't force them to see reason.

Still, when the Prince brought up the upcoming army, his hands had a slight tremble to them as he pressed them to the table. The consequences of his actions are catching up to him. *What might we find if we decided not to fight? Would they be willing to take the Prince as payment for his supposed crimes?*

The idea makes me smile, something Anneliese doesn't miss as she watches me across the table. I glance away but can still feel her gaze burning into me. What's she planning for me? Is there any way I might be able to strike first? Not without Tristan's help.

"Do you not require your military councilman to discuss any strategies?" asks a man towards the end of the table. "How serious is the Naicroft threat?"

My muscles tense at the idea of Captain Wimark being invited back in, but it might give Tristan an opening. I don't know if he'd take it or not, but it would exist if he wanted to.

"Wimark is fine where he is," the Prince says. He glances at the door, his shoulders tight.

Anneliese gives him the same dark smile she often shows me.

"Unfortunately for us, Naicroft is much more of a threat than I would like. Their army is bigger than ours, should they choose to use it all against us. I was sent there to help procure peace, but it was not peace they wanted."

Is Captain Wimark the reason why Anneliese has been able to get such a firm grasp on the Prince? I glance at the closed door and back at the sweating Prince. What did he do to ruin any peace negotiations *and* send their army marching our way? That sounds like more than just a failed marriage proposal.

"What do you propose then in regard to your problem, *Prince?*"

I don't catch who said it, but the Prince is out of his chair so fast that it clatters to the floor despite being made of heavy wood.

"Do you dare mock me?" he demands, face turning red.

"Do not bother yourself with them," Anneliese says as she places her hand on his arm with a smile. His eyes grow unfocused as she continues talking. "Let them know your grand plan."

"My—my plan is." He sways on his feet and moves out of her reach, shaking his head as though to get Anneliese's magic out of it. "We will meet the army where it is. We will not wait for them to meet us here and risk so many civilians. We will have to send a contingent group out to meet them on the road."

"Are you not concerned that they will be able to take down the men you dispatch and continue moving forward without your knowledge?" Anneliese gives me a knowing smile and trails her hand down the Prince's sleeve. He shudders.

The woman is insane. There's really no other option. How can she think she can get away with all these levels of manipulation? The Prince obviously doesn't want to give her what she wants but she just keeps pushing. What will happen if he's able to get Captain Wimark moved out of the castle? Will she still be able to maintain her control over him? If he's on his own, it's possible we could sway him away from her. There's no way he can like working with her.

The Prince shakes his head again. "No, that will not be possible. You forget, I've spent much time with these people. I know they wouldn't expect us to do anything so daring. They still believe my father rules, and he was not known for having an offensive nature."

"Who would you send then?" the Fae man next to me asks.

The Prince must see his moment because his mouth opens with glee before Anneliese stops him.

"We'll have to think on that before we send any men," she says quickly. "We would hate to risk the future of our country on any hasty decisions." She reaches to grab the Prince's hand and he yanks it away from her.

"I have a few men I am already considering though," the Prince says, his gaze flickering toward the door.

"And you really believe this will eliminate the threat? There are no worries about enacting a bigger war with this kind of action?" someone else asks.

"No. This should clear it all up."

I shake my head. The Prince is dreaming if he thinks a small group will take down his inconvenient neighbors.

"And what about the humans?" Ry asks.

I gasp, staring at him with wide eyes. Doesn't he realize how careful he needs to be around the Fae? We're not welcome here, not really. We don't have an army to back us up if the Prince decides there's no longer a need for a human within the castle.

"The humans are nothing to us," Anneliese says without even glancing at Ry. "We will take care of the issue as it comes to us. There is no need to negotiate with them."

The Prince's face grows red. "You are overreaching your station," he hisses at Anneliese.

She reaches a hand for him, and he pulls away. "I am simply trying to help you."

"I do not need help; I am the King." He straightens his shoulders, but still looks more like a boy playing dress-up than an actual king.

"I did not mean to distress you," she says while trying to touch him again. "I only want to help. After all, this is a job we will soon be doing together."

The Prince stands up so fast his chair clatters to the ground. "That will never be an option."

"But I thought—"

"You have done your best to wheedle, but it will never work." The Prince pulls on his tunic to smooth out the creases. "There will be no arrangement between us, Anneliese. You will never be my bride."

Her face goes red as she rises to her feet. Her hands twitch, but the Prince doesn't allow her to get close to him. No one does as she rushes from the room, her skirts swishing behind her.

"If we could discuss the situation with the humans again," Ry tries again.

"This meeting is over," the Prince says, not even glancing toward Ry. "We will continue forward in getting a group together to take out the army. We shall meet again when this disaster has been taken care of."

Ry hisses between his teeth, but I'm the only one who hears it as everyone else gets up to leave and the sound of wood scraping on wood fills the room. I give him a warning glance as he stands. If he does anything rash now, it could ruin our future ability to look like we're serious in front of the Fae. I'd really like to be invited back to the council when Tristan is in charge again. If he's ever in charge again.

I should go right back to Tristan and let him know what happened, but once again I'm tempted to follow Anneliese instead. She's hiding more than the terrible things I can already see. And there's so much of that.

Jaw clenched, I follow her from the room. The hallway still has several other Fae in it, but her dark red dress is hard to miss. My boots are soft against the stone as I take the same left that she did, going further into the castle than I've been before.

A hand grips my arm and yanks me back. I twist in agitation and find Ry staring down at me, his face screwed up in a scowl.

"What do you think you're doing?" he asks in a tight whisper.

"Leave me alone." I turn to get a glimpse of Anneliese, but she's disappeared down the hallway. I heave an exasperated breath as I wrench myself out of his grip. "What is your problem?"

He grabs me again and pulls me back towards the more familiar parts of the castle.

"You can't follow her, Mariel. Do you want to get yourself killed?"

"If I did, it would be my own business," I hiss back at him. "You don't get to decide for me."

The words feel funny in my mouth after all times I've tried to tell him what to do. Fat lot of good that's done either of us. I don't know if him following me ruined his life, or the times that he didn't. Either way, it's a mess that I've helped create.

"I'm not trying to decide for you. I'm trying to help you make a better choice. If you want to follow her, that's fine, but do it with a *plan.* Unless getting yourself killed is what you're after. If that's the case, let me know and I'll leave you alone." He thrusts me into the hallway, the bright torch-light casting his face in shadow. "There's so much about this world that you don't understand."

I cross my arms over my chest, trying not to look like a petulant child but I know I'm failing. There's a lot I don't know, but I've spent months thinking about this place. About him. I want to understand the castle and the Fae but in this moment all I can think about is how I can't even understand him anymore. How could he work with the rebellion? After everything they've taken from me, they've taken him too. My eyes burn and I have to look away at him before tears can fall.

"We're here for a reason, Mariel. Don't mess it up. Ask me for help if you need it."

"Would you even give it to me, or would you ask the rebellion for permission?" I keep my voice hard so my tears can stay tightly locked up.

Ry's jaw drops. "Is that really what you think? Mariel, the rebellion saved me. That doesn't mean they own me."

"You're going to be just like Zale," I whisper.

Ry grabs my hands, holding them firmly between his own. "That's not going to happen. The rebellion will only come between us if you let it."

I war with myself, not sure what I'm more upset about. I did this to him. I forced him into this position and now I'm mad at him for taking it? If I don't know him, it's only because of everything I've put him through since we left our ship.

I don't say anything and Ry sighs. He lets go of my hands, shoulders tight.

With a last look at me, he strides away, looking like he's lived in the castle all his life. There's so much that's happened to us since we started this journey. I have to believe that there's some way to get me back my friend. There's just too much I have to do and I wish he wasn't on my list. I wish we were just fixed.

"Ry, wait!" I chase after him, ready to say I'm sorry, ready to let the rebellion issue go, but he's already gone.

FIFTEEN

Tristan actually laughs out loud when I tell him about the Prince and Anneliese.

"They're playing a vicious game," he says with a smile as he invites me to sit with him on his chair again. "Perhaps we need not worry about them as much as I thought. They could take care of each other for us."

I bite my lip to try and stifle the disagreement coursing through me, but it doesn't work. "Perhaps Anneliese will take care of the Prince, but *who* will take care of Anneliese?"

"You give her too much credit. She has her eye on the throne. She's not as smart as you think she is."

I raise my brow at him, and he shrugs. After what I've seen from her firsthand, I'd have to be a fool to dismiss her so quickly. Why does Tristan find it so easy?

"You're not interested at all in what she's up to?"

He sighs. "Mostly, I find myself being grateful that she has moved her focus onto my brother."

"She could still be a threat." I wiggle off his lap and he grunts in protest.

I pace in front of the fireplace, tapping my finger against my cheek.

She's trying to manipulate the Prince like she did with Tristan, this much I already know. He's more aware of her power than Tristan was though and seems to be doing his best to avoid it. Now that I think of it, he looked *scared* of it. I can't say I blame him. Not having control over your own mind would be terrifying. Is that how she was able to get Captain Wimark on the council? One little touch from her and she was able to make all her dreams come true? It's highly possible and would explain why the Prince is more familiar with her 'work.' How was she able to succeed in that, yet not becoming his bride?

Tristan watches me think with heavy eyes. He doesn't believe me in this one, but that's okay. He doesn't have to believe me to be helpful. He's proven that in the past.

Before I can create a rut in the carpet with my pacing, Tristan slides from the chair onto the floor, blocking my next step. With a gentle hand, he guides me to my knees, then lies across the carpet, and I follow suit. How can I not, when I want nothing more than to be as close to him as possible? Focusing on the issues at hand is a task to be reckoned with when he's this close as well, but I know he can help me.

I thrust my fists into the rug. "Will you help me figure out what she's up to?"

"What about your issues with the Seafolk? Are you not more worried about your cause to help them and the humans?" Tristan asks, taking my fist in his hand to massage it.

"Finding out what she's up to will help them, I guarantee it."

Tristan gives me a long look. "Your guarantees have not paid out well in the past."

I know he's talking about what happened with my brother, and that's something I'll have to accept. I didn't know him well. I thought I did, but he changed too much when he came here. Just like Ry. Just like me. But I'm doing better, and Ry will too. We're going to make it out of this, even if Zale couldn't.

"This time, I promise it will be different. She's up to something. I can *feel* it. And she's not just some pretty courtier looking to find the best match. There's something else behind it all." I grab his hand in mine. "Will you help me?"

He shakes his head, but a gentle smile grows on his face. "Have I not shown you enough by not for you to trust me? I will always help you, even if I'm not sure why I am doing it."

That's good enough for me.

I throw my arms around his neck, nestling a kiss against his cheek. He wraps his arms around my waist, pulling me closer to him. This is it. This is what makes being here so much better than anything at home.

~

Unfortunately for Tristan, I won't stay distracted by him for long. He's right, I need to remember why I'm here. I'm fighting for my family and friends that cannot fight for themselves, I'm fighting for the Seafolk that are so easily forgotten by their counterparts on land. The stakes are far too high for me to forget I'm here to take action, and not to get caught up in rekindling what I thought I'd lost with Tristan.

I'm not just Mariel anymore. I haven't been for a long time.

"We need to figure out how to get things moving and I think we might have an opening."

"Moving?" Tristan asks. His face screws up with confusion as I slide out of his all-too-distracting arms.

"Moving in your direction, moving so that my people get what they need. Captain Wimark is most likely going to be leaving soon on a little trip, and that's going to leave Anneliese exposed and the Prince ready to act." I climb to my feet, excitement pouring through my blood.

Tristan rolls over, his elbows holding him up as he looks at me. "Just because Captain Wimark will be gone doesn't make them any less dangerous."

"I know, but it means their muscle won't be here to help them and we have to take all the wins we can get."

Tristan reaches for my leg, but I step out of his reach.

"I want to support you, and I will, but this seems a little hasty," he says with a groan.

"I know, but that's the only way it can work. We have to take them by surprise." And not just them, either. If I let myself think about it too much, I'll scare myself out of it. I need less time to come up with the worst-case scenarios, and the biggest potential heart tug is one I can easily take care of. "And I think we need to do this without Ry."

Tristan sits up, his brows pulling down. "Without Ry? Isn't he your friend? Plus, he's our connection to the rebellion, and we want them as an option for backup. If you alienate him now, they might not help us when you want them to."

"I know, I know." I wince. He's not making this any easier on me.

I don't know how to say anything else without losing it. . Ry's been through a lot. I know he has. And I've done this to him by leaving him behind. Now he's hurt, and he needs help and it's all because of me. I should be able to do this little thing for him. I should be able to let things go. I owe him that.

"He has experienced much since you saw him last," Tristan tries to reason. "It makes sense that you would not feel as close to him as you once did."

"That's not it." I feel the wind being taken from my sails and my chest deflates. "It almost feels like he's my enemy. He's working with the rebellion!"

Tristan climbs to his feet and grabs my hand. "I think this is more about you trying to figure out who he is now than it is about how you feel."

"I know how I feel."

Tristan squeezes my hand and I pull it away. "There has been a lot for you to take in. It's okay if it takes a while for you to come around. But Ry is on our team, and we need to keep him there. Like I said, he is our connection to the rebellion. We might need them later."

"So we should make sure Ry stays unaware that he's not included then."

Tristan shakes his head, but I won't be budged in this. There's something weird there and if he's around I won't be able to do anything. I want to trust him, but he's just so different now. He feels too much like how Zale used to. I do my best to ignore the sharp pang in my chest at the thought of my brother.

Plus, what better way to save him from himself than by keeping him out of direct action.

I grab a piece of sweet bread off the little table beside his chair and take a bite of victory. This has to work. It's what's best for everyone.

∽

As I predicted, the Prince finds a way to get Captain Wimark on the team sent to deal with the issues at the border. With him gone, I feel much more confident skulking around the castle. Not that Anneliese isn't a threat of her own, but I don't have to worry about being locked up again.

My hand trails over my wrist where scars still pepper my skin from when I got out of my manacles and wince. I don't ever want to face prison again.

Captain Wimark has only been gone a few hours when I take up the task of finding Anneliese. Tristan still isn't completely on board, otherwise, I would have left immediately. Instead, I had to wait for him to be called away before I could get started.

I feel more confident as I march through the corridors that had previously been strange to me. Things look more familiar now after my last time in the castle and I find my way to Anneliese's rooms with no trouble.

Pressing my ear to the door, there's only silence, but that doesn't mean no one is inside. I bite my lip and ease the door open gently. I only open it enough for a small crack of dancing light to come through. Anneliese must have the fireflies in her room again.

All the Fae are capable of magic, yet Anneliese seems to be the only one interested in wielding it. Tristan said it takes a physical toll. Is Anneliese the only one interested in paying it? If we continue closer to war, I doubt that will continue to be the case. What will Tristan do if he is pushed into it?

When it stays silent inside, I open the door a crack further to get a better view of the room. Lights dance across the ceiling, but the many seats where Anneliese's ladies have sat are empty. I scan the room for a desk or some papers or anywhere I could find some evidence of what she's up to, but it's still just an elaborate sitting room. Nothing about it looks like it's made for anything other than light gossip and giggling. No wonder why she's been able to get away with things so well. She's played at being demure for so long that no one even questions it anymore. It makes me want to throw up. How can they be so oblivious?

I push my way into Anneliese's room with my heart in my throat as I wait to be discovered. The last thing I want is for Anneliese to know that I'm on to her. When only silence greets me, my chest loosens a little as I creep across the soft rugs thrown across the hard stone with light feet. The air here is warmer than in the hallway, clotting in my lungs and making my breath come in tight gasps. Moving out of the main room, I find Anneliese's bed and poke around it. I lift the mattress and toss aside the blankets, hoping to find anything, any scrap of paper that could tell me her plans. But despite my prodding, there's nothing. *Ship.* She's too smart for that. I'm going to have to catch her in the act.

With a sigh, I put her bed back in order and slide out of the room, closing the door behind me. I'm not able to fully breathe again until I hear the solid click of it closing, and even then, I'm quick to get out of eye-line of her room.

Now on to the more arduous task of finding her.

It would probably be a tall order to hope Anneliese might have left with Captain Wimark. No, if she's not sitting around with her ladies, she's up to something.

I'd ask Tristan where he thinks she might be, but he's been busy with his military duties. And there's a part of me that doesn't like the idea of him knowing where she could be because he's kept tabs on her. Not only has he kept tabs on her, but he hasn't come to the same conclusions that I have. I know they've had a history, but that combined with their more recent, and brief, engagement makes me want to shy away. So it's up to me.

I pause as I pass the door to the Well of Truth. This is where Tristan saved my life, and I knew once and for all that I could trust him. Everything changed in this room. I find myself wanting to go in.

Pushing the door open, a blast of warm, moist air hits my face. The water is still within the tiled lip of the well. I kneel by the water, careful not to fall in, and take a swim again. There's nothing that I'm hiding this time. This world knows who I am and *what* I am. So much has changed.

It's hard to imagine the girl I was before. To think about when finding Zale was the only goal I had, and I was willing to do anything to make that happen. Now that dream is gone, and I've become an advocate for so much more. It's not just about me anymore, even though I've started to become one for myself. I have so many people depending on me now. I don't think I could ever go back to that quiet life I lived before.

I back out the door and close it behind me, letting out a relieved sigh. I'm not sure how, but this is going to make things pull together, I can just feel it.

"Mariel?"

And my relief is short-lived as I turn to face the accusing frown Ry gives me.

"Can I help you?" the words come out sharp, doing little to hide how irritated being around him makes me.

"What were you doing in there?" he asks, peering around me.

I stomp down the hall before he can open the door and figure out what's waiting inside. "What does it matter to you?"

He blows out an exasperated breath as he jogs to catch up with me. "Why wouldn't it matter to me?" He grabs my hand and forces me to stop. "Maybe I haven't shown it well the last few days, but I care about you. No matter what's happened between us, I will always care."

"That's why you're rude and accusatory about everything I do?" I tug my hand out of his grip.

He rubs his hand across his forehead. "I'm not trying to be. It's just... it's been rough here."

Guilt gnaws at my chest. "I know. I mean, I don't know. I can't imagine what you've been through. I never should have—"

"I don't want to talk about that, not now. I'm trying to make sure you really think before you act. It's not your strongest suit and being here puts us in real danger. I know that better than anyone."

I brace my fist against my hip. "I'm not a baby, Ry. I'm not just jumping into things. I'm doing what I have to do, same as you."

"I don't want you to get hurt like me." Ry's eyes crinkle as he reaches for me again. He doesn't go so far as to grab me, his hand hanging in the hair between us. "I want to protect you."

"I don't need you to protect me. I'm here to help you. You let your anger dictate your decisions. You refuse to work with me and Tristan to do what we're here to do." I can feel my face growing red and I can't tell if it's because I'm angry or because I want to cry.

Ry shakes his head. "You've got this all wrong. And I'm hesitant to work with you because I don't think you're making the right choice. You have so much trust for these people, trust I don't think they've earned."

"You only think that because you've been working with the rebellion," I point out.

His face twists. "They *saved* me, Mariel. I owe them everything for that."

"You don't have to owe them blind loyalty." I can't help the personal pain that comes out of my mouth. There was a time when his loyalty belonged to *me*. Have things really changed that much?

"It's not blind." He stops talking and we shift to the side of the hallway as two Fae women in long orange dresses drift through. The stone wall digs into my back as I turn to face him again. "I've seen the dark side of them, Mariel. I've seen things you could only dream of."

"You talk like I'm stupid. I know what they can do. I've seen it too. But look at you. I know you wouldn't be all fixed up if it wasn't for them."

Ry clamps his mouth shut as though he can hide his fixed teeth. "One right doesn't make up for a million wrongs."

"Maybe not, but it should count for moving in the right direction and seeing that there's good in them just like there's bad in us." My chest grows tight, and I want to run away again. Talking with Ry brings everything to the surface that I would rather forget.

"Does this mean you won't tell me what you're up to?" he asks, by-passing my argument entirely.

I fold my arms across my chest. "Not if you're going to try and stop me."

"Try me." He gives me a smile that almost looks like it used to, and I'm instantly transported back to before all of this happened.

"Okay. Let's do it."

"Okay. I'm in." He stares into my eyes, as he does his best to erase the last few months. "I've always been in. What's happened here won't change that."

"You wouldn't toss us all away over some teeth?"

He smiles again, revealing his fixed mouth in its full glory. "Not even for teeth. Now let's do whatever your plan is before I can wise up and stop you."

I give him a grin. "Just remember you asked for it."

SIXTEEN

Ry is true to his word in helping me take down Anneliese. His only problem is that she's dangerous all on her own, something I'm already too familiar with.

"Even without Captain Wimark, she's a force of her own. I don't want to see you get hurt, Mariel."

It feels weird to have the words I think about him be used against me. I can take care of myself. Haven't I proved that already? *I'm* the one who made it home. I owe him that same opportunity. "It's worth the risk. We may never get as good of an opportunity again."

He gives me a tight nod and we move through the hallway at a quick, but casual clip, just in case anyone happens to be watching us. We pass by the great hall where a few people eat from steaming bowls of soup. I can't imagine Anneliese deigning to join them. She's more of a big occasion or nothing kind of woman. I give everyone a closer look anyway though, just in case one of her ladies might be in there. But there's no sign of them, either.

"Where else do they gather?" Ry asks me as we move back into the hall.

"How would I know? You're the one walking around like you've been here a million times." I can't keep the bite out of my voice. I thought this would be so much easier and I don't like having Ry here to see me fail.

"You know I haven't. I've just learned that if I walk like I belong, no one questions it."

I want to stick my tongue out at him but refrain as another group of Fae moves through the hallway. My gaze trails after them, their skirts swishing against the tile. I nod towards them to Ry, and he gives me a tight nod back. We may not know where to go, but we can follow people that do.

We keep our steps even and our expressions light in case they look back at us, but the women are so caught up in their own conversation that they barely pay us any attention at all.

It's easy to stay close to them until they decide to leave the castle and our trail ends.

"It was a good idea," Ry says, giving me a pat on the arm. "Maybe the next group will be more helpful."

We stand before the large double doors of the main entrance. I watch the group until the doors block them from view. Where the heck could Anneliese be? Where are any of them? The castle is full of people, yet it feels so empty. Maybe it's because I'm looking in the wrong places.

With a tight grimace, I grab Ry's arm and pull him back from the door. "I think I know where to look."

It's the only other place in the castle that I have familiarity with, but not in a good way. Ry's steps slow as we near the tight twist of stairs that will bring us to the dungeon as realization dawns on him about where we're going.

"Come on. It's basically the last place we have to look." I

try to keep my voice light, but there's nothing that feels good about going back here.

He freezes in place, toe at the top of the steps. "I can't do it. I won't go in there again."

"Okay." I try to rethink how this will be without him and just how much danger I'm putting myself in. "That's totally okay. You can wait for me here. Tell Tristan if it seems like I've been gone too long."

I take the first step into the dark and my stomach sinks. Memories I've been avoiding threaten to take over and drown me in the amount of unpleasantness I've survived.

Ry grabs me before I can take another step. "It's not safe for either of us to go down there. I...I think we should wait for Tristan."

Hearing his name on Ry's lips makes me want to smile. There wasn't a hint of malice about it at all. Maybe there's hope for them to work together after all.

"We can't wait for him," I point out even though it pains me. "We all need to pull our weight and do our part, and this is mine right now. I can handle it."

I take another step forward, dragging Ry closer to the edge. His fingers tighten into my arm as his whole body goes rigid.

"Please, Mariel." His eyes are wide with panic. "I can't do this."

"You don't have to." I pat his hand and try to move his fingers away, but his grip is too right.

He shakes his head. "I would never forgive myself if something happened to you because I was too afraid to move. If you're going, I'm going." The silent *"or none of us have to go"* hangs in the air between us, but I ignore it.

"Perfect. Let's go." I take another step forward, but he still doesn't move down one at all. His body hangs at an angle as he does his best to keep a good grip on me and the bright hallway above us.

It's like trudging through sand to get any sort of momentum, but eventually, he's forced to move with me when I get too far down. His grip on me stays painfully tight and I'm sure I'll be feeling his fingers on my skin for weeks.

The darkness closes in around us as we follow the twist in the stairs and leave the torches of the main hallway behind. I'm tempted to go back up and steal one for our journey, but I don't think I would ever get Ry to come back down with me if I gave him the chance to go back now.

Our feet on the stone and the hollowness of our breaths is the only sound as we travel further beneath the castle. This felt like the beginning of the end of my last adventure, perhaps it will be the same now. Maybe we'll get lucky and Anneliese will be hanging out in one of the cells and we can close the door and forget all about her. But that would be too easy, and I'm not sure my conscience would allow me to kill anyone, even her. Maybe her.

The flickering light of a candle greets us as we reach the bottom of the stairs. It sits at the desk where the guard was that Tristan had to argue with before, but now the chair is empty, the post abandoned.

Ice travels through my veins as we step closer. Why isn't the dungeon being monitored? It seems like a place where someone would always have to be keeping watch.

There's a shuffle in the dark behind the desk, and I grab Ry with a death grip of my own.

"What now?" he whispers, leaning closer to me until we're huddled together.

My mind and my body tell me to run, but I have to swallow down my fear. I grab the candle off the desk and move into the oppressive darkness.

"Now we search."

The first cells we pass are empty, although one has a slight gleam of reflection in the back behind the bars that could be a forgotten bowl or the eyes of a rat. We don't linger long enough to find out. Sweat trickles down my back. The farther we go, the harder it is not to remember the time when I've been a prisoner myself. I can't imagine how much worse it is for Ry. Is it really worth it to put ourselves through this? Maybe we could have waited in her room for her to come back. Sure, that would have eliminated the element of surprise, but we would have felt safe. Not that it would be hard to feel safer anywhere but here.

The cell doors switch from bars to wood and it's harder to tell if there's anyone on the other side anymore. We could be completely surrounded and not even know it.

Once the thought enters my brain, I can't shake it loose. I feel like I can hear breathing behind every door as twenty soldiers prepare to take us prisoner. Panic creeps under my skin, growing like a weed until my legs are shaking and the candle shifts so violently in my hand that it threatens to go out.

"Mariel?"

Ry's voice breaks the spell of fear and allows reason to inch its way back into my body. Slowly my shaking grows less until I'm able to move forward again.

We're about halfway through the cells when I wonder if I should admit defeat. This would have been a weird place for Anneliese to hide and I can't see her going this far back even if she did come down here.

A loud thump comes from behind the door to our right and my breath stops in my lungs. My hand not holding the candle tightens into a fist as I inch closer to the door.

"Careful," Ry hisses.

As though I need the warning.

I knock against the door and clear my throat. "Anneliese?"

A deep, rasping laugh comes from the crack under the door. I'm torn between wanting to press my ear to the gap to hear better and running away.

"It's not her," Ry says as he pulls me back. "She wouldn't be locked up down here anyway."

"Of course not." The voice chuckles. "This is where she locks *us* up."

"Anneliese locked you in here?" I ask, moving closer to the door again.

"This is where I was sent when she had no use for me anymore."

"And what *was* your use for her?"

Ry keeps his hand on my arm but doesn't try to stop me as I go down on my knees to hear the voice better.

The man's laugh is loud before it turns into a fit of coughing. "She does not need us to comply. One touch is all it takes and then we run to do her bidding. She would not like us spilling her secrets though, so we were sent to live out the rest of our days down here. Cozy, no?"

I'm beginning to wonder if he'll have any real possibility of helping us. Has he been down here long enough that he's started to lose his mind?

"What did you do for her?" I try again. I've watched Anneliese use her magic before, it wouldn't surprise me if she'd done it on this man. But what could she have made him do that would have made her nervous enough to lock him down here to never tell anyone what he'd done?

"Come closer," he whispers.

Ry shakes his head as I comply.

"Closer."

My face is almost flush with the gap now as I crouch on the floor. Ry's hand tightens on my arm, ready to pull me away. Scuffling comes from under the door as the man on the other side inches closer to me as well.

It's like I can feel him breathing, even though I know that's not possible with the width of the door between us. Still, the air moves like a spider over my face and my body twitches to get away.

He laughs again, the sound close enough that we could be face to face.

"I killed the King."

My body grows cold as Ry yanks me away and the man's laugh echoes through the dungeon. Footsteps echo through the darkness from the other end of the dungeon and Ry pulls harder on me to move. The man doesn't stop laughing as Ry forces me past the desk and up the stairs. I don't think I take a breath until I'm in the relative safety of the hallway where the torches are bright, and I can hear Fae talking in another room.

"Well, that was a bust, we spent all that time searching just to find a crazy guy in the dungeon," Ry says as he leans against the wall. He looks as pale as I feel, both of us rattled by the stranger in the dark.

I shake my head. "I disagree. Now we know it was Anneliese's plot to kill the King."

"You're really going to trust that guy?" Ry pushes away from the wall and storms down the hallway, putting more distance between us and the prison.

"Why wouldn't I? What does he have to lose by telling us she forced him to kill the King?" I keep my voice down as we pass a room filled with Fae.

Ry scoffs at me. "You're looking at it the wrong way. It's not what he has to lose, it's what he has to gain. You're a sympathetic ear, someone who might give him his freedom if you feel like he's been unfairly locked up."

"I wouldn't do that." I stumble to keep up with Ry's increasing pace.

"Maybe you wouldn't, but he doesn't know that."

I can't believe Ry is so ready to disregard our first big lead. I don't care what he says, I believe that man. How easy would it have been for Anneliese to give him a friendly touch and then he's waking up from a nightmare, covered in the King's blood? I've seen her work her dark magic before. I know she can do it.

I have to tell Tristan. I'm not sure what he can do with that information, since he's been effectively strong-armed out of everything, but he has to know. He has to know that that witch killed his father.

My feet take me to Tristan's room, the only path I've been able to really memorize. Ry sighs, but he follows me anyway.

The door is ajar when we stop in front of his room. There's no hint of light inside, no crackling of the fire he usually makes sure is busy in the grate. Ry moves to go inside but I grab him and give him a tight shake of my head. If someone is in there, I don't think it's Tristan.

Rather than wait for what could be a trap or an errant maid, I motion for Ry to turn around and we move back toward our rooms. I'm not sure I want to be with Ry the doubter right now, but I know I don't want to be alone, so when we get to our rooms, I nod for him to come with me into mine.

Everything looks the same as it did when I was here before, but there's something in the air that feels different and I'm glad I'm not alone. I sit, back rigid, on the side of the bed and Ry joins me. The mattress sinks under our weight, cradling us like my hammock back home.

It makes an ache bloom in my chest and all I want is to be able to go home. But I can't. How could I look my father in the face again after I allowed his son to be killed? I may have brought him back, but then I just as quickly took him away again, permanently this time. I can never go home now. How can he look at me when I can barely even look at myself?

Tears prick the corner of my eyes, and a sniffle grows in my nose. Maybe I should have been alone in here after all.

"Are we just waiting for Tristan now?" Ry asks, completely oblivious to my struggle.

"Yeah. I'm sure he'll know what to do next." If I don't think of something first.

He can't pretend Anneliese isn't a viable threat now. She's been the mastermind behind all of this. But what is her angle? She didn't need to kill the King to become queen. She already had that set up with Tristan. But as soon as he was dead, she moved on to the Prince, who clearly doesn't want her. There has to be something I'm missing.

"I'll have to tell the rebellion," Ry says as he leans back on the bed. "They put me here to gather information for them and I've done a poor job of that thus far."

I lean back next to him with a huff. "They're really good at putting people in the castle, much worse at extracting them. I'm not sure how much they really care about the information they send people for."

Maybe that's being unfair. They didn't care about *me*, but I also wasn't really working for them. All I wanted was Zale. They wanted him too, but they were working on their own pretenses. I was just a bonus.

"Azalea will want to know."

I can't think about that girl. I can't think about the visible strain of heartbreak that is probably making its way across her body as she mourns my brother.

"What will she do when you tell her?"

He lifts a shoulder noncommittally. "Maybe nothing. She has no interest in punishing the king killer."

"So why the rush to tell her?"

"It's an important piece of politics. The rebellion will need to know it when they make their next move."

I shake my head. I don't want the rebellion to get more involved. I know why we need them, but my interest in having allies only goes so far.

I'm saved from having to say anything else by Tristan opening the door. Sweat covers his body and his hair hangs damp in his face.

I rush from the bed to look him over for anything else. "What happened to you?"

"Just a bit of training, nothing I could not handle." He offers me a grin and I raise my brow. We have different ideas about what he can handle.

"This looks more like punishment than training," Ry counters.

Tristan closes the door with a solid click. "That was more than likely part of it. No one on the field liked that I had made a bid for king. Not that they understand that it was given to me. No, they only understand my less than favorable birth."

"I guess we won't be finding any allies there then." Sure, Azalea and her followers could hardly be replaced at this point, and of course I haven't forgotten that Tristan's team betrayed us in the past, but I would prefer almost anyone else over the rebellion.

"After what happened with my men, I did not think we would. I still have a job to do, regardless of what they think of me."

And that's what makes Tristan a better man. Even beaten down he gives me a smile as he wipes the sweat from his brow.

"We did work of our own while you were gone." My chest feels bubbly in my eagerness to please him.

He leans against the wall, and I wait for the warm smile he saves just for me, but it doesn't come. Instead, his face is stern as he turns towards me.

"You were not supposed to do anything that could get you in trouble. I wanted you to stay right here and wait."

"I can't just wait around for you. People have died." An unspoken *my brother has died*, hangs in the air between us. "I have to be able to do something. So, we did."

Tristan pinches his lips together. "At least you made it back safely."

"We were going to follow Anneliese and see what she was up to." Tristan opens his mouth to interrupt me, but I talk faster. "But we couldn't find her. She wasn't in any of her usual haunts, so we decided to search the dungeon."

"Such a reasonable decision," Tristan says dryly.

"Well, it turns out it was the right thing to do. Did you know she has prisoners of her own down there?" My grin just about splits my cheeks.

Tristan frowns. "That is not possible. She has no control over that."

"Well, whether she did it or she got Wimark to do her dirty work for her, she has a prisoner sitting in the cells right now. And do you know what he said?"

"What did he say?" Tristan refuses to rise to my level of enthusiasm and Ry just watches us with a tired expression.

"He said he was in prison for killing the king."

Silence permeates the room as Tristan stands in shock for a second. He shakes his head, sweat dripping from the ends of his hair.

"How can that be? An investigation is currently underway to find the killer. If she knew who did it, she would have used that information to her advantage."

"Not in this case." I bounce from foot to foot as I deliver the final blow. "Because this man says it was Anneliese who *made* him do it."

I know Tristan understands my meaning as his face goes pale. "You are sure of this? You trust this man?"

"I told her not to," Ry grunts.

"We are fortunate you are here to be the voice of reason." The words are right, but the way Tristan delivers them makes Ry flinch. "What you're saying is serious. Anneliese would never recover from this kind of betrayal."

"Is it really so crazy to think?" I have no trouble believing that Anneliese is a murdering psychopath.

Tristan slides to the floor, bracing his head in his hand. "You do not know her as I do."

"If you don't think she's capable of this, then I don't think you know her at all."

"It is not that." Tristan looks at me, the color coming back to his face. "I know what she can do. I just don't want to believe her capable of killing my father."

Sympathy finally finds a crack to worm its way into my heart. I don't know what I would do if someone I grew up with had killed my father without so much as blinking. The betrayal would sink deep even if I knew they were capable of terrible things.

"What do we do now?" Ry asks, not interested in working around Tristan's emotions.

"I need to talk to this prisoner myself."

Tristan rises to his feet and takes my hand in his for a moment before throwing open the door.

CHAPTER
SEVENTEEN

Tristan moves like a man possessed as he traverses the hallway. It's a struggle to keep up with him and I'm sure we look comical to anyone who might see us. Thankfully we don't pass any other Fae as Tristan takes us back to the prison.

There's no hesitation in him as he takes the stairs, forcing Ry and I to push past ours much quicker than we did last time as we follow him.

As we reach the bottom of the stairs, the corridor is devoid of light, and I curse myself for not leaving the candle where I found it when it was time for us to leave. Tristan whispers something in the dark, and a spark bursts from his hand to hover in the air beside us, bringing illumination to the nearest space around us.

My chest feels tight. This might be the first time I've ever seen Tristan use his magic. I know he has some, every Fae does. It's another thing entirely to see this difference between us so plainly. Why didn't he use it when we were on the road? It could have either proved handy, or made me run away faster.

"Which cell was it?" His voice is deeper than usual as a hint of gruffness enters it.

"Down here." Ry takes the lead, pushing farther into the dungeon despite the sweat beading on the back of his neck just from being here.

The excitement I felt earlier fades now that I'm back in the dungeon. How could such a feeling exist here when the air is chilled by the despair of its prisoners?

I clench my hands together to keep from falling apart. I did this before, and I can do it now.

"This one." Ry points to a door.

The light bobs over, illuminating the disturbed ground from my time on the floor. Tristan's face is tight as he grabs the knob and tries to jerk it open. But the lock holding our informant prisoner holds fast even as his face turns red from the amount of force he applies to it. I place a gentle hand on his shoulder, and he shrugs it off even as he moves out of the way for me to work.

I grab a pin out of my pocket and jimmy the lock open, trying not to let my mind wander over the many times I've done this with Zale. The door pops open with a squeak, revealing darkness inside.

Tristan's touch is gentle as he moves past me into the room, his light following him. My breath catches in my throat. The room is empty. There's no man waiting in the darkness to tell us Anneliese's secrets. A dark crimson stain mars the stone floor, glistening as the light moves over it.

"We're too late," Ry says. He slams his fist into the wooden door, causing a crack to form in the middle of it.

Tristan shakes his head. "This blood is fresh."

I don't want to look stupid, but I have to say the words out loud anyway. "She killed him?"

"There's no way she was going to let him live after he'd

killed the King for her. I have no idea why she kept him down here as long as she did," Ry says.

"She must have had someone watching him." Tristan dips his fingers into the blood, watching as it drips back into the puddle. "You finding him in the first place had to have been an accident. She would not have allowed the same occurrence twice."

"Do you believe us?" My chest grows tight as he rises to his feet and wipes his hand off on a cloth pulled from his pocket.

"If this room had been empty, I would have had a hard time believing it—"

"But I wouldn't lie to you—"

Tristan holds a hand up and I clamp my jaw shut. "I have believed much more unbelievable things from you in the past, so I would have found a way. However, this blood is much more incriminating than the man himself. I have no choice but to believe you."

"So, you agree that Anneliese is our enemy?" Ry asks from the doorway.

"Anneliese has always been our enemy in some form or another. I didn't want to believe that she could be capable of such an act. I have no choice but to believe that now."

It's the wrong place and the wrong moment for it, but my chest feels warm as Tristan gives us a tight nod and we make our way out of the dungeon. He believes me. He really believes me. And I solved the puzzle, with help of course. I'm still not sure about the why, but I have the who and that feels just as important.

Maybe I'm finding a place here after all.

I EXPECT Tristan to go back to our rooms so we can discuss what this means and what our next step should be, but he breezes past that hallway. His face is hard and his footsteps heavy upon the stone floor as he marches to the council room.

Captain Wimark isn't there to stop him this time and he throws the doors open so hard that they smack against the wall. The gathered Fae look up at him in varying degrees of shock, except for the Prince whose face is made of stone. He looks bored as Tristan stalks closer to him. No one moves to stop him, their chairs acting as their prisons as he grabs the Prince by the throat.

"Did you know about this?" Tristan demands as he lifts the Prince from his chair. "Tell me you did not know, for you'd hate to see what I will do if you did."

I scan the seats, looking for Anneliese's devilish face. "She's not here."

That seems to knock him out of the trance of his anger, and he takes his attention off the Prince to look at the rest of the council gathered around the table. Slowly he sets the Prince down. His hands shake as he adjusts his tunic, but his face remains bored as he looks at Tristan.

"Would you care to explain why you are interrupting this private meeting?" He tilts his head up so he can look down his nose at us. He's trying to look powerful, but it just looks like a boy pretending.

"Did you know that Anneliese was the one who murdered our father?" Tristan asks. Gasps echo through the room and several people shake their heads at him like he's gone mad.

I want to step up and support him, but I don't think that will help right now. No matter my supposed position on the council, I'm still just a human to them.

"I think you need more rest. What you are saying is a

serious accusation." The Prince's lips curl into a mocking smile. "I know it has been hard for you since the King died. He was your last leverage to power and now you're left with nothing. Be grateful though, because thanks to that fact, no one would possibly believe the killer was you."

Tristan slams a fist down on the table, rattling the cups on it. "I am telling you who the killer is. This is not speculation; this is the truth. Are you going to do your job and detain the killer?"

The Prince adjusts his cup on the table. "I could not hold her even if I wanted to. She has left with my men to take care of the situation at the border. I expect her back in a few days."

It's all too convenient. *Did she only leave for the troops when she realized she'd been found out? What is the long game with that though?* When she comes back, we'll be right here to accuse her all over again. The evidence might not be fresh anymore, but it will still be the same as it was before. She's not going to be able to get away with this.

"You still trust this witch to do your bidding?" Tristan's voice goes dangerously low.

"You do not control me, Tristan. You are nothing but my bastard brother. You are not the King; you are not even a prince. You do not get to stand there in the middle of *my* meeting and dictate to me what I should do." The Prince's face grows to the shade of a beet as his volume increases.

"Are you so proud that you will accept no help at all?" Tristan demands. "I am telling you that she is the one responsible, and you refuse to accept it because you are not the one who found her out. Unless you were the one who told her to do it in the first place."

"You are out of line," The Prince spits the words out. "I would never have killed my father."

I believe him, but not because of some great emotional

connection. As I stand here watching him, every moment shows a scared boy underneath the trappings of a prince. He would not have been brave enough to take the steps necessary to kill his father.

Tristan laughs, the sound deep and cutting. "Maybe you did not do it yourself, but you wanted to. You wanted to the minute you found out he wanted to replace you with me."

He clenches his hands into tight fists as he faces Tristan. "You will leave immediately, or you will be forced to do so. The King may have given you privileges beyond your birth, but you will remember your place. If you ever address me so informally again, it will be you who is detained."

"And you will remember that the King desired me to take his place instead of you and you had to form a coup to even get this far." Tristan's smile is grim as he turns. He gives me a nod and we leave the room, whispers springing up in our wake.

"Is that it then?" I ask when we're far enough away from the council room that I don't have to worry about them hearing us. "You accused Anneliese, and that was enough?"

Tristan grabs my hand, winding his fingers through mine. "That is all I had to do. The council will do the rest. Anneliese never belonged there, not while my father ruled. Her presence will have bothered him regardless of what she did. To know that she could be behind his death? They will not let that go quietly."

"But she's not even here, so what does it matter?"

"Oh, it matters." He pushes the door open to the Great Hall. "Regardless of her being here or not, William will have a hard time controlling the council after that. They will not be so quick to do his bidding."

That might be a good thing, but there are so many negative aspects to that. Has Tristan not considered that we are at war? A many-sided war if the Prince is to be believed. My family is fighting it on the water right now, and the Prince has sent men to deal with the other half, and we're creating a civil war right in the middle of it. I'm not sure how smart all of this is right now. I may not have been taught and trained to rule a country, but it doesn't take a genius to see where they should be placing their focus.

A blast of warm air filled with the scent of roasting meat hits my face as we enter the hall. Fae sit in clumped groups around the wooden tables as they enjoy a midday meal. Several wave to Tristan and he gives them a broad grin as he finds a place for us to sit. It's strange to see people happy to see Tristan. I haven't seen that since we met up with his men and that was a lie. We haven't talked about it, but I wonder how much that still bothers him and if he misses the closeness he had.

Tristan secures us a plate full of the glorious meal and digs in without waiting for me. Juices run down his chin as he eats the meat and he grabs his napkin to soak it up. My stomach rumbles as I settle beside him,

"Are you sure this is a good idea?" I whisper to him.

His eating slows and he gives me a thoughtful look. "I thought you might be hungry."

"No, not lunch. Everything that we're doing with the council. Should we be sowing the seeds of discontent right now? There could be a bad war coming, and your country is in complete disarray."

"I'm not sure *complete* is the right word for it. We'll manage. If things get really bad, I'll always be here to help." He picks up his fork again and shovels potatoes into his waiting mouth.

"That may not necessarily be true. At the moment, the Prince is very capable of kicking you out and is already threatening to do so. If he does that then you can't help at all."

Tristan puts the fork down and reaches for my hand despite all the Fae that will see him doing so. "This is necessary, and this is the right moment. We must make the council uneasy about his presence, or else his position will only become more secure."

"I thought you never wanted to be King."

He leans back with a sigh, the bench squeaking beneath him. "It's true that I never wanted any of this, but that doesn't mean that I cannot do what is right. I loved my father. Even if I didn't want to do what he asked of me, I still loved him. You should have seen him when I finally agreed to stay, it was as though the stars had aligned just for him. I could never go back on our agreement after that. Even in death, I must strive to give him that same happiness."

I understand but I don't. Tristan and the Prince were both the King's sons. Would he really have favored Tristan so highly over the Prince? My father had two sons and I never felt like he loved one more than the other. Even when he thought Zale was dead, he never even let his mourning affect the rest of us. He still made sure we were taken care of.

"Did your father not love the Prince?" I have to know even if the question is rude.

Tristan tightens his grip around my hand. "Of course, he loved William, but things were different, harder. His mother made it that way."

"What could she have done that would make him not care for his own child?" It sounds ridiculous to me.

"When she found out about my existence, she kept William from my father. She whispered lies in his ear so that when he did see his father he would resent and hate him. Can you imagine the pain that would come from your child hating you? My mother on the other hand...” He hesitates.

I've never heard him speak of his mother before and I squeeze his hand in encouragement.

“Despite the fact that she could never be his wife, she loved him. She loved him enough to give him what he really needed even when he didn't want to accept it. That is why I never had a title or a place here, because she wanted to make sure that his place as king was always secure. I was taught to look up to him, and to think of him as a great king. You tell me how that would affect your emotions between your two children.”

“But he was the king, surely he could have taken the Prince away from her and done as he pleased with him,” I point out.

Tristan shakes his head. “Court politics are complicated and it would not have looked good if he were to be found removing a child from its mother, even his own. And so, William was raised in such a way that would tear them apart forever, as you can see by the man he became. He was never allowed to be trained to be King and as such does not know what to do with the title now that he has it.”

“But you weren't trained to be King either.”

He tilts his head at me with a smile. “That may be so, but I have trained with the King's military and held positions of power within it. That is already far more than my brother has done.”

I chew my bottom lip but let the moment pass. Tristan thinks he's ready and that should be all that matters. What do I really know about any of that anyway? I came from a ship. I wasn't prepared for anything life has thrown at me. That hasn't stopped me from achieving my goals. I *was* able to bring Zale home, even if he didn't stay there.

"I'm worried about Captain Wimark and Anneliese being together. Do you think she went with him to the front?" I pick at my plate even as my stomach rumbles.

"She would never do that." Tristan's shoulders relax, the idea not something that remotely concerns him. "She's not one to get her hands dirty."

"I think you need to reconsider her. If you don't, she'll constantly have the upper hand on us."

Plus, I'm tired of being the only one to be looking at her critically. She's a monster and I know it. Why doesn't he realize that?

He taps his fork against his plate as he studies me. "Perhaps you're right."

"If I *am* right, we need to act. I don't want to be under her thumb again."

"And what do you suggest?" He tilts his head. He studies me like it's the first time he's ever seen me.

I hate the words that I have to say before they even come out of my mouth. Nothing about them feels right and yet it's the best option we have. "I think we need to form a harder alliance with the rebellion and with the Seafolk. We might even be able to use the sea beasts to our advantage if we can pick the battlefield."

"The battlefield? What is it you think you need to prepare for?"

"I think Anneliese will do anything to achieve her ends, and I'm pretty sure those include her desire to become Queen. You're only focused on the Prince, but she's flitting around in the shadows making everything happen. Without her, he has far less power, and without him, she is back to having none at all."

"I feel like you are reaching here. My brother has thrust her away. He does not care for her and will not allow her to be Queen."

"But that hasn't stopped them from being aligned anyway."

He frowns and pushes his plate away, a potato rolling free with the movement.

"I think it would be best to prepared, even if it comes to nothing." I have to press my advantage now. He is so close to seeing reason with me.

"You want to prepare for battle?"

"Like I said, it would be better to be prepared."

Tristan stands, the bench scuffing along the floor as he does. "I think you are jumping to too many conclusions. We'll be fine. We need to keep our focus on William."

I'm going to have to do this without him then.

EIGHTEEN

My body feels tight as I stand outside Ry's room, but I know this is what I have to do. Tristan may not listen to me, but Ry will. Maybe not about other things, but definitely about preparing against Captain Wimark. Still, in too many ways, he feels like a stranger now for me to feel completely comfortable bringing him into the fold with me.

The knock is soft, so quiet he might miss it. But the door swings open almost immediately as though he knew I was standing there.

"Mariel." He leans against the door frame as he studies my face.

"I think we have some planning to do." I push by him into the room, and he watches me with startled eyes.

"Planning?"

I lean against the small desk set up against the wall. "Planning. I think Anneliese and Captain Wimark are up to something and I won't let them succeed."

Ry barks out a laugh. "That's an ambitious goal."

"You were with me before when we were looking for

evidence. Without us no one would know that she orchestrated the King's death. Will you be with me now?"

He crosses his arms over his chest, his new muscles flexing. "I am always with you, Mariel. I want to fix this mess as much as you do."

"I think we need to prepare for battle. That's what Captain Wimark is best at, and I think Anneliese will use it as her final coup to grab power. Especially since Tristan told me that she's the Prince's cousin. That puts her in line to the throne all on her own, even if it is remote. I think she'll use that to her advantage."

My fingernails dig into the wood as I wait for him to respond. He could just as easily think I'm jumping to conclusions like Tristan. But every time I say the words out loud, they feel more real than before. They never feel crazy or a step too far. That must be a sign.

Ry purses his lips as he thinks my words over. He gives me a nod and the tightness in my chest eases. "That gives her plenty of motive. I think you're right and it would be smart to get a leg up on her plans. What did you have in mind?"

I tell him about working with the Seafolk and the rebellion like I told Tristan, and Ry uncrosses his arms and flexes his fists.

"I think we should go a step further. The banished will want their part in this, too. We're going to need everybody we can get."

The tightness eases its way back in. "The banished wouldn't be ready for something like that. We can't bring them in so unprepared. It would be a bloodbath."

I can't bring anyone else I know and love into this fight. I need them safe, and safe means far away.

"You're being narrow-minded. We didn't know what we were doing when we first came here either."

"And look where that got us!" The words explode out of me, ripping through my chest. "Zale is *dead*, and you were almost that way yourself. How much more do we need to put our people through? We don't belong here. We never did."

"Then what do you want Mariel? You want to fight for them and get Tristan his throne and then go back home? The Seafolk won't thank you for that solution, and neither will the humans. We all want more. Keeping that out of their reach won't save them. It will only convince another Zale to leave home someday looking for freedom." He comes closer to me, leaning against the desk so that our hands are almost touching. "We all want more now, and we've had it so close to being in our grasp. It would be cruel of you to take that away now."

My eyes burn but I refuse to let tears fall. "I'm not taking anything away. I'm giving them life and I'm giving the fight to those who are better prepared."

"They'll never be prepared if you don't let them learn." He covers my hand with his. "You have to let them fight for themselves, Mariel."

I bite my lip to keep myself from exploding. "I think we should keep them as a last resort."

It's the only sort of concession I'll make, and the words are a lie as they leave my mouth. I have zero intention of ever bringing the rest of my family into this. They deserve better and I'll bring it to them. I want the first time they step on land to do it as free men, not fighting for the Fae. I can't risk them. Not after losing Zale already.

"I'm not sure any of this has gone to plan. This could be our last resort." He squeezes my hand as though that will make everything better.

"I'll send them a letter." The lie feels safe as I say it, lessening the pressure pushing through me. "They can be prepared to be called in, but only as a last resort."

Ry nods, an easy smile breaking across his face. "It feels good to be doing something."

I can't imagine what it's been like for him to have had zero control over his life this whole time. Still, I won't let him hurt the rest of my family just to satisfy his need for revenge.

"I'm sure the rebellion will feel the same way."

He reaches behind me and pulls a few sheets of paper off the desk, handing them to me as he takes one for himself. "The rebellion will be thrilled. We must let them know as soon as possible."

He turns and begins scratching out a note on the paper, his words forming a thick scrawl. I hesitate, not just because there's only one quill, but because I have no idea what to say. If I write something to the banished here, Ry will see my lie, and what do I say to the Seafolk? *I came to make peace for you but that hasn't worked out so prepare yourself for battle?* It feels wrong. It feels way too much like failure, the taste of it bitter in my mouth.

And then I'm out of time as Ry hands me the quill and folds up his missive for the rebellion.

"What did you say to them?" Maybe his answer will help move me in the right direction.

He runs his hand down the folded page. "I told them that it's time."

Yeah, that's not going to help me at all.

He leaves with his letter, squeezing my shoulder as he passes, and I still hesitate with the quill in my hand. I know what I want to write my family. I want to tell them that this exercise has been a failure and they should prepare for the worst. I want to ask them to send a letter back to let me know they're okay. I want to ignore them altogether, so I don't have to know how they felt when Zale came home. None of those options will work, and all of them are completely self-serving. I have to be better than that now.

The letter to the Seafolk comes much easier.

I have tried to make the Fae see reason with your plight, but even when they are facing attacks from your people due to them becoming displaced by the sea beasts, they still refuse to budge. However, in a lucky twist of fate for us, they are being faced with an enemy at another border right now, one that is determined to march straight to the capitol. We are hoping to use this to our advantage to force the Fae to work with us. Either they will need us as allies, or we will work to pin them against the wall until they agree to our terms. Will you fight with us?

I have no problem putting them in a tight position. There's no love lost between me and the Seafolk. Maybe if they had been more of our allies from the beginning I would have felt differently, but because they kept their distance until they absolutely needed us, I don't feel bad asking them to fight.

My hand shakes as I finally decide what I want to say to my father.

Please forgive me. Know that I tried my best and it wasn't good enough. All I wanted to do was save him. I just wasn't smart enough or fast enough. Please... please forgive me.

It's not anything like Ry wants, but I feel better once the words leave me. It's what I should have done from the beginning. Zale's body never should have returned home without some sort of note from me. I can't be that coward anymore.

My heart already feels lighter just by getting the words down. I should have done this a long time ago.

～

THE HALLWAY IS empty as I come out with my letters, Ry already long gone. He probably doesn't have to send them the way I do. He could just walk to the rebellion and hand them over himself.

I hate how much that thought tears through my chest. I shouldn't care so much. I should be happy that he found someone to help him when I couldn't. It shouldn't feel like a betrayal, but I can't help feeling like it is. I've been replaced and I only have myself to blame.

A messenger boy runs through the hallway with a bag filled with letters at his hip, his soft feet quiet against the stone despite how fast he moves.

I wave him over and he stops, his forehead creasing into a frown until I show him the letters. He shoves them down into his bag and holds out an open palm to me. I stare at it, and he stares at me, confusion rippling through both of us.

"Let me handle that."

My chest feels buoyant as Tristan strides toward us. He places a few coins into the boy's hand with a smile the boy doesn't return as he speeds off through the halls once more.

"Sorry, I didn't know you had to pay him." I feel stupid admitting it out loud. Too much of this world is still foreign to me. Will I ever find my footing here?

"It's no matter." Tristan turns his smile on me, and my stomach curdles. I don't deserve it. "I told you I would help you here, and I'm glad to do it. You should have let me know you wanted to send letters."

"I didn't think you'd like it." The truth has always been something forced out of me when I'm with him.

"I would never stop you from communicating with your family." He grabs my hand, his body feeling too warm against my skin. "Come with me."

I don't put up a fight as he drags me through the castle. I'm torn in too many ways, and I don't know what to do.

Just once, can't the answer be easy? Can't there just be one clear choice for me to follow?

I crane my neck to find Ry as we go, but he's fully disappeared. I probably won't find out what his letter says until the rebellion shows up at our doorstep.

"I thought you might need a break from all this tension, and I knew just where to take you," Tristan says leaning closer to my ear like we're sharing a secret. "I know being here has been hard, and your help has been invaluable."

My body tingles from his attention and his contact. The strength of his hand transports my mind away from my troubles until all I can focus on is him.

He leads me through the maze of the castle and down a steep flight of stairs. Burrowing deeper into the stone feels dangerous, but I let him guide me, anyway. I know he wouldn't do anything to hurt me. It's taken a long time for me to fully grasp that, no matter how many times he tried to tell me he was there for me. I have nothing to fear from him. He's not going to lead me down and lock me in the dungeon.

"I should have taken you here before, but I forgot all about it until this morning." His voice is giddy as the stairs under our feet grow slick and a green film of moss covers them.

The tingle of salt tickles the back of my nose and my heartbeat quickens. He squeezes my hand even tighter and helps me down the last few steps that are completely covered in the green slime.

He lights a torch and holds it up, swinging it around in an attempt to show me the cavernous space around us. "What do you think?"

I couldn't speak even if I wanted to, even if I knew what I wanted to say. He's taken us to a massive cave under the castle. With Tristan's torch and the faint daylight in the back of the space, I can still barely see all of it. The ceiling reaches so high that it feels like the whole castle could fit inside. The ground is a mass of rocks and sand that I stumble over as I get to the best part of the whole room. Just a little further in, lapping against the rocks, is seawater.

"One of my ancestors decided he needed quicker access to the sea and had this built for him. I bet it used to store some incredible boats," Tristan says, his face wistful as he stares out at the black water. "I used to think if I wandered around in here, I'd find the tunnels that would bring me back to our home under the earth, but there are none here. At least none for a curious boy to find."

"I'm surprised they wanted to be closer to the sea, since they can barely stand to be on it at all with the amount of garbage still soaking in it." I dip my hand into the water and shudder at the coolness from the cave soaking into my bones.

The pebbles skitter under him as he sits on a larger rock. "I do not believe my kind always knew how the pollution affected them. Their vendetta against humans and their creations was not initially because of how it affected them. It was simply because that is what they believed was right."

"So, your ancestors loved the sea despite how it hurt them?" I can completely relate with that feeling, but with more than just the water.

"We do not always make the best choices where our hearts are concerned." Tristan turns to look at me, his eyes almost black from the shadows of the torchlight. "I have been there myself."

My breath catches in my throat. "And what has touched your heart hard enough to convince you to make bad decisions?"

"I would not call them bad decisions, but definitely

ones that have left me vulnerable because of my need to protect." He reaches for my hand and the cool water presses between our palms as we connect. "Just as my ancestor felt the need to be close to the water, I feel the need to be close to you, Mariel. No matter the potential to hurt me. Without you, the rest of it does not matter anymore."

I lean closer to him, wanting to reassure him with my presence where words feel impossible. He matches my movements until our faces are next to each other and he presses a kiss to my forehead.

"I will make sure you are taken care of. Whatever comes next, you *will* survive this, Mariel."

My fingers shake as I place my hands on either side of his face. His face is a mass of shadow and the air between us is a twist of salt and promises. I pull his face to mine and press my lips to his, letting the rhythm between us take physical form. His hands fall to my waist, gripping me and pulling me closer to him as though his will alone can protect me from what comes next. I tangle my hands in his hair, letting the thick strands twist around my fingers. He kneels on the rocks beside me, pulling me flush against his chest. Our heartbeats mingle into one as we consume each other. Our kiss is full of hope and desperation, the same cocktail that brought us together in the first place.

Tears threaten to fall, my face burning as my mind makes this into a goodbye. To give in to each other feels like giving into our fear that this is it.

I bury my face into his neck before he can see the redness taking over my face and breathe in the strong leather smell of him and the ocean beside us. His grip on me loosens and he uses one hand to trail up and down my spine.

"Thank you," I breathe into his neck. "For bringing me here."

"This part of the castle feels like it belongs to you. How could I not bring you here?" He presses a kiss to the top of my head. "When I am King, I think I will officially give it to you. I can have a plaque made or something."

"A plaque?" I chuckle at the idea.

"Yeah. It can say: Mariel's Grotto."

Laughter fills my chest, pushing the tears away. "You're ridiculous."

"Only when it comes to you."

We stay pressed together, letting silence be our only witness. This man is a gift. Without him I would never have made it this far. He's made everything possible for me. He's risked everything to make sure I was safe. I don't deserve him.

I have to save him, too.

NINETEEN

There's levity in my step as we climb the stairs back to civilization. Getting in touch with my roots was just what I needed to pull myself out of the blackness that was threatening to take over. Either that or the attention that Tristan so liberally bestowed. My lips still feel warm and a little swollen, but I love it.

He leaves me outside my bedroom door with promises to get good rest, which I have every intention of doing until I enter my room and my brain starts functioning again.

There's ocean access right under our feet.

Honestly, the Prince is lucky the Seafolk didn't know about it before because I bet that's where the kelpies would have decided to come up first. But they don't, yet. I lunge for my desk and scribble out another note. This will make working with the Seafolk so much easier. This will make our battle much more possible. I wasn't sure before how we were going to get everyone far enough away from the castle to get to the water, but now I don't have to. It's been here all along.

Excitement runs through me in waves as a plan of real possibilities comes together in my mind. All we have to do is wait for the Prince to fail, which is something that I can almost plan on now. He may have been raised to be king, but he doesn't have the mind for it. If he can't handle Anneliese and Captain Wimark, he couldn't handle a whole country. It's almost sad, but I can't linger in those emotions because I'm still trying to do my best for Tristan. His military background will be invaluable in holding the country together, and I want to help him however I can.

So, I wait for the Prince to fail, the army comes marching, and I find a way to get the rebellion, the Seafolk, and the remaining Fae to fight together to save the country. It might be a hard sell to the rebellion, but I'll find a way to convince them it's in their best interest. The civil war that is very possible without the already established monarchy would not end in the rebellion's favor. At least helping Tristan, who already believes humans deserve better, would prove their worth to a monarch ready to listen. That counts for something. They can believe in that right?

I scratch out another note, leaning over my desk as the excitement running through my blood makes me shaky and unable to slow down to sit. But the Seafolk need to know right away. I've given them the perfect place to gather. This grotto could change the tide of the whole battle. And how could the Fae not see how important we are after we help them survive? They'll have to come around to us.

For the first time since I've been here, I feel like I'm pulling my weight. I'm proving myself and doing what I set out to accomplish. I can have pride in myself. I can feel like I'm worth something.

My feet skid along the smooth stone in the hallway as I search for another messenger boy. Instead, I hit the all-too-solid body of Ry as he approaches my room.

He grips my shoulders to steady me, watching me with a side smile and a raised brow. "Going somewhere?"

"Just trying to mail this letter." My voice is breathless with excitement and I'm sure my face is completely flushed.

He tilts his head as he studies me. "You're awfully excited over a letter."

"Help me mail it, and I'll fill you in."

I grin at him, and he gives me a nod before looping my arm through his and starting off on my original quest.

"So what's got you so worked up? Something to do with that Fae boy?" His grip on my arm tightens as he mentions Tristan, and I tense at the off hand reminder that he isn't just some boy. Tristan will be King.

I resist the urge to bite my lip. I have nothing to hide. "He showed me something that I think will pull everything together."

"He's been holding out on us?" He breathes out a dry laugh. "Why doesn't that surprise me?"

"He wasn't holding out. I don't think he knew how perfect it was. Plus, he told me he forgot all about it."

I refuse to let Ry's words penetrate my brain and work their way into my doubts. I don't need to doubt Tristan. He's proved himself over and over to me. He's solid.

"Sure, he did. Now, what did he 'forget all about'?"

I lean closer to him, his shoulder jutting into my throat as I try to whisper in his ear. I'm not sure how much of a secret this place is, but I don't want word of it to start circulating through the castle because I'm too stupid to keep my mouth closed.

"There's access to the ocean under the castle."

Ry's eyes grow wide. "Are you serious? That's a big deal, Mariel. That could change everything." His voice grows louder as the excitement gets to him too.

"That's what I thought. That's why I have to let the Seafolk know." As I say it out loud, I realize how big of a betrayal this might be to Tristan. Even as Ry's eyes gleam and I feel like I'm moving forward, it occurs to me that the Seafolk could choose to use this to attack the Fae later. But it's worth it to have them as allies now. I have to believe that, or else drown in the undertow of uncertainty.

"And the banished," Ry says. His tone is unbudging, so I choose not to mention that I have no interest in involving them.

I have to juggle what's best for everybody. Ry just doesn't understand.

"Well, now we know where the fight will be," he says with a grin that reveals his fixed teeth that gleam bright against his dark skin. "That solves that little puzzle."

"Right!"

I'm glad he sees it my way. If he can understand it so quickly, I hope that Tristan can too.

"I'll update the rebellion. They'll love this. We're bringing the battle home. That will give us the largest population ready to fight," he muses.

As he mentions the largest population, my excitement fades a little. He's right, we're going to need more people. We have no idea what to expect from the invaders, and Captain Wimark will undoubtedly have more tricks up his sleeve that we need to be prepared for. We're going to need more than just the Seafolk and the rebellion. But not the banished. We're not desperate enough for them just yet.

"I'll talk to Tristan and see what military he can drum up here. He must still have some contacts." It would have been a lot better if he still had his men to rely on. I'm sure he'll think the same thing. It seems like the thing I'm best at is reminding those I care for about their pain.

"And I'll talk to Azalea."

"Good." I'm glad Ry is here to handle the rebellion. I don't know if I can look into her sunken face again. I can't face the very real consequences of my failures that close.

Ry takes my letter and continues searching for a messenger boy on his way to the rebellion headquarters while I pivot to go back for Tristan.

It seems ridiculous that I didn't think of the possibilities while I was with him. I needed a moment for it all to come together in my mind. I want to blame lack of sleep or training, but I know most of it is because of my own hesitation to get everyone involved. I need to accept that this is what's happening and move forward with it. Denying it won't help any of us and I'm a fool if I think I can save all of them. But I might be able to save my own people. And that has to count for something when it's finally time for me to go back home. It hurts my heart to think about leaving, but I know that will be what's best for Tristan. I'll have done what I wanted to do and then I'll have to leave him behind to do what is best for his country.

I know I won't be seen as a hero, far from it, but that's okay. I don't need them to think of me that way. I just want to know I can go home someday. Is that too much to ask? The darkest parts of my heart say yes.

Speeding past the Great Hall, my gaze snags on the back of Tristan's tunic and I hesitate instead of going to him right away. He's talking to a man I don't recognize.

"It has been a lot for us to adjust to. You have to realize that. You had been gone for years and then you were back, but you were back and tangled up with the human. I am not sure how you thought you were going to be getting our support. You put us in an impossible position."

I hesitate, hiding against the wall to hear better. My chest hurts as this Fae says the things I've been thinking. I shouldn't be here. Not when it comes to Tristan. We should have stayed apart if he really wanted to take the throne like his father wanted. I'm holding him back. And how can he ever *really* choose me if he has the throne dangling over his head? That will always come between us.

"You have to understand her part in this," Tristan says. "She is not a random human I decided to drag around."

"Sure, sure. We just do not understand how any of this came to be. It feels irreconcilable."

There's a long period of silence and I'm not sure what I'm expecting Tristan to say. I don't expect him to choose me, but I want to hear him do it anyway. I want to pretend that I'm more important even though I shouldn't be. I should leave now to protect him, but I can't. I have to help the Seafolk and my family and keep Ry out of too much trouble. I can't do that if I leave.

"You know that William is not the right choice. What I do should have no bearing on that," Tristan finally says.

"It does not feel like we have another choice," the man says with a sigh. "You want us to ignore everything and look at you the way your father did, but we cannot. In many ways, he was blinded to your faults by love."

"And you are blinded to William's faults because of his birth," Tristan snaps.

The stone wall digs into my back as I press harder against it. I want to sink into it and disappear.

"He has been our prince from the beginning. Do you really expect us to forget that?"

"No, I just thought you would be more willing to follow my father's wishes."

"Do not let this come between us." There's a clapping sound like he's put his hand on Tristan's shoulder. "Try to see it from our perspective. Your father never made things completely official. That puts us in a bad position right away. We are trying to do what we think is best for the whole country, not just what you want."

Footsteps stomp across the floor. "That is the same

thing I want." Tristan's voice grows louder, and I have nowhere to hide. "You are a fool if you think William will not run this country into the ground. It has already begun."

He rounds the corner as he exits the room, his eyes growing wide as they land on me.

"Tristan please come back. We need to talk about this more," the man calls from inside the room.

"Go now," Tristan mouths at me.

I turn and run, not sure where I'm going but hoping I can get away from the pain in my chest.

SOMEWHAT IRONICALLY, I find myself back at the water. Now that I know it's here, I can't help but be drawn to it. I throw a rock into the lapping sea, the sound clattering through the high roof of the cavern.

Tears burn down my cheeks in a solid river that I don't bother wiping away.

So much of this pain feels like my fault. If I wasn't here, Tristan could have been king already. People wouldn't be so confused about him. Ry wouldn't be in this mess if I'd never come here. I wouldn't even have been able to bring Zale home to start his strike that led to this mess if I hadn't come here.

All I've wanted was to save everyone. I want to help them and protect them, often from themselves. But what have I really accomplished? There's just a string of broken people fanning out behind me, and I have no idea how to help them anymore.

It would have been better if I'd never come.

"Mariel?" Tristan's voice echoes through the cavern as he makes his way down the stairs. "I thought I might find you here."

How many places did he really have to look? I wipe my tears away with the palm of my hand, but I know it's useless. I won't be able to hide that I was crying from him.

"I never wanted you to hear that," he says as he reaches the stony beach. "I know you already carry so much on your shoulders, and I did not want to add to it."

"You wanted to lie to me instead?" I toss another rock into the water.

The rocks shift as he comes to sit next to me, his arm sweeping around my waist. "I never lied to you. I did not think their opinions were important."

"How could you not?" I slide out of his grip. "I'm keeping you back and everyone knows it."

"That's not true. If they could not accept me as king because of you then they were just looking for excuses. If they really wanted me as king, you would not even be a factor in their decision-making." Tristan clenches his hands into fists. "No matter what my brother does, they will always prefer him to me."

"I don't see how that can be true. He's so stupid and self-absorbed. Can't they see that?" *How can they not see what I see in Tristan? How can they not believe in him?* I'm willing to do whatever it takes to support him, and they can't even consider him because of something as meaning-less as his birth. It's beyond stupid.

He stares out at the dark water with a frown. "We all have our demons, Mariel. This one is mine."

Maybe I shouldn't have been so quick to pull away from him. I want to get closer again, but I don't. To do that would be selfish and I need to think about what's right for everyone, even when Tristan won't. So instead, we sit by each other watching the waves in silence.

After a while, he reaches over and takes my hand where it's pressed into the rocks. He squeezes it tight, conveying all the emotions he cannot say. That we both cannot say. We cannot escape our fates. I always knew that. We've been fooling ourselves, and the knowledge that it cannot continue threatens to break my heart.

How could I not want to be with this man, regardless of if he's Fae or not? Tristan is solid and so capable. He'd help me with anything, even to his own detriment. Even now he's fighting his own two-front battle to try and keep me safe from the opinions of his people. He's a better man than I deserve.

"I came up with an idea," I tell him to break the silence and pull away from thoughts of what I'll never be able to have.

He raises a brow as he looks at me. "Why should I be surprised?"

"Well, I never would have even known to think about it without you." I knock into his shoulder with a smile that does its best to ease the tension in my heart. "I think you've found the missing piece that will make our battle possible."

"Is that so?" His grin grows wider. "And what is it that I've done that will turn the tides for us?"

"It's this." I gesture with an open hand at the space around us. "We needed the Seafolk as allies and you've found how we'll actually be able to use them."

I watch the emotions war on his face as he drifts between delighted and conflicted.

"Did I say something wrong?" The emotions of earlier threaten to rip me under with their strong pull.

"No." He shakes his head, hair falling across his forehead. "It is a lot of me to take in. This place has been such a closely guarded secret. I imagine it has been that way for a reason and I am somehow disappointing my ancestors."

"I think your father would want you to win the fight that is coming. I don't think he would hold you back from using your best chance even if it did reveal a secret or two." I try to give him a reassuring smile, but his face grows darker. "Plus, it will be a great way of convincing the Seafolk that they are our allies. It's a little give and take that will allow you to hide bigger secrets later if you want."

He sighs and runs his hands through his hair. "You do not need to convince me. I know that this is a good option, this is something I will need to figure out for myself."

"So don't tell anyone?" I can't help the wince that runs through my face.

Tristan grabs my shoulder. "Who did you tell?"

"I— it was just Ry." Tristan relaxes until I open my mouth and mumble out the rest. "And he was going to tell the rebellion."

Tristan jumps to his feet, rocks skittering in his wake as he paces along the water's edge. "You have given all of our enemies easy access to us, and you did not think this would be something you should ask me about first?"

"I wasn't thinking of them as our enemies." I struggle to my feet, tripping over my skirt as I try to keep up with his pace. "I was thinking of our *allies*. They get to know our secrets."

Tristan looks at me with a sad smile. "This just shows how different our worlds are that you would think that. Allies quickly become dangerous enemies when you give them your secrets. Plus, the rebellion has always been our enemy. That is why they are called the *rebellion*."

His logic sinks my stomach like a stone. There's no argument to be had here; he's not wrong. I already know that my brother has killed many of his people in the name of the rebellion, something he never had to stand trial for. Although, he was punished just the same.

He stops his pacing to stand in front of me and I have to

stop short before I walk into his chest. "I know you meant well, and I will figure out a way to fix this."

"Or you could let me fix it." If I move fast, I might be able to get Ry and tell him to stop. And I never mailed the letter. It could be easy...ish.

He chuckles. "This is my area. I can handle it."

I grind my teeth together, but his laughing makes me want to throw more rocks. This was my moment to prove myself and to really do something big for this battle and he can't see that at all. My cheeks burn as I shove my embarrassment down, letting anger take its place. "Or maybe you could admit that I didn't do too bad and that my idea is a good one. You just don't want to believe it could be because it's mine."

"That is not true, I—"

"You say that I act without thinking, and maybe that's true, but I think this is a good idea no matter what you say, and I think maybe you're the one that isn't thinking." I poke him in the chest, and he steps back, mouth dropping. I want his reaction to make me feel better, but it doesn't. Hurting him doesn't change the hurt inside me.

"I did not mean to offend you. I just think I might know a little better than you right now."

"I've been sitting around waiting to be useful and I finally found something that I thought would make me useful to you and to the Seafolk and to my own father. I have to do something right or I'll never be able to go home. Why can't you see that what I'm doing is what's best? All it does is reveal a little hole under the castle that I'm sure you can block up or post guards or something that would negate any advantage it would give anyone later. This isn't a bad thing. This is a great thing." I stand up taller and brace my fists on my hips. "And I'm proud of it."

He stares at me slack-jawed. I've never talked to him

like this before. But I always ran away before and that isn't an option anymore. Running away won't solve my problems. They've all come to the castle with me.

"Mariel, I—"

"I don't want to hear you doubt my ideas anymore." I don't need to try and catch Ry and fix things. The more he didn't like the plan, the more it felt right to me. I don't need to feel bad about it.

He can't look at me like the council would. I'm not just a helpless human. I'm more than useful, and I'm going to force him to see that.

"Okay." He holds his hands up in surrender. "Maybe I was a little hasty when I said it wouldn't work and would cause issues for us. You're right, those are issues we can tackle later."

I give him a curt nod even as excitement builds in my chest. I've won this round. I did it.

"So how would you like to handle the next step?"

He frowns and begins pacing again. "I don't doubt that William's attempt to stop the army will fail, but I'm not sure how you intend to get the army down into the grotto. I would not leave my castle so undefended for them to march straight through."

"No, you're right, that wouldn't work." I chew on my bottom lip and brace my chin against my knuckles. "But what if we could use the sea beasts?"

His forehead crinkles as he glances back at me. "What do you mean?"

"I mean, they are already a problem, why not make them the army's problem instead of ours?" I jump from foot to foot as my idea takes hold. "I'm sure the Seafolk could find a way to guide the beasts here and then when the army came, we'd have monsters waiting."

"Waiting to destroy the castle," Tristan comments

dryly.

"Wouldn't that be worth the risk if it meant that you would be secure in your kingdom? Who would dare attack the nation that could command the beast of the sea to rise on their behalf?" I'm sure I look half-crazed as I grab his tunic and pull him closer to me. "It would make you look beyond powerful. It would give you all the respect your father wanted for you."

I know I've gone too far when he jerks away from me. He takes two steps and keeps his back to me. "This plan would only work if there were no Fae among the army that could talk to the beasts themselves."

"Can they do that?" I can't begin to imagine how useful that would have been on the ship.

"Of course. All of us have our own magic. You have seen Anneliese's."

A bitter taste runs through my mouth. I *have* seen Anneliese's magic. It's a dark thing that I don't see any positive ways to use. The way she can just take away some-one's free will... I couldn't do it.

"What about you?" I've never asked him about anything that made him distinctly Fae before. I know we're different and that was as much as I needed to know. I want to know him better, regardless of our differences.

He kicks at the rocks. "What about me?"

"What's your big bad magic?" I try to tease because there's no way it could be worse than what Anneliese does.

Tristan's face goes dark, and I know I've said the wrong thing. "I would rather not talk about it. I don't even use it."

"Is it really that bad?"

He looks at me with a grimace and I know I've done it again.

"My magic is one that no one can survive. It is a dark cloud of death."

CHAPTER

TWENTY

Tristan's words echo through my mind long after he leaves me in my room to process. He's such a good man that I can't imagine his magic being something so dark. I can't imagine what it would have been like to discover what he can do. Did he harm someone close to him as a child?

I climb into the bed, but I just feel restless. It feels wrong to have left Tristan the way I did. He was hurting and I knew it and I still let him walk away.

But I'm afraid.

I don't think I want to find out more about his magic. I'm sure that's not what he'll want to talk about either, but that gate has already been opened and we'll have to talk about it at some point. Even just as far as to talk about why we need allies when he could take out the whole army. Or why Captain Wimark was sent to disperse the enemy when Tristan could have done it without even trying. Do they not know about his magic? I would have to think they don't based on how they treat him. There's no way I could be that disrespectful to someone who could easily wipe me out.

Digging my fingers into the rough weave of the blanket covering the bed, I try to find a way to pull back and to settle my emotions. This shouldn't feel like so much to learn. This really shouldn't change anything between us. It's not like the first time I found out about his magic was because he had used it and we were surrounded by the dead. No, I should be far more worried about how my plan will work if someone has the magic to communicate with the sea beasts. It seems like a stretch considering the Fae can barely tolerate going near the water at all, but still, it could happen.

Despite all of Tristan's misgivings, I know I need to do something about putting our plan in order. If he doesn't want to use his magic to give us the advantage, we're going to have to find another way. The way that I've discovered.

I grab a fresh sheet of paper from the desk for a missive to the Seafolk. I give them directions as best as I can imagine to the grotto considering I've never seen it from the outside and explain how we want the sea beasts herded there to take care of the impending battle.

It seems like a bit of a stretch that they could get the sea beasts to do anything, because if they could, they wouldn't have sent me to deal with the politics of what the banished were up to. Plus, there's the small issue of how we'll get the beasts to leave when everything is over. I doubt Tristan wants a kraken hanging out beneath the castle, ready to take it down whenever the mood strikes. But that can all be figured out later. We have to survive this first.

This time when I open the door, a messenger is working his way down our hallway and it's an easy thing to hand over my letter.

My chest feels like it's full of a thousand butterflies as I lean against the door. But the damage is done now. No matter how much Tristan doesn't like it, my plan is moving forward. I just hope it's as successful as I think it will be. I hope that in the end, he's proud of me.

I hope *I* can be proud of me.

TRISTAN LOOKS haggard when he knocks on my door later. His hair's a mess, and his tunic is wrenched to the side like he's been in a fight.

I jump out of bed and let him inside quickly, my gaze roving over him to catalog what else might be wrong. He gives me a wry smile as he collapses into the chair, letting me examine him better.

"What happened to you?" I ask when I notice a cut behind his ear that is still dripping blood and looks suspiciously like it came from a blade. I wrap my arms around my chest as the cold night air seeps into my bones.

"I attempted to tell William our findings about Anneliese and the King." He runs his hand through his hair, smearing his hand with blood. "As soon as I brought up our father's death, William refused to listen to anything else. He wasn't here when it happened and is more than happy to believe I was somehow involved in it, even though he can't prove it."

I look around the room for something to clean him up with and land on the water pitcher beside the bed. I wet a handkerchief and work on cleaning up his hand and neck.

"It went that well then?"

He grabs my hand to still my movements. "I think it is safe to say that he is not interested in that scenario. He has no other option, no one else even remotely close to having been capable of committing the crime, but he will not charge her with it either."

"What a snake," I murmur as I wipe clean all the lines in

his palm.

He shakes his head. "I do not think that's it."

"Then what could it be? If he's not in on it with her, then why hasn't he charged her? You saw the way he looked at her at the council meeting. If he really hated her, then why doesn't he move now that he has an opportunity to get rid of her?" I know I would. I would have her arrested in a second just so that I would never have to deal with her stupid beautiful face or her condescending smile again. "Is he in on it?"

"I do not believe my brother capable of plotting to kill my father, not to mention the fact that he was not even here when it happened."

"Well, isn't that convenient," I grumble as I work at the cut behind his ear.

"Either way, we cannot rely on William to remove Annelise. Whatever we plan next, we have to account for her being around."

"To mess everything up."

He tilts his head to the side, out of my reach. "You are becoming quite the little saber."

I bare my teeth at him, and he laughs, reaching out to cup the back of my head. He pulls me closer to him and presses his lips to mine. A smile works its way across my mouth until he ends up kissing my teeth.

"It only seems appropriate that I become a saber since it's what drew us together in the first place." Sometimes being in that forest feels like years ago. What would our lives have been like if that big cat hadn't attacked Ry and me? Would I have ever met Tristan? He probably wouldn't have become my ally. I might just owe that saber everything.

Tristan smiles back at me and leans further against the chair. He sighs, picking dried blood from under his finger-nails. "I think you will need to keep channeling that saber in the days ahead."

"I think I can handle whatever comes next." As long as it falls neatly within the parameter of our plans.

"I hope so. There is a battle coming, something you have never experienced before."

I open my mouth to refute him, but no words come. He's right. I've never been in a real battle where people are doing their best to kill each other. I've been in *fights* before, but those were mostly verbal with the occasional punching and almost always with my brothers. This really will be different. But I can do it. I can be strong.

"Any words of advice?" I swing around the chair to sit on his lap, giving him a smile that softens my question.

He picks up a lock of my hair, twisting it around my finger. "I would rather that you hid until it was over."

"Do you think I'm not brave enough to fight?" My chest burns and I try to stand up and move away but he keeps me locked in place.

"It's not that. You are one of the bravest people I know. How many have you met that would be willing to leave their homes behind to come somewhere entirely new where the world is out to get them? I don't know many who would even try, let alone stay. You fight for us every day, even when you do not have to. What could be braver than that?"

I look into his calm sea eyes, wanting to refute him. He doesn't live inside my head, so he doesn't know how hard this is for me. But maybe that's part of the point. It's hard and I've continued to do it anyway. I'm scared but I haven't run away for home. Maybe I am a little brave.

I tuck myself against his shoulder, breathing in the heavy scent of him by his neck. "If you know how brave I am, then you must know how stubborn I am. I want to live in a way that I can look back on with pride. Self-respect. There's no way I'm going to hide somewhere until it's all over. This is my battle too."

Somewhere along the line that really became true. Land may not be where I belong, but I will fight for this nation. For Tristan. For the possibility of freedom for my people. For the Seafolk that trusted me enough to send me here on their behalf. I belong here now.

He runs his hands through my long blonde hair, working out the little tangles along the way. "I know. Just please tell me you have some experience with a sword."

I don't think I've ever even touched a sword, let alone learned how to use one. "I had that trident before."

"And that is the only weapon you know how to use?" His hand on my back stills and I know I've said the wrong thing.

"I wouldn't say I *know* how to use it. Ry gave it to me when we were separated. You were the first enemy I even had the chance to use it on."

I want him to laugh at how ridiculous that is, but his chest goes still under my body.

"Mariel."

"Hmm?" I close my eyes and push my face further into his neck. I just know I don't want to hear whatever he has to say.

"We have work to do."

~

HE TAKES me to a training yard filled with sand and lined with wooden racks full of weapons just outside the castle.

Fae with thick, corded muscles swing heavy broadswords at each other in circles drawn in chalk.

"Welcome to your worst nightmare," Tristan says, and this time he smiles but it does nothing to calm my nerves that have settled like a rock in my belly.

He steps up to a rack of weapons, examining a few of them before setting them carefully back in place. "If you are going to fight in this battle, you will need to learn to use a sword. If you cannot, then I cannot risk you being on the battleground. You will only end up being a distraction to me, and I do not think I need to tell you how dangerous a distraction can be."

I frown, but there's nothing I can say to refute it. I can see how he would feel the need to protect me if I couldn't protect myself, but I don't like thinking about how useless I would be. Will pushing to be present for the fighting end up getting me killed?

If I linger in those thoughts, I *will* end up running away.

"So, I will see how quickly you can be trained, and then we will go from there."

He picks up a small blade that lingers somewhere between dagger and actual sword. He hands it to me and my fingers curl instinctively around the leather grip. It's a lot heavier than I was expecting, my arms dipping with the weight, but I quickly hold it upright so Tristan doesn't think I'm too weak to use it. He watches me with narrowed eyes and shakes his head, muttering something under his breath as he examines the weapons again.

"I think this one will work." I swing the sword through the air, muscles screaming as I stop its trajectory and bring it back up.

"Do you really think you could hold it for hours without tiring?"

How do I tell him I'm already tired? Still, I keep the sword from shaking as I give him a falsely bright grin. "How hard could it be?"

"Mariel, this is not the time for joking. If it's too heavy, we will find you something else."

I look down at the small blade. Could there really be something smaller than this? If there is, I don't want to be the weakling that has to trade for it. I'm strong enough for this blade. Or at least I can be by the time I have to use it.

"It'll be fine, so show me how to use it."

He walks us over to one of the chalk circles closer to the side and picks a wooden sword from the rack for himself to use.

"Shouldn't I get one of those too?"

He shakes his head. "We do not have time for you to practice with a weapon you will never use. You need to spend all your time getting comfortable with the real thing."

"Then shouldn't you use the real thing to practice with me?"

He grins, rolling his shoulders out. "I would not want to hurt you."

His confidence makes me grit my teeth and heft my sword higher. My shoulders already ache as we circle around each other. Sweat drips from my temples as the midday sun beats down on us. Tristan's easy smile is in place as he casually lunges forward. I move the sword just in time to deflect but he swings around and catches me behind the knee on the other side.

"You have to move quicker," he says as he watches me wince with each step. "Your enemy will not wait for you to recover before they strike."

"You don't say."

My cheekiness makes his smile grow wider and strikes a

chord of irritation in me. I swing my sword around to catch him in the side, but he dances out of reach. Moving forward, I try again to the same effect. His easy pace and complete lack of concern over my attempts encourages anger to grow in my chest. I strike and strike and strike again. My arms flail as I try to reach him, but he easily moves out of harm's way every time. Sweat pours down my temples and my spine. The sword grows heavier with every swing and nearly pulls me forward with its weight as I attempt to hit Tristan.

He taps me on the side, on the leg, my arm, and once even my neck. He's able to move past my efforts with barely a thought and completely eviscerates me. My face is red as he motions for me to put the sword down. I thrust it into the earth, eager to be rid of it.

"Do you see now why I was so worried about you fighting?" he asks me, sinking onto his knees and sending a puff of sand into the air. As if he needs to recover.

I grind my teeth together. "I always understood why you were worried, but that doesn't change what I need to do."

"Not even this?" he gestures to the ring.

"Not even this. I won't hide somewhere and wait for it to be over." There's no way I could do something like that. I need to be in control of my destiny, not waiting for him to figure it out for me.

He shakes his head but moves to stand anyway. "Then I guess I need to find you a better weapon."

It takes us all afternoon as we try out option after option, but he finally finds something he feels comfortable with me using. My arms are complete jelly at this point, but even so, I can lift the dagger he offers me.

"It is not an offensive weapon, that is for sure," he says before I can complain. "However, it can be useful to defend yourself and I don't see you being part of the heavy fighting anyway."

I want to argue with him about it, but I can't. If I were to be in the thick of the fighting, that would be the end of it for me. I wouldn't have to worry about what my father would think of me when I came home because I wouldn't be alive to experience it.

"Okay, so I take this dagger, and then what?"

"You can be somewhere close to the battle without being a part of it and if someone comes too close, you stick them. Remember, it's better for you to accept a slice to get a stab in than to wait for the perfect moment. Using a dagger means you are likely to get hurt too."

"Lovely."

Tristan puts his wooden sword away and gives me a grin. "I am not sure what else you hope to accomplish, but that is the best I can offer given your... talents."

"Are you saying I'm hopeless with a blade?"

"Let us just say that your lack of training really comes through."

I nudge him with my shoulder, wanting to be grumpy with him but I can't help but laugh. He laughs with me and the sound of it is so good to hear as his deep rumble spreads through the training space. How often have I even been able to hear him really truly happy? It hasn't been a part of our relationship thus far. Things have been too chaotic for these brief moments of levity.

"You have the dagger so we can both feel appeased that you have something to defend yourself, but don't get so cocky that you decide to join the real fighting," he says as he watches me slip the dagger into my pocket. "If you are ever attacked though, go for the underarm. It's less protected and is often a death blow. Behind the knee works well too.

But seriously, stay out of the real fighting if you can manage it.”

“There’s no worries about that. I choose life.”

“Of course you do.” He smiles at me again as he loops his arm around my shoulders and my heart threatens to melt onto the floor. “And I am glad to hear it.”

CHAPTER

TWENTY-ONE

espite the late hour, I can't sleep. I sit up in the bed and spin the dagger around between my fingers. The mix of metal and wood warm and chill my fingers in the dagger's endless procession. It's like my body recognizes what my brain refuses to: my days are numbered.

All too soon my plan will come together, and we'll be forced to fight. Even though I promised Tristan that I wouldn't get too involved, I know it's a daydream to think I won't be a part of it at all. The odds of this conflict leaving me as a corpse are very high.

Will Zale be there waiting for me when it's time to cross over?

Even though I wasn't directly involved in his death, the guilt still follows me, and I can't help but wonder if he holds me responsible anyway. He had a whole future here one he was so excited to live out and that's all gone now. *What would have happened if it had been me the crowd took in vengeance instead of him? Would he be with Azalea now, happy?* I'm sure he would. And I don't think he would have

225

taken any time to worry about how to help the Fae defend their borders.

Was he a better man than me?

That's a question better left to someone else.

I sink farther into the plush mattress, letting it swallow me up in the scent of jasmine that wafts out of the pillows, wishing it could lull me into sleep with its rich comfort. The candle on my nightstand flickers as it burns down, casting deep shadows across the walls.

Rolling to the side, I place my dagger on the nightstand, watching the candle flame's reflection flicker along the length of the blade.

Footsteps clatter down the hall outside my door and I bolt upright. Men's voices yell to each other and my chest grows tight. Could this be it? Has the battle finally been brought to our door?

I fling the blankets off me and slide over to the door, my white nightgown trailing around my legs. Tristan made sure I had more clothing brought in, but I still can't get used to it. One or two tunics were more than enough for me back home.

Pressing my ear to the crack between the door and the frame I try to still my breathing so I can hear something other than it but there's only silence. Whatever was happening, they've already left my section of the castle.

Curiosity and a lack of sleep have me tugging on the door handle before I can think better of it. I don't want to stay in bed hoping I can sleep when there's something going on. I'd like to think I'm doing great spy work and Tristan will applaud my efforts to find out information for us, but I know that's not true. It's not even a very good dream. Tristan would want me to have nothing to do with this.

The hallway is empty when I open the door. If I hadn't

been awake when I heard the noises, I might have chalked it all up to a dream with how peaceful everything feels. I creep past Ry's room, considering waking him up to come with me and then thinking better of it. If he's getting sleep after having to deal with the rebellion, then that's the best thing he could be doing. Following me around will only expose him to more trouble.

The farther I get away from my room, the more it feels like there was never anything outside my door. There's only quiet all around as the castle sleeps. But I know I heard voices. I know there were men in this hallway only seconds ago. So where could they have gone?

My feet are quiet against the stone as I keep moving forward. I trail my hand against the wall, letting the rough surface keep me grounded. It isn't until I get to the stairs to the dungeon that I hear the Fae moving again.

There's the barest flicker of torchlight coming up from the dark stairwell, just enough that I don't have to worry that the sounds I'm hearing are the ghosts of tenants' past.

I move carefully onto the steps, watching my feet to make sure I don't make any noise to draw attention this way.

"She said to prepare." A man's voice drifts up the stairs and I slink back against the wall. "I cannot wait to see the look on the Prince's face when she comes to take what is rightly hers."

"Hush up," says another man. "She said to *prepare*, not draw attention. The last thing we need is to give away her plans before she can enact them."

"Do you really think she would make us walk into the lake and drown ourselves if we fail?"

"That is what she said. I think you would be a fool to doubt her."

Anneliese? What could she be planning? I thought she

went into hiding after everything that happened with the Prince. I know I would have wanted to. A rejection like that is not something so easily walked away from. If Tristan had ever done that to me… I would have been rowing my way back home right now, no matter how long it took.

"Still, I think she is not as heartless as she wants us all to believe," says the first man.

"Then you are definitely a fool."

"If I am such a fool, then why are we working to make her Queen?"

It's a good question, one I would ask anyone who was working with her. It doesn't take long of being in her presence to know she's a snake.

"She is the best option we have. There is no way I would want to take on the army she is bringing with her."

I move farther down the stairs, wanting to see what these men are doing for Anneliese in the dungeon. They've already gotten rid of the evidence of her crimes, what more could they need to do down here? It's just a bunch of empty and abandoned cells. I keep my back tight against the wall as it curves around the stairs.

"Just think, if the Prince had never tried to make a marriage alliance with Naicroft in the first place, Annelise would have never been able to utilize them for her own interests. It was a genius move."

"I wouldn't say that. It weakens our border no matter what. Now they know how much our country is suffering after the death of our king."

"They could have assumed we were suffering on their own. It does not take a genius to figure that out when a king is assassinated."

"Still."

I reach the last curve of the stairs, my body tight as I

lean around the stone column to get a glimpse of Anneliese's men.

There's only two of them despite the commotion they made traveling past my door. The 'fool' is a slight man who holds the torch as his much larger companion moves full canvas bags into the jail cell closest to the stairs. I stop breathing as the fool looks my way and I tuck my head back around the corner where they can't see me.

"What is she going to do with all this?" the slender man asks.

The big one grunts as he heaves a bag up onto his shoulder. "I would prefer not to know. Nothing good comes out of knowing her plans before she is ready to share them."

"You are not curious at all?"

"Curiosity is a good way to get yourself killed," the big one says in a voice like gravel as he heaves the bag into the cell. "If you do not wish to end up like her other allies, you would do well to learn how to keep your mouth closed."

I peek around just in time to see the small man frown, his face turning red. "I didn't think I needed to watch myself when it was just you and me down here. Anneliese is still far away. Do we really need to be afraid of her when she's not even close to us?"

"That woman is a demon. You should pray every night that she doesn't take too close of an interest in you." The big man's voice is softer as he watches the small one shrink into himself with embarrassment. "Let's finish the job and get out of here. The sooner we can wipe our hands of this, the better."

The slight man sniffs and nods, all the youthful emotions he had earlier completely snuffed out.

There are only a few more bags sitting on the desk and the big man moves fast, so I start working my way back up the stairs before they can finish and find me watching them. I'll have to come back later to see what they were up to.

Maybe I've found another way to take down Anneliese after all.

~

IF I THOUGHT SLEEPING WAS HARD BEFORE, it's near to impossible now that I'm actively waiting. I'm not sure how long I should wait before going back to the dungeon. The last thing I want is to get caught snooping down there. It would be far too easy for them to shove me into a cell and never be heard from again.

I can't help but be giddy. Tristan may not think I can do much as a lowly human but look how much I've been able to figure out while he manages the politics. If I had waited around like he wanted, where would we be? Still trying to figure out what route to take forward. Instead, I've given us one. I've been brilliant if I say so myself.

I wrap myself tighter into my blankets, letting the pressure soothe me. Closing my eyes, I rest my head against the pillow and think about how proud I would imagine Zale would be of me. We disagreed about how to do this, but I think he would be pleased that I kept up his cause after his death.

When I can't take it anymore, I finally leap out of bed and head over to Ry's room. I'm going to need help and he's the closest option.

I rap my knuckles against the door and his face is shocked when he opens it to find me.

"It's the middle of the night, what are you doing here?" he asks, doing his best to smooth the surprised creases in his forehead back out.

"I need you to come with me. I discovered something earlier and I want to check it out."

His eyes narrow as he watches me, and he shifts onto his back foot. "I'm not sure now is the best time."

"Of course, it is. What, do you have something better to do?" I try to laugh but it dies on my lips as his face remains serious.

"Actually, I have company."

"Company?" Who does he even know that he could invite here, let alone actually be allowed inside?

Ry sighs and holds the door wider. "Just come in."

I frown at him as I cross the threshold but freeze in my steps as soon as I see who's sitting on the bed. "Azalea?"

She looks worse than I remember. Her clothing and guards hang on her like she's playing dress up and dark circles form rings under her eyes. Her skin is sallow and the smirk she gives me has none of the earlier confidence that would have made me uneasy just a few months ago.

"Welcome to the party," she says, her gaze flicking back over to Ry.

"When she heard about your plan, she wanted to come and strategize together." Ry stands in the middle of the room, equidistant from both of us. "We wanted to give this fight its best chance."

I curl my hands into fists, as I try to understand what he's saying. "Don't you think your strategizing would work better with me and Tristan? Plus, don't you think she might get in trouble for being here?"

Ry looks away from me and it's all the answer I need. We may be working together, but he still doesn't trust us. There's a part of me that understands why he would have a hard time working with us, but the larger part of me wants to feel betrayed about losing my friend once again.

"What issues do you have with the plan?" I try to move forward and keep this at the business level between us.

"There's a few things that trouble us," Azalea says, her voice rougher than it used to be. "For instance, your hopes that the sea beasts will work with us..."

"I don't expect them to work *with* us, but I'm hoping they can be used to our advantage. We wouldn't have to fight as hard if they were here to take down the army."

"We wouldn't be able to fight at all," Ry says. "We'd be hiding from the beasts just like the enemy."

I clamp my jaw tight, anger coursing through my veins like blood. I didn't expect Ry to have the same hangups as Tristan. How can no one see what a good idea it is? Having the sea beasts fight for us could save so many men. That's all I want. I want to win, and I want everyone to live. This feels like the best option for that outcome, no matter what they say.

Crossing my arms over my chest, I dig my nails into my skin to keep myself from exploding.

"We worry that we'll lose too many men to the monsters if they are invited into the castle," Azalea says. Her voice is as firm as any general. "They are far too wild to be useful for us. We should stick with the Seafolk and leave the beasts alone."

"We can't just ignore that the beasts are out there. Leaving them alone isn't an option when they refuse to leave us alone. I watched one take down a whole ship in minutes and there have been reports that others are finding their way onto land. They're a part of this fight whether they realize it or not and I would rather have them distracted out here than be given the option to take down my father's ship."

Ry's eyes soften as he watches me, my breathing

coming in short pants as I do my best to keep the tears away. "I know how worried you must be—"

"Do you? Because it's been a while since I've felt like you know me at all."

Ry gapes at me, his jaw hanging open. "Is that really how you feel?"

"How could I feel any differently? I'm so sorry about what happened to you, that was never what I wanted, but you can't keep pushing me away. There's been a growing wedge between us since you came back." I try to relax my arms, but they refuse to budge.

"I'm not... I'm not trying to push you away. I'm trying to protect you. From yourself a lot of the time, if I'm being honest. I don't want what happened to me to happen to you." He glances at the floor. "I'll do anything I can to keep you safe."

His confession knocks the wind out of my sails. My brain can't find words to respond to him and snags instead on Azalea still sitting on the bed, watching our interaction with unabashed interest.

"You don't need to worry about keeping me safe. I can take care of myself." I stand taller, straightening out my back as though that could smooth out the worries and anxiety we've both carried. "So next time, let me know if you hate my plan."

"We don't hate your plan," Ry says as he runs his hand over his tight curls. "We just aren't sure if it's the *right* plan."

"Isn't that the same thing?"

"No, it just means maybe we should consider other options before we go for the sea beast idea. I think that should be our last resort."

"They're too uncontrollable and unpredictable," Azalea

pipes up. "How would you remove the creatures after the battle?"

"I..." I didn't think about that. Maybe Tristan wouldn't mind having some monsters in his basement. It seems like a pretty Fae thing to do. He can swap out Anneliese for one of them.

Azalea slides off the bed. "And what will you do if they decide we are the better meal?"

"If we know the beast is there, why would we approach it?" Finally, a question I feel like I can answer.

She shakes her head. "Because someone will have to lead the enemy down there, probably a lot of someones. How will you keep them safe from the monster?"

And just like that, I'm adrift again.

"We're not saying it isn't any interesting idea," Ry says, trying to step in as my face grows redder. "But like I said, it might not be the *right* plan."

Tears burn in the back of my eyes, and I want to run away. When will someone believe in me? Do I look so stupid that no one thinks I can strategize? And all this so they can say they don't actually have a better idea; they just don't like mine. What am I supposed to do with that? It's hard not to take it personally. To not hear them saying that I'm the issue they have with the plan instead of the plan itself.

"If you're so smart, then what's your brilliant idea?" My voice is harsh and biting as I use it to keep my tears at bay. I'd much rather show my anger than my devastation.

Ry chews his cheek for a minute. "As I said, we're not sure what the right plan should be. That's what we wanted to talk about. Do you have any other thoughts?"

It feels more like he's trying to appease me than that he's interested in my thoughts. "There's no other big solution hiding around here. The sea beasts are the only creatures we could use instead of our people."

"Mariel, I think you underestimate how much people want to fight. They've been suffering for a long time. If you don't give them someone to hit, they're going to hit the people you want to protect." Ry raises a brow at me, and I don't have to be a genius to know he's talking about Tristan.

"You really think they would hurt Tristan? Even if he was doing good things for them?" I just know Tristan wouldn't be a king like his father or any of the kings that came before him.

Azalea chuckles. "First of all, I'm not sure I believe your precious Captain will do anything good for us. He has yet to prove himself. Second, they definitely would. There is no relationship between the humans and the Fae. You know that. They're not going to go down easy and accept a new oppressor without a fight. Not when they know the turmoil that's been going on."

"And how would they know that?"

Ry avoids my accusatory gaze. "I was asked to be the human representative. That's what I'm trying my best to do." He looks up at me, his face hard. "I have to look out for them first, Mariel. I'm surprised you're not doing the same."

"That *is* what I'm doing." I take a step back as Azalea comes closer to me.

"Is that so? How is it exactly that you think you're accomplishing that? By treating them like babies?"

"They *are* babies compared to this world. They know nothing about it! *I* knew nothing about it and neither did Ry, and look where that got us." I hate how my voice rises, determined to let the emotions out somehow. "They're not ready for this fight. They're not ready to be here. And if you two were being honest with yourselves, you'd know that."

Ry frowns. "I think you're making a pretty big generalization."

"How many more people that you love need to die before you realize I'm right?"

Silence descends on the room with only the crackling of the fire to break it up. Azalea and Ry won't look at me and my chest puffs up the barest amount. I've gotten them. How can they argue that point? It's nothing but facts. The awful terrible facts that we still carry the scars of.

"They should be allowed to die for a cause they care about," Ry finally whispers.

"Is that your plan, then? Send the banished and the Fae out together to fight the army?"

Ry shifts on his feet.

"What?"

He looks at Azalea who gives me a hard look. "We don't intend for them to fight at all."

"At all?"

My stomach sinks like a rock. That's been part of the plan the whole time. The Fae invited us here for peace talks, this is part of the peace.

"This isn't our fight. We can wait until we have one clear enemy."

"Not your—" I can't think. Nothing about this feels right. "Is that what you're going to tell the council then?"

Ry purses his lips. "The council doesn't want us here in the first place. Our opinion hasn't been asked once, and I don't think they've thought twice about using us."

"What about when we were down in the grotto? I thought we were on the same page then?" I have to get him to see that he believes what I do.

"Azalea helped me realize how ridiculous it all is," Ry says.

I glance over to catch her feline smile curling across her too-thin face. "Of course she did."

"I don't know why you're surprised," she says. "The rebellion has always existed to get humans back on land, fighting the foreign enemy does nothing for us."

"Does nothing for you? Have you considered that it might give humanity a better place and more respect from the Fae? Right now, we have nothing to offer them except our work on the sea. Don't you want to be able to give them more?" I don't know why I'm arguing this now. I don't want them to fight. Ry and Azalea have me so turned around I don't know what I'm doing.

"We don't *want* their respect," Azalea practically spits. "Why would we want them to respect us? They should give us equality regardless of what they think of us. We're people, we're not just some animals that they can push away from their *perfect* world."

"It's hardly perfect," I point out. "They lost half their population to an illness. That doesn't sound like their world exists without flaws."

Azalea smiles and it makes my stomach turn. "Let's just say that that illness had a little help."

Ship. "Did you—"

"No, no." She waves away my concerns, but the smile stays in place. "That was long before my time. But the rebellion has had a hand in things for quite a while."

I glance at Ry, hoping to see the same level of horror that's coursing through me, but his face is like stone. I wrap my arms around my side and wish that I had gone for Tristan first. I wish I didn't know any of this. I would rather live in ignorance than know that my brother was involved in such evil. There's a reason I've never tried to find out all of what he did for the rebellion as their 'hand.'

"I don't think we're going to be able to find a way to agree." My voice is quiet as I back towards the door. "I'm just going to go back about my business."

"Don't be like that, Mariel." Ry reaches for me, but I flinch and he pulls back his hand. "You have to understand what we're saying just a little bit. I'm only trying to help you."

"Maybe a little bit." I wrap my fingers around the cool door handle. "But never enough to justify what you two have done."

I launch myself out the door before they can stop me, my heart a mess that feels like it will never recover.

TWENTY-TWO

After everything, all I want to do is collapse into bed. The excitement that carried me through has evaporated into dust. I consider finding Tristan for a brief moment, but my room is too close to be interested in roaming around the castle to find him again.

However, Tristan's smell hits me with a blast of earth and pine when I open the door. I wonder if I'm already dreaming before I catch sight of him sprawled out on the bed.

"Hey." He gives me a big smile that hits me square in the chest. "I know it is late, but I finished my meetings and I just wanted to see you."

I scurry across the room and leap onto the bed, curling into his arms. Pressing my face against his neck, I breathe him in to calm my racing heart. He wraps his arms around me, and I feel safe in this cocoon of our own making.

"Glad to know the feeling was mutual." I can hear the smile in his voice, and it makes me want to snuggle deeper into him.

He lets me stay like that for a long time, just breathing him in until my heart stops racing and my mind calms down. He trails his fingers over my back in small circles, the movement reminding me of being on the boat.

"Somehow I do not think that this reaction is entirely to do with me," he whispers into my hair. "What happened while I was gone?"

I don't want to think about it anymore. I don't want to rehash what Azalea and Ry have been up to, or even think about the betrayal they suggested. Shaking my head, I press even farther into his body as though I could disappear if I could only get close enough.

"I cannot help you unless you tell me."

As if he could help me at all. These are human problems and human business. He couldn't force Ry to change his mind any more than I could. At least I had a history with him on my side and even that wasn't enough.

But there *is* something I can tell him.

"I followed Anneliese's men earlier tonight. They were unloading some heavy bags into the dungeons. I never had a chance to check it out and see what was inside them."

"And that is what has made you so upset?" he asks, and I can just imagine the dubious look on his face.

Shifting in his arms, I pull my face back so I can see him. My body immediately misses his warmth. "Don't worry about that. What do you think Anneliese was having brought into the castle?"

"More bath soap?" he asks, wincing when I give him a hard look.

"Can you take this seriously?"

I can't take one more person doubting my ability to think critically or be responsible. If he can't understand what I'm asking him, I might just scream. Not might, I definitely will. I'm capable and observant. I could be such an asset to him if he only let me.

"Okay." He sits up and runs his hand through his hair

until it sticks up at a million different angles. "What would she be bringing into the castle?"

"Not only is she bringing something into the castle, but I think I know where she went."

Tristan doesn't bother trying to hide his grin. "She has gone to ground. After the display between her and William, I doubt we shall see much of her for a long time."

The urge to scream bubbles back up again as I shake my head. "She's not hiding and licking her wounds. She's been planning."

"Planning what?" Tristan frowns.

"I think she's going to make a play for the throne."

He laughs. "She cannot do that. She would have to be insane to think she could skip the line of succession like that."

"Is it really insanity if she's part of that line? She seems to think that she is owed the throne just as much as any of you."

Tristan winces. "I mean, she is William's cousin, but her mother is related to his mother. That is not part of the King's line. So, her place in the succession is not exactly close. It is not like she is next after me."

Interesting. From the way she talked, and the men talked about her, I would have expected her to be much closer. What makes her think she can make such a huge power play if she's not even close to inheriting the throne?

A sick feeling grows in my stomach. "When was the last time you saw the others that stand closer to inheriting the throne?"

"Years probably. It is not like we are all extremely fond of each other or anything. They are the ones that I thought would come to the initial council meeting and never showed up."

I bite my bottom lip, letting my teeth dig in to the point

of pain. How long has she been playing this game? Is it possible that she's been working her way up the line, eliminating the competition, one by one while no one was watching? If so, it would explain her desire to get close to both Tristan and the Prince. She'd have to be close to them to take them out. But both of them know her powers too well to let themselves get close enough to her for her to be able to make any kind of serious move. Except Tristan did…

"Did Anneliese ever use her magic on you while you were…" I have to swallow before I can force the word out. "Engaged?"

He glances away from me, keeping his gaze trained on the fire in the grate. "There was a moment when she tried, but I threatened her with my own magic and that was enough for her to back off."

"Your magic is something she fears even though you never use it?" I can't help my curiosity. This is the part of him that he's kept the closest tabs on and never shared with me.

"Every time it has come out the results have been… devastating."

His face grows even more distant. I reach out and grab his cold hand, squeezing my life into it. He doesn't respond, his mind somewhere in the past where I can't reach him.

"So." I have to move forward to draw him back out of his stupor. "Do you think it could be possible that Anneliese has been quietly making her way up the list?"

She just slipped up with Tristan and the Prince never let her get close enough to even try. It's possible.

He frowns. "I think we would have heard something."

"Or she could have been taking up residence at the castle to make sure no one did. You weren't here so you can't really speak to it. She's been squatting here like a spider in its web with none of your family the wiser."

It all makes sense. Anneliese is much smarter than to randomly act for no reason. It never made sense to me that she'd dumped Tristan for the Prince who obviously didn't want her. Now it's all coming together. She was removing the competition and now there's few enough left that it was time to act.

I hate how brilliant she is.

Tristan's forehead wrinkles as he thinks it over. "If that is the case, then she would have had to be working on this plan for years."

"That doesn't seem like it's a big enough deterrent to rule it out."

"No, maybe not." He scratches his chin. "But you have very little evidence for this."

"I know her."

"So do I."

"Not as well as I do." She's never hidden herself from me. She's never had to pretend to be demure and ladylike. I saw her true colors right away. She tried to poison me almost immediately, so...

"Let us say that that is what is happening, what would you have us do about it? We are already preparing for a battle."

I lean closer to him. "You need to understand what battle you're actually preparing for."

He frowns and I scramble to keep him with me.

"If you know exactly what you're fighting, you'll never be caught off guard." And with Anneliese we can never afford to be caught off guard.

"I will think about it," he says as he lays back on the bed.

I don't get what there is to think about. We already know Anneliese is shady. She's already tried to work things over with him. What more does he need to know? I don't understand because personally, I find nothing about Anneliese redeemable at all. She's nothing but a spider.

"Let us just take the rest of this night," Tristan says, patting the bed next to him. "Can we pretend for just a few hours like this is not the end?"

The end. It seems so final. How can he think that way?

His eyes crinkle at the corners as he looks at me and despite the anxiety bubbling in my chest from everything we've been through tonight, I curl up next to him. He wraps his arm around me and breathes deep into my hair. I sync my breathing with his, feeling our chests move together.

It's crazy how far we've come. Even crazier is the fact that a part of me has always wanted to love him. We've been drawn together since I set foot on land, and he's been my undeniable ally ever since. I couldn't have gotten through any of this without him.

I want to be able to stay like this forever, the two of us connected and close, but it feels like time is running out. He cannot be king with me beside him. His people would never accept that. Surely, he knows that too. I'm deluding myself and bringing him down with me.

A tear slips down my cheek and I'm glad Tristan can't see it. He wants to pretend that we can have each other for these last few hours of the night, and I want to let him. I want to give him that peace. That's what my love should be good for.

When he kisses the side of my face, I keep all my doubts and worries bottled up and instead twist my head further to make contact with his lips. I'll face the future tomorrow, but right now I'll hide in the dark with him.

Tristan's arm over my chest is a heavy weight as daylight finds me. I want to snuggle in closer to him, but I know we have to get moving. I've already lost precious time with figuring out what Anneliese was bringing into the castle. I can't continue to lie around with love as my shield any longer.

Rolling on my side, Tristan's face is so peaceful in the weak light. All the stress lines are smoothed out and he looks younger without the weight of the kingdom pulling him down. I run my fingers through his hair, letting the silky strands drift over my skin. He stirs from sleep, giving me a small smile as he finds his way to consciousness.

"What an excellent night," he sighs as he swings his arms out in a wide stretch. "I can take on the world now."

"Good, because I'm pretty sure that's what you're going to have to do." I slide out of the bed despite him trying to catch me and pull me back. "We have work to do."

He groans, burying his face in a pillow. "I was hoping to forget about that for just a little longer."

"Sorry I couldn't indulge you this time." I really am, too.

He lays on his side as he watches me pull on my boots. "Thank you for staying with me last night."

"It's not like I could exactly leave," I tell him with a grin. "You were in *my* room."

"I am nothing if not strategic."

I laugh and reach out to pull him from the bed. He groans as his feet hit the floor and pulls me into a tight embrace.

"You smell so good, like salt and sun," he says into my hair.

"Better than garbage and sweat." I have to bring us back to reality before I can forget what I decided and what I have to do next. Tristan is always my weak spot and I've become his too. I can't allow this anymore.

"Tristan?"

"Hmm?"

"There's something you should know."

I feel his arms tighten around me as he braces himself. "And what would that be?"

"I..." I don't want to tell him. I don't want to stop this. If I were just a little more selfish, I could have everything. But I'm not and I couldn't do it to Tristan. I swallow down the growing lump in my throat and try again. "You should know, if you're going to be King, I will leave you to that endeavor."

"What do you mean?" His voice has a harder edge to it as he tries to understand.

"I mean, I'll go back to the ships with my father. I can't stay here with you if you become king."

"I did not know you hated the idea of me being king so much." His arms feel limp around my body, and I don't dare try to look up at his face or I'll never finish.

"It's not that. I want what's best for you and I know if you were king, that wouldn't be me. I would get out of your way so that you could have the trust and the support of the Fae that you would need. We both know they don't want to see a human anywhere near the throne."

He releases me completely and takes a step back, his thighs hitting the edge of the bed. "And what if I do not care about that? Do I not have a say in what happens?"

"Would you make the right choice?"

He looks away from me and my chest grows tight.

"I am a grown man. I am perfectly capable of making the right choices, of making sacrifices. What do you think my whole life has been? You asked about my magic, did you know that such a power would have given me access immediately to higher ranks and perhaps even preference over my brother, but I kept it inside instead because it was the right thing to do? Do you think I liked being stationed at a post no one else wanted because my superiors saw me as useless?"

I step closer to him, but he moves away, shifting around me until he's closest to the door.

He shakes his head. "You talk of doing the right thing, but have you stopped to consider the fact that you might not be? I think you are hiding from me because what we have scares you."

"I'm not afraid." My hands curl into fists and I'm glad to have the space between us. "I'm trying to do what's best for you. You know the Fae would never accept you with me beside you."

"You don't know that. You're so busy making speculations that you cannot see what is right in front of you. Everything will be well with the Fae because that is what I wish. When we defeat this army, the Fae would have to be crazy to not accept me and you by extension."

I chew on the inside of my cheek. He might be right. He might garner enough respect and reliability that the Fae would take him even with me involved, but that's a risk I don't want to take. I'm not going to be the reason he cannot be king.

Tristan stares at me and I give him a sad smile. He blows out a long breath, knowing I'm not going to give in. He shakes his head, his hair falling over his forehead as his eyes grow dark.

He yanks the door open without looking back at me. "I have work to do," he says before slamming the door closed behind him.

TWENTY-THREE

The back of my throat feels scratchy, and my eyes burn but I refuse to cry. I refuse to cry over a decision that will be best for both of us. He has to know I'm right and if he doesn't now then he will later. Someday he'll understand that I did this for him. Someday he'll know that my decision here shows just how much I care about him.

Swallowing down the thick lump in my throat, I wait a few more minutes before I leave the room to make sure I don't run into Tristan. Not that I'm afraid to see him, I just don't want to continue what we started in my room out in the hall. I doubt showing my emotions so clearly would ever help the Fae come around to me being with Tristan. *No, it's much better to just wait.*

When I leave the room though, I feel lost.

I'm alone in the castle. I have no allies to turn to for help. Ry and Tristan are out. I thought I would always have them to turn to, so their loss is felt deep within me in a solid ache. Especially Tristan's. His loss is what's best for him, but that doesn't make me miss him any less.

I wrap my arms around my waist and curl into myself.

My breathing feels sharp and jagged, but I close my eyes and force it back to normal. It takes a few minutes in which I worry that someone will come around the corner and see me, but I'm blissfully uninterrupted until I've squashed my emotions back down.

I'll have time to deal with all of this later, but not now.

My legs shake as I move toward the dungeons. I won't have someone to watch my back, but there's nothing I can do about that. It'll be better to know what's down there than to sit around feeling sorry for myself that I've lost all my allies in one fell swoop.

A chill seeps through my boots and into my bones as I take the stairs down to the cells. Darkness presses in on all sides and as I come around the first turn in the staircase, I realize there's no torch left at the bottom. Anneliese's men must have taken it with them. I guess it makes sense. Why would they leave a torch burning down here when there's no one there? No prisoners and no guards means no light. But it also means no one to catch me.

Still, there will be nothing to catch me doing if I can't find any light down here.

With the utter darkness pressing down on me, my heart beats a rapid clip by the time I get to the bottom of the stairs. I stumble forward with my arms extended, hoping to find the desk before it finds me. Instead, my hip hits against the corner of it and I whisper a bleak curse into the emptiness. Without taking any time to assess the damage, I run my hands over the top of the desk hoping to find a stray candle. The desktop is empty and the pain in my hip feels even more acute with nothing to show for my efforts.

Kicking the back end of the desk, I add toe pain to my mounting list of discomforts, but the movement causes the drawers to slide open in a clatter of rolling objects. I sidle around the desk, careful to avoid knocking against it again, finding the open drawers and pick through the contents. My fingers curl around a slender piece of wood and I know I've won.

I pull it out and strike it against the side of the desk and fire explodes into existence. With the new light, I find a torch on the wall and press my match against it so that it can flare to life. Blowing out the match before it can burn me, the light from the torch is enough for me to navigate into the first cell with.

Expecting to find a pile of heavy sacks, the breath knocks out of my lungs as I take in the empty cell. My footsteps are loud in the silence as I go further inside. I look around the space once more, but all that's there are damp stone walls and their matching floors.

Stumbling back against the wall, I slide down until I'm sitting on the floor, and bury my face in my knees.

"What am I even doing here?"

My voice breaks the silence and breaks the dam holding my tears at bay. I sob into my knees, letting my tears drip down onto my thighs.

What could I have done better? I've been running since I got here trying to patch everything up and protect everyone I love and all I've done is drive them all away. Not only that, but I've let Anneliese's secrets pass through my fingers all for the selfishness of having a moment with Tristan. I can't get that time back and the worst part is that I don't know that I would want to. I might never have a moment like that again.

Letting my hands drop to the floor, I let the coolness of the rocks seep deeper into my bones and numb my pain. But the ground is rough under my fingers, even rougher than I would expect with the stone floor.

Sniffing, I lift my head off my knees and look at the floor beside me. A fine layer of black covers the stone in uneven patches. I rub the tears from my eyes to be able to see better. Crouching closer to the ground, the smell of sulfur takes over the air. I take a pinch of the powder and rub it between my fingers. A spark flashes from my fingers and burns where they were touching the powder.

I scramble backward, the friction of my feet causing more sparks to flash in the cell.

My chest heaves with quick breaths as I stare at the seemingly innocent floor in front of me. Those men were moving bags and bags of this, and not little ones either. What is Anneliese planning on blowing up?

With extreme care, I scoop up all the black powder I can find. I hold my breath as though that will help the powder stay stagnant and not explode.

It seems so innocuous, just a little black pile in my hand, but my fingers still hurt from where it sparked earlier. There's nowhere safe to put it unless I'm willing to let it disperse in my pocket, which feels far too dangerous and not at all productive. I'm left to hold it as I back out of the cell while carefully making sure my feet don't provide any friction for powder that might be left behind.

I can't breathe fully until I'm making my way up the stairs. I didn't bother extinguishing the torch. It didn't feel worth the risk with explosives in my hand and I doubt anyone will think it was me down here anyway. They'd have to remember I'm here to be able to throw blame in my direction.

This changes things, though, and whether they like it or not, Ry and Tristan are going to have to work with me. We have to figure out where Anneliese took the powder before she has time to use it.

～

I'M NOT sure what worries me more, the black powder or having to see Ry or Tristan again. My heart is a heavy lump in my chest as I make my way through the dark hallways as morning threatens to rear its head. I know I need them, but after everything that was said, I wish I didn't. Neither of them is a good option to talk to.

Despite the internal battle, my feet carry me to Tristan's door and the decision is made. I knock on the door, a sound far too loud in the silent air.

There's the sound of scrambling and something falling over, and then Tristan yanks the door open. The room behind him is pitch black, but even so it feels dangerous inside, like the shadows are watching.

"Mariel, I did not expect to see you so soon." He leans against the door frame, his hair ruffled and red circles forming under his eyes.

I'm not sure what to say. I know this is a pivotal moment. Should I apologize for what I said earlier? That feels like a step in the wrong direction when I still mean what I said. Staying away from him would be much better in the long run, probably for both of us, but if I ignore our fight then I know this weird distance between us will only grow.

I try to speak but nothing comes out and I have to cough to clear my throat before trying again. Tristan raises a brow at me but allows me a moment to be able to continue.

"I found something."

Tristan chuckles and runs his hand through his hair. "Why am I not surprised? You couldn't just sleep like a normal girl?"

"I couldn't sleep," I confess with a frown as my chest grows tighter. "So, I went to see what Anneliese was up to."

Tristan's head jerks up and he looks around the hall to

make sure we're alone. I wait for him to invite me inside to continue but he looks back at his room with a frown before gesturing for me to continue.

"And the items she was moving were already gone."

His shoulders relax and the tension ebbs away from the corners of his eyes. "Well, that takes care of that then."

"I was still curious about what she was moving though, so I decided to see if anything was left behind."

Tristan pinches the bridge of his nose with a pained expression. "Of course you did."

"And I found something."

I hold out my hand, the black powder looking so innocent as it sits in the well of my palm. Tristan frowns, stooping down closer to me to get a better look at it. Behind him, the shadows in his room seem to follow his actions like a cloak and darkness trickles into the hallway with us.

"Black powder?" Tristan asks, not noticing the shadow's movement. He steps closer and takes a deep inhale. "Definitely black powder. You found this in the dungeon?"

I nod, keeping a careful eye on the shifting darkness behind him.

He groans and punches the door frame, causing both me and the shadows to flinch. "This makes things a lot more complicated. Did you see how many bags of it they had?"

"A lot. I didn't stop to count them though."

Tristan glances at me and I try to make it look like I'm paying attention to him and not to the darkness in the room beyond.

"If she only had four, that would be more than enough to take down a castle wall."

Of course, it would be because why would Anneliese ever do anything normally? Want to take over a country? Just take down the castle wall and march right in.

"What do we do then?" It's not like there was a trail. We can't just waltz around and hope we run into her men.

Tristan winces. "I think we might have to use your plan after all."

"Excuse me?" There's no way he just said that.

"If she is not going to respect the castle, then we will not be able to either. We are going to need your plan to make sure that there is a nice surprise waiting for her when she blasts her way in."

"Does this mean you believe me now?"

He reaches for my hand, but the shadows move closer and I'm afraid to take it. Plus, just that small touch could make me go back on everything I've been trying to do. He lets his hand fall with a sigh. "There is no innocent reason for having black powder. I am not sure if she is a deceitful as you think, but she has definitely been up to something."

It's not the best admission, but I'll take it. It's closer than he's come in a while to agreeing with me.

He looks behind him with a frown before turning back to me. "I'm not sure if you should come in."

"But you want me to come in?" I can't help the grin that tugs at the side of my mouth.

This is not the right time for it, but I do like knowing he wants to be with me. No matter what happens, I always want to know that there was care and affection between us.

"Yes, but I... I lost myself for a little while there and now it is not safe."

His confession makes me grateful I didn't take his hand even though I wanted to. What might the shadows have done?

"Is it..." My voice grows softer. "Is it your magic?"

He winces and the darkness surges. "I never meant for you to see it."

I peer through the shadows, seeing for the first time

that there is still a candle lit on his desk. His room isn't dark at all, all of this is him.

"I don't want you to have to hide from me."

Taking a deep breath, I reach out for his hand even though I know I'm making this harder for both of us. This is the first time I've seen his magic, and I can't reject him for it. This is a part of him like being human is a part of me. I must trust that he won't hurt me, no matter what he's said about what his magic can do.

He hesitates and I see in his eyes the desire to take my hand warring with the worry of what his magic can do.

"You won't hurt me."

I don't know if that's true, but just saying it out loud changes everything for him. He takes a step forward and the shadows stay behind, trapped behind the doorway. He slides his hand into mine and his skin is cold. Far too cold and clammy, like the hand of death itself.

It's hard not to shudder as he squeezes me, his face torn between joy and pain. His hand slowly warms, and I feel weaker like he's leached life out of me to do it.

His magic has to be pretty powerful to have that effect even when he's trying to keep it at bay. What could he do if he was actually trying? A shudder runs down my back and Tristan uses the motion to pull me into his body. He presses my face into his neck, breathing deeply into my hair.

I can feel the shadows drift away as he calms himself, the sensation as tangible as when a fire is lit. My chest eases without the pressure of the darkness and I feel like I can breathe.

"Thank you," he whispers, "for not being afraid of me."

"I know you wouldn't try to hurt me." My voice is muffled against his neck, but by the way his fingers tighten around me, I know he heard me.

He presses his lips to the top of my head. "No one has

come this close to me when my magic has been released since the first time. No one ever trusts me with the darkness around."

"Maybe if they had, you wouldn't fear what it can do so much." This isn't the right time, but it makes me angry to think of Tristan as just a boy being rejected by the adults around him because of their fear.

He sighs. "No, I am right to fear it. It's a power that only brings destruction, but with you it feels like I control it instead of the other way around."

"Why was it out now?" After all this time of being with him, it seems strange that tonight would be the time it chose to make an appearance.

"It...I..." His chest grows tight where it's pressed against mine. "After what you said, I lost it for a while."

Has he been sitting in the darkness this whole time, letting his magic brood and marinate and take him down? I want to reach out and take his face in my hands and tell him I didn't mean what I said before. But I can't. I *do* mean what I said, and there's a part of me that worries that if I move, his magic will take it as an invitation.

"It hasn't happened in years; this isn't something you need to fear from me." He struggles to sound reassuring while death presses against his back.

"I don't think keeping it trapped has been doing you any favors." All it seems to have done is make him afraid of himself. Maybe that's the real reason he took that post in the middle of nowhere to 'protect the King's Forest.' Maybe he thought if he was alone, he didn't need to worry about hurting someone. Instead of discovering this part of himself, he's shunned it completely. If only Anneliese had done the same.

"It is much safer that way."

Maybe he's right and it is safer, but how would he even

know? He doesn't. His magic could be waiting to do so much more and instead take form of death because that's the only way to do anything at all. He won't let it do anything else.

But this isn't the moment to pressure him into changing the way he's been thinking his whole life.

I wrap my arms around his back, keeping my flinch inside as the shadows pulse against my exposed skin. He groans and crushes me against him. His strength is almost too much for me as the shadows creep closer and I'm completely stuck and pinned against him. I close my eyes so I can't see anything and focus on my breathing and on the smell of Tristan that fills me.

There's nothing in this space but he and I. There's no room for anything but the pine smell of him and the love I carry inside. I trust him. I've learned to trust him above anyone else. I can trust him here, with this. I can trust him even as death threatens to engulf us both. He won't let it touch me without succumbing to it himself. We're in this together.

"Mariel," he whispers, and it sends tingles all through me, dropping low in my stomach. "Mariel, I'm sorry I let myself get out of control. I never should have let your words affect me so. I should have been more willing to fight for you and less willing to fall into grief. I just... I know things have been *unusual* lately and I don't want to lose you because of it. I do not want us to become so engulfed in what's happening now that you think this is our whole future. It's not. I won't let it be. I don't want to even consider a future where you're not by my side."

His deep voice runs through me like honey as he holds me tight. *Is he right? Have I been too hasty to decide things will never work?* I just want what is best for him, and I know myself better than he knows me. It won't be me. I will never be the best answer. But that doesn't mean I can't be *something* for him. I want to be with him. That hasn't changed.

"I don't want to bring you down." My voice is quiet with the very real threat of tears hovering behind them. "I want you to have everything you want. I want you to have what your father wanted."

"I cannot have what I want if you're not here with me."

This man, this *Fae* is going to wreck me. How can he feel this way about me after everything? I've brought him nothing but chaos and disruption. That's all I can offer him for as long as he stays with me. And yet, here he is telling me not to leave, to stay and continue to cause confusion and disruption.

I turn my face to his shoulder, and he adjusts until he can press his cold lips against mine. My hands grip the back of his head, pulling his face tighter against me. He shudders against me, and I know we both needed this. We both needed a moment of connection.

"Mariel!" Ry's voice echoes off the stone walls as he runs around the corner.

Tristan and I don't immediately spring away from each other, it's not like Ry doesn't know parts of our history together. He squeezes my waist before I turn and face Ry.

His face is red and his chest heaves like he's been running for a long time. He presses a hand against the wall and leans over to catch his breath.

"They're here."

TWENTY-FOUR

I grab Ry by the shoulder, forcing him to look at me. "Who's here?"

There are far too many possible answers to that question for comfort.

"The Seafolk. They got your letter and they're waiting in the grotto," he pants, sweat trickling down his temple. He must have run all the stairs down and back to get this news.

I glance at Tristan, and he gives me a tight nod. This is my business to attend to.

"Take me to them." I straighten my spine as though that will make me look older and more serious. I doubt it will work when I have to face the Seafolk and confess how little I've been up to. Glancing back at Tristan, I'm glad to see the shadows inside his room have abated.

"Are you coming with us?" I ask.

He hesitates, hands clenching and unclenching. "Are you sure?"

"Of course." I reach for his hand and he's slow to give it to me.

Ry watches us with a slight smirk, but I don't want to know what he's thinking.

"Trouble in paradise?" he asks, standing taller as the red fades from his cheeks.

"The Seafolk have never liked the Fae much," Tristan admits as we trod through the halls and toward the grotto.

Ry laughs. "Another thing we have in common."

"Would you knock it off?" I let go of Tristan to give Ry a shove.

He places his hand over mine to keep it against his arm. "I'm not trying to be antagonistic, just realistic. Having something in common is a good thing."

"Not when it hurts our cause."

"You seem to forget." His dark eyes grow serious as he stares down at me. "That our cause is not saving the Fae. It is merely giving them a reason to help save us."

"We all have to work together Ry, there's nothing wron—"

"There is everything wrong with it." Ry glances at Tristan with a frown. "They kept the peace between each other by treating us like children. That will all end now."

I yank my hand away from Ry and move faster to keep out of his reach. "Can you wait to pick another fight until after we've won the war?"

Ry clamps his mouth shut, but I know this is far from over. The banished and the Seafolk are fighting for their rights. Their rights to land and to safe water. I hope Tristan realizes how serious they are.

A SMILE STRETCHES my mouth wide as the first wave of salty air hits my face. Despite the darkness, the grotto is definitely my favorite part of the castle. Water drips down the stone walls where they sweat just as much as Tristan. I take a deep breath as my feet hit the stony beach. How could I not love this touch and taste of my home?

Today though it looks far too much like my home for comfort. The stretch of beach is covered by the lithe bodies of the Seafolk, their multicolored tails rippling in the torchlight. They slide onto shore, shaking the water from their bodies. As they do, their tails shorten and split into legs that let them come further up the beach. Behind them, the water is filled with all-too-familiar boats.

"Ry, you said it was the Seafolk that had arrived." I try to keep my jaw from dropping as the noise of men and Seafolk fills the vast space.

He grins at me, hanging off the railing of the stairs as he takes in the view. "Aren't we all kind of sea folk?"

"You know that's not what your answer meant." I scowl at him but refrain from knocking him off the stairs.

I'm looking at my worst nightmare become a reality. How could Ry be so happy about this? Everyone I've ever loved is waiting for me on those boats. My father... Alon... how will I face them? The choice not to has been taken from me by Ry's thoughtlessness.

Tristan rests his hand on my back, ushering me the rest of the way down the stairs. As soon as my toes hit the sand, I want to crumple. I'm not sure I'm strong enough for what is waiting for me.

"Mariel." Isla sits on the beach holding a trident longer than I am tall. Her skin is even greyer than the last time I saw her. Things must not have improved in the oceans while I've been here. "We received your missive and are here to fight." She glances at Tristan behind me, the shells woven into her hair clacking together. "You had better remember this."

"I hope that we will always have peace between us and

a further desire to work together when I am King," Tristan says carefully.

His stance is too casual as I watch him, and I realize he's scared. How could he not be when he's so completely outnumbered? If he remains unwilling to use his magic, the Seafolk and the banished could take him down without a second thought.

Isla laughs. "You had better remember the sacrifices we have made for you and the agreements we kept with your father."

Tristan's eyes go wide.

"Yes, we know all about you, the King's beloved bastard son. It is good to see you taking some initiative for yourself now that he has passed."

Tristan's fists clench and he hides them behind his back. "Let us not forget that we still have a battle to win before we can be anything for each other."

Isla nods, a smile still playing across her grey lips. Worry puckers at the back of my mind but I force it to subside. There's nothing I can do to help either of them, and it's not a fight I want to get involved in anyway. We can wait and see how things continue to play out. It's not necessary for us all to be best friends right away.

Something splashes into the water, and I force my gaze up beyond the Seafolk and towards the men in the boats. Pain hits me in the gut as I recognize the ship at the front and its sunburst painted on the side.

It takes everything in me not to fall to my knees as I watch my father's head bob in the water as he swims closer. His eyes never leave me as he reaches the shore, his body pale like he's seeing a ghost. I guess after what happened to Zale, it makes sense. He's probably wished the worst for me this whole time.

Tristan glances between me and my father, his hand

drifting toward the knife he keeps in his boot. He wouldn't have had time to do anything with it anyway, as my father flings his sopping wet body onto mine, crushing me against him as his shoulders shake.

"I never thought I'd see you again." His voice is hoarse as he tugs me tighter against his shoulder. "After Zale came home... I've spent every day praying that I would never see another boat on the horizon."

Tears squeeze out as I tremble. Of course he never wanted me to come home. I knew he would have to feel that way. How could he not after what happened to Zale? Especially after I didn't come home to explain or send a letter or anything. I let him down in the worst way.

I did this to myself.

"To see you now..." He draws a haggard breath. "Is better than I could have imagined."

My spine stiffens in shock. "You—you want to see me?"

He pulls me away so I can see his face, wet with tears. "Of course I want to see you. How could you ever doubt my love for you?"

I can't hold back the torrent of emotion that takes over me and I weep into his shoulder. This is probably the last thing I should be doing as a leader, but I can't help it. Let them lose respect for me if it means I get my family back.

After a few minutes, Tristan clears his throat and I know its time to pull back and get to work. My father looks from me to Tristan, a frown marring his face as he wipes his face. He looks past him and sees Ry and his face lights up again.

It makes my heart hurt to know how much pain I've caused him. This must be so hard to see us, knowing he'll never see Zale again.

"So," Tristan says as he glances between the ships and

the Seafolk. "You've come, but did you come prepared to fight?"

"If you mean to ask if we bring the monsters, then no," Isla says, looking directly at me. "To get close enough to one to lure it here would have meant death. It was not something I was willing to risk my people on."

I grind my teeth. No wonder the banished are here then. Without the beasts to take down the army, we'll need every able person we can find.

Beside me, my father moves from foot to foot, watching the sand shift beneath him. It's his first time on land and despite the seriousness of the situation, he's childlike as he discovers this new world.

"Did you tell the banished to come?" I hiss at Ry. I understand why he would have. I get the logistics of it, but I still hate it. How can I look at my father and think he's ready for war when he can't even stand straight on unmoving ground yet?

He shrugs. "We needed them, Mariel, and they wanted to fight. All I had to do was tell them what we were planning."

Tristan puts a hand on my shoulder to steady me, as though he can read the murderous thoughts flitting through my mind. My father notices the action and his frown deepens.

"We understand the beasts aren't here, but that will mean you will have to fight even harder." My voice warbles and I have to take a deep breath to steady it. I can't help but look at every ship and wonder who will be left after all of this. Will it even be worth it?

"There's an army coming," I say. "One that is determined to change this country and make it impossible for any of us to come peacefully to land ever again. I know you don't like the Fae and hold them responsible for a lot of the ills we have had to bear, but if we want a chance for something more, this is it. This is the only chance you will see in your lifetime, so use it well."

The grotto is silent as the last echoes of my voice drift away. I'm not sure what I expected, but it's hard to keep my back straight and not slink away as the silence continues.

"We're ready to fight with you," my father finally says in a voice that carries strength despite the slump of his shoulders. "We're ready to continue what Zale started."

Isla looks at my father and then at the boats behind him. "And we will fight if it means the humans will hold up their end of the bargain and keep our waters clear so the beasts will sleep once more."

I can tell by the way my father looks at Ry that this isn't something he's shared with him. How could he get the banished to want to fight with us if they knew that they would still need to be on the water doing the same tasks they've done for generations? They wouldn't do it. Why risk death to go back to your same life?

Luckily Tristan sees the look on my father's face too and steps in. "When I am king at the end of this battle, I will see that all of us are able to live as they desire. There will be a way made so the waters can be cleaned, and the men can live on land. Those points do not have to be mutually exclusive."

I purse my lips. I hope Tristan is able to do that. He stands on the beach like a king, but he hasn't been tried yet. If I thought *I* was going to be a problem for him politically, then what would this promise to *all* the humans mean?

I hope he knows what he's doing.

There's some discussion between the men about whether all the humans should come on land or if they should stay on their boats. The plan is still to get the army to come down here, even though there's no great beast waiting for them. That's what we'll have to be. At least down here we still have the Seafolk to fight with us. That's more than what we would have outside the castle. In the end, it's decided that some men will come on land and the rest will stay where they are. None of them are trained enough for hand-to-hand combat and will need the leverage of their ships to give them an advantage.

My father is one that has chosen to stay, something that makes me want to scream. I can't protect him on land. I can't protect any of them from what will come next. It's too much of a burden to bear. I don't know how Tristan manages it. No wonder he didn't want me involved in the fighting and tried to train me. Maybe he worries more than he shows.

"I brought something for you," my father says, reaching into a sopping wet bag at his feet. "We found it after you and Zale had left. I think he intended it to be our new symbol when all of this was over, but it feels right for you to have it now."

He pulls out a carving that makes my breath stop in my chest. It's not a sunburst like the one on the side of our ship, but something else entirely. It's a dark circle with black tendrils spreading from it, and it looks like the inky darkness that happens when the moon crosses in front of the sun. He hands it to me and it's heavy in my arms. This feels right. I've never seen a more accurate depiction of what my heart and mind feel like right now. How did Zale know?

"This shouldn't be a symbol just for us," I tell him, hugging the carving to my chest. "This is all of us now. We're all about to be reborn."

I hold it out for all men the men watching, my arms shaking as they cheer.

TWENTY-FIVE

Tristan doesn't stay with us long, and instead goes to the council room to see if he can find out how far away the battle is. Despite sending Captain Wimark to deal with the army, the Prince kept his head enough to track of their movements himself.

My body shakes as I settle into the sand with my father, Ry, and the Seafolk woman. This feels like a weird dream and not the reality of my life. It gets even worse when they begin plotting battle strategy.

I wish they'd been able to wrangle a sea beast up here. It would have eliminated so much of this stress and would have made my father safe somewhere else.

I guess some of my dreams were just too big.

"You haven't been trained to fight. It makes no sense for you to be on the ground with us," Isla says, her trident glinting wickedly in the light. "You will only get in our way."

"We're far more agile than you on land," Ry points out. "And the humans that have been living here have had to fight, so they're no strangers to what we're about to do."

"How many humans have been living here?" my father

asks. He disguises it as a serious question, but I know him well enough to sense the war between tension and eagerness hiding underneath. He must be thinking about Zale.

We all look at Ry, waiting for the answer. He shifts and keeps his attention focused on the boats behind us. "There are enough."

"If we're going to be working together then we need to know more than just that 'there are enough,'" I point out. Ry frowns at me, but I'm not the only one who needs to know. "We're allies now. Surely that must mean something to the rebellion."

"It's not my information to share." Ry sticks out his chin.

"Did you send for Azalea?" I ask, moving past the temptation to tease him about his position in the rebellion.

He looks at me with sharp eyes. "Of course I did. But it's not like she can just sneak in whenever she wants."

Someone behind me asks, "Are you sure about that?"

I try not to jump as I turn to find Azalea standing there. She gives me a wink and settles into the circle we've made.

"You want to know numbers?" she asks my father and Isla.

"Why the need for secrecy if we will be fighting side by side?" Isla asks, her voice raspy. "Are your people any better than mine?"

"Your people have somewhere to hide if this all goes south. Mine will be left exposed," Azalea points out.

She glances from me to my father and back to me. I watch her eyes widen slightly as she realizes we're related. Glancing down at her hand, I notice she still wears the ring on her gaunt finger.

"They won't be left exposed," my father says. "They'll always be welcome with us."

Azalea laughs. "I don't think many would be happy

about such an offer. The whole reason they're here is to avoid the sea. Many of them have never even been on the sea before."

My jaw goes slack. How long has the rebellion been here that they've been able to make such lives for themselves? Babies have been born here on land and haven't been discovered yet. Suddenly I'm glad Tristan isn't here. Not that I think he would hurt them, but I don't need to see how much this deception hurts *him*. He's been tasked with protecting the Fae and there's been a whole human colony hiding under their nose the whole time. At least he wasn't assigned to the capital. This isn't *really* his failure. He just might not see it that way.

"What are you saying then?" I ask her, finally finding my voice. "Is the rebellion going to join us or not? Are you so scared of failure that you'll guarantee it for the rest of us?"

Azalea scowls. "That's not what I'm saying."

"Then what *are* you saying?"

"I'm saying we need some kind of agreement about what will happen to us should things not work out." She slaps her thigh. "It's not unreasonable to want safety for my people."

"But you didn't want what I offered," my father says, crossing his arms over his chest.

She sighs. "There has to be another way that isn't giving up on everything we've been working for."

When she says it like that, I can almost understand her point. She wants to fight for more but doesn't want to risk giving up what they've already gained. That's not so crazy. It's just not something we can help her with.

"If we fail, none of us will be in a power to help you." She's asking us to do the impossible when we will be at our weakest.

"Not all of you." Azalea turns her attention to Isla. "You know the sea better than any of us." She ignores my father's grunt of disagreement. "Surely there's some place outside of Fae reach where we could go."

"And how would you propose to get there?" Isla smiles, revealing a row of sharp teeth. "How far can you swim?"

"Have you seen the ships?" she asks. "If this fails, I vote that humanity, all of us, start over again somewhere else."

Isla shakes her head. "If you are suggesting giving up on your ocean work, then we will not help you. That's the only reason for our involvement now. The ocean cannot be left like this. Every day that work is not done my people grow weaker and the beasts grow angrier."

"I understand but—"

"Do you? Do you really?" Isla pulls her torso up higher so that she towers over us. "Have you held a dying baby that has been poisoned by the trash settling lower and lower in the ocean every day? Have you had to watch your city destroyed because the beasts have awoken and are looking for souls to punish? What have you had to experience, young human, that would give you an understanding of my pain?"

Azalea is silent for a moment, and I don't expect her to speak, but with a curt nod, she decides to share her story anyway.

"There are many that I have had to watch die over the years. Always from Fae problems, always because of laws we had no choice in. All they wanted was a better life, a way for them to be able to choose their fate, but all they got was a bloody and drawn-out death. Not only that, but I had to watch my husband, my love..." She has to swallow before she can finish. "I never got to say goodbye to him, only got to see his body once before he was returned to the sea. I had to watch him leave knowing I would never get to mourn him as is our custom. So yes, I know of your suffering."

I bite my bottom lip. I've never gotten to hear her talk about Zale that way. I knew his death caused her pain; I knew she was suffering. I should have tried to do something for her. I shouldn't have hidden in the castle from all the hurt his death caused. I've been a coward. I didn't even know they were married. I thought the ring on her finger was only a promise.

"I'm sorry about your husband. Such a loss is a hard one and will leave its mark on you forever," my father says.

Azalea glances at him and I wonder if I should say something. He doesn't even know he's sitting with Zale's widow right now. Would it give him some comfort to know that, or would it feel worse to know that Zale kept so much of his life hidden from us?

"Yes, and that is why we must make sure there are contingency plans in place in case we fail. It has happened before, and it can happen now."

Isla nods, her seashells clacking. "We will help you. We will bring you to a secret place if we are able."

Azalea gives her a grim smile. "Thank you. Now we can talk."

They move through the battle plan, discussing how everyone can be used best. It's painful and I wish I had left with Tristan. When he appears at the top of the stairs, it takes everything in me not to run to him and beg him to stop all of this. But it can't be stopped now. Even I know that.

Tristan's face is as hard as granite as he reaches us. "They've already been sighted in the valley. This battle will be upon us now."

Everyone pauses to take in this information before they all spring into action and move to their assigned places. My father grips me by the arm and pulls me into him, crushing me in a tight hug.

"We'll make it through this," he whispers to me.

I return his embrace. "I know we will."

He gives me a long look before turning back for the ships to make sure all the banished are in place. Ry watches him go, his face mirroring the pain inside me. This is our family. This is all we have left, and it could all be gone today.

"Do you have your dagger?" Tristan asks me. I shake my head and he gives me a hard look. "You should *always* have it on you. I'll go get it; you stay right here."

He points at the beach like I won't understand him. I give him a weak smile and he leaps back up the stairs. He's right, I should have had it. Then he wouldn't be exhausting his strength before we've even started.

"Mariel," Ry whispers, grabbing my arm once Tristan is out of sight. "We need to go."

I scowl at him. "Didn't you just hear Tristan? I'm supposed to stay right here."

"I don't care what Tristan wants. I have a plan already to keep you safe, but we need to leave *right now*." Ry gives my arm a tug, but I don't budge.

All around us, the beach is awash with activity as the Seafolk take up their places and the banished position their boats. The air is filled with their loud, deep voices, adding a tinge of confusion to the air.

"I can't leave, Ry. I need to stay here so Tristan can find me."

"You don't understand, Mariel. You're not going to be here for Tristan, you're not going to be here for the battle. I've found a way to keep you safe, but you need to come with me right now." His voice grows desperate as he grabs my arm.

His words plunk against my mind like stones, and I feel like I'm wading through seaweed to try and make sense of them.

"What are you talking about?"

Ry glances at all the movement around us and pulls me closer to him, pitching his voice low so only I can hear. "I made a deal with the rebellion. That's why I've been working for them. It's all been for this. They have a safe house and that's where you're going to stay."

"No." I pull out of his grip. "I'm not leaving to hide."

He gives me a pleading look. "I did this for you. All of this." He gestures at all the people around us in movement. "You need to trust me now."

"No," I repeat. "You don't get to choose that for me. I'm not going."

"Don't be dense, Mariel. I made this deal for you; you have to take it!" His voice rises but no one notices with all the other noises in the grotto. "Everything I've done here has been for you. I just want to save you."

"I never asked you to do that!"

I'm sure my face is getting red. In so many ways I feel like I'm back on my father's boat praying he doesn't bring up how we both know he feels. I thought that was over between us. In every way he's acted, it seemed like it was. And now... I don't know how to handle this turnaround. I just want to run away.

I search the stairs, but Tristan still isn't back yet.

"You may not have asked me, but I was never going to wait around for you to. I would be waiting our whole lives for you to realize what was right in front of you." He takes my hands, clasping them in his. The rough callouses from his years at sea rub against the back of my hands. "Choose *me*, Mariel. Run away with *me*."

"I could never run away." My voice breaks as he looks

away. "I could never ask others to fight in a battle that I helped to bring upon them. This is my fight, whether you like it or not. I will not hide like an old woman, and I will not leave Tristan."

Ry's hands fall to his side. He shakes his head. His face turns red, and his shoulders slump and he stumbles backward.

"Okay. If this is what you want, then we'll fight. I'll fight for you, Mariel. Then you'll see."

I reach out to grab him, to make him understand that that isn't what I meant, but he sprints across the beach, sand and rocks flying up behind him.

This isn't how this was supposed to go at all. He was never supposed to even *be* here. I did this to him. I turned him into this. If I had just been better prepared or been more able to tell him how I felt... But there were a few moments when I wondered and that was all it took for me to hold back.

But I have Tristan now. Ry knows that. How could he think I'd abandon him?

All I want to do kick the sand or yell at Ry or just do something. But I can't. I especially can't on this beach with everyone watching. Even if only one person is watching it would still be too many eyes on me for a moment of such strong weakness.

A rumble shakes the beach, rocking me out of my thoughts as the shouting men go silent. Rocks rain from the ceiling and the smell of the black powder I found with Ry permeates the air in a rush. The battle is here.

TWENTY-SIX

The silence only lasts a second before the noise becomes louder than it was before as everyone springs into action. Dust falls from the ceiling of the grotto as the heavy rumbling continues overhead.

How many men has Anneliese brought that they were able to infiltrate the castle so quickly? My heart is a tight knot in my chest as I stare out at the ships, all perfectly lined up now under Tristan's direction. How many of them will be left at the end of this?

I feel exposed standing on the beach with no weapon and no Tristan. I'm useless and in the way like this. I need to get off the beach, but this is where Tristan told me to wait. If I move and he comes back for me then I've only created more problems for him.

Dancing back and forth on numb feet, I'm not sure what to do. Then a glance at the stairs takes care of that for me.

Fae in silver armor descend the stairs. They march in time, shaking the metal stairs and filling the grotto with the sounds of every step.

I try to swallow the lump in my throat, but I can't.

277

Around me, the Seafolk have moved into position. They brandish their weapons, hissing as the soldiers come closer.

This is the wrong place for me. I can't be on the front line. I won't make it. Not without a weapon and after practicing with Tristan, probably not with a weapon either.

A quick glance around the beach gives me nothing. The stairs are the only way in unless I want to swim out of the grotto, which I definitely don't. I don't know what's at the other end. It could be miles before I reach land I can climb out on and that's only if no beasts are waiting for me out in the dark water.

This is it. I'm stuck here, pinned between the oncoming Fae and our small army. Tristan won't be able to reach me here. *Maybe I should have left when I had the chance.*

No, that's a coward's thought and I will not go out that way. I can be scared, but I don't have to choose the coward's path. I may not belong right here, but that doesn't mean I'm going to hide or cry. I can stand my ground. I can do my best to fight. And I can go down like a warrior.

"Here." The Seafolk man next to me hands me the shining hilt of a weapon. "You look like you need this more than I do."

"Thanks."

My hands close around the smooth handle and I heft it in front of me. Shock almost makes me drop it as I realize I'm holding onto a trident. Memories of those moments in the woods flood through me, making my knees weak.

The first line of the Fae army reaches the bottom of the stairs and I hold my trident higher. This is it. I have to be strong now.

All around me the Seafolk scream, a tight hoarse sound that reverberates through the grotto. I join them, transferring my fear into the noise.

The Seafolk man shoves me behind him right before the

first clang of weapons fills the air. Tucked between the Seafolk with their scaled legs and armored torsos, I'm safer here than when I was standing alone on the beach. I hold my trident up, ready for my turn as the fighting continues in front of me. The clash of weapons and the screams of dying men take over my senses. I glance down as water soaks into my boots only to find that the water is still far behind me, and a river of blood is slowly making its way past me.

Bile rises up my throat and I have to swallow it back down. I don't have time to be squeamish now. I need to be ready for when the Seafolk in front of me fall and it's my turn to fight.

Unsurprisingly, just thinking that doesn't turn me into a warrior. The trident shakes with my hands and my feet are numb. A stiff breeze could knock me over, let alone a weapon.

I look up, keeping my sightline above the blood, hoping to see Tristan. If I can just see Tristan in this writhing mass of fighting men, I might be able to pull myself together.

But he's not here.

If I had just kept the dagger on me, he'd still be here. Instead I had to forget it and he's left wandering around to find it. But maybe this is a good thing. He's safely away from the fight. Maybe this will have saved his life. He'll get to go on and be king because he didn't have to fight in this battle.

That's a good thing.

I have to think of it that way because otherwise, my mind will take me down.

The Seafolk man in front of me falters and the sword of the Fae in front of him slashes through to me. Lifting my trident, I use it to hook the sword and knock it out of his hands. He looks at me with his impossibly beautiful face, shock rippling through his eyes before he's stabbed in the belly by the Seafolk man beside me. His hands struggle to grip the dagger, growing slippery with his own blood, but the Seafolk man yanks it back out. The Fae collapses in front of us and the next one takes his place.

Again, and again, and again, they just keep coming, surging forward as they look for any breaks in our line. The sounds of battle drown out my heartbeat and I stop hoping to see Tristan, my focus finally melding with what is happening in front of me. It will take my full concentration to survive this, and I *will* survive this.

Behind us, the boats sit waiting. Some of the ships with canons use them to blast holes in the beach, but their accuracy is hard to predict. After one hits the fighting Seafolk, I don't hear another cannon blast again. We're on our own on this one.

The stairs shine like a school of fish as more and more of the Fae wait on them for their turn. I expected the Seafolk to be clumsy on the land, making them more susceptible to the Fae, but they hold their own spectacularly. Despite being out of the water, they fight fluidly and with no hesitation. Their weapons, normally saved for much harsher creatures, find purchase in the Fae with ease, biting through their armor like it's made of paper.

The line behind me pushes forward, eager to be part of the fight. I stumble on the rocks but keep my trident up, using it to keep myself upright as well. I knock aside another sword that reaches through to me. A feeling of power travels up my arms with each interaction. I may be just one of the banished, hiding here on land as we try to find our place, but that doesn't mean I can't fight. And I'm fighting for the most important thing of all: family. Both my father behind me and Tristan somewhere above me. They're all my family now and I won't let them down.

My arms shake as I bring my trident up to block another attack. The sounds of battle and death rattle the air around me. Screams echo deep in my mind as soldiers around me lose their lives. Metal clashes as I make contact and my muscles scream as I try to wrench the sword out of the Fae's grip. The Seafolk man in front of me succumbs to another attack and I'm left vulnerable to the Fae whose grip is better than the others who lay at our feet. The Fae gives me a sly grin under his shining silver helmet as he pulls his sword out of my trident's prongs.

My body feels cold as he advances. The trident was never meant for close encounters. I hold my trident up and grit my teeth. He swings his sword high, and I press forward with the trident, but it glances off his armor and I'm left even closer to his attack. I refuse to flinch as the sword comes down, inching toward my exposed neck.

But the blow never comes.

The Fae screams as blood trickles between the plates of his armor. Blood bubbles from his lips as he's thrust aside. I take a step back, ready to fight this new foe, but it's Tristan who stands on the other side.

"When I told you to stand here and wait for me, I didn't think you would take it so literally," he says as he hands me my dagger with a smile.

I want to fling myself at him and thank him for rescuing me, but I know it's not the right moment. Instead I position the dagger in my left hand with my trident in the right. He turns and behind him, I can see more Fae, and a sight that makes my jaw drop. *Humans.* So many of them descend the stairs behind the Fae as they attack their rear. Azalea pulled through.

Their faces shine with grim determination as they finally take on an enemy they've been dreaming of for years. There are so many Fae, but there are even more of us.

On the boats behind me, I hear the banished yell their encouragement to the rebellion and my chest swells with pride.

Tristan swings around to protect my front from the oncoming Fae, his sword moving faster than I can keep track of as he takes on multiple enemies at once. Everything about him is smooth as he keeps us all alive. He knocks swords aside to deliver killing blows to their underarms, necks, and livers.

The dagger is warm in my hand. I keep the trident in my other, not willing to let go of a single weapon after the panic of having none.

Confidence fills me with every swing. We're going to survive this. Almost all of us will make it. Tristan will become king. Everything will work out the way he's dreamed. And it's all been made possible by my people. Humans and Seafolk will have bought the Fae this victory and they will be forced to remember it.

Crackling fills the air, raising the hair on my arm like a summer storm. I glance at the roof of the grotto, but no clouds fill the space. How could they in here? And yet the feeling is uncanny.

Magic.

Tristan said the Fae would come with magic and it seems they've seen the same thing I have and are ready to use it.

Lightning plunges into the ships, catching two of them on fire as the men aboard scream. I feel the tug to go and help them, but I know there's nothing I can do. The flames have already grown too big, and the men begin jumping overboard. I'm forced to watch as several of the ships of the banished are taken from them by a Fae too cowardly to show his face. Too cowardly to even attack those right in front of him.

Pressure builds in my chest, forcing a scream between my lips as I lunge with my dagger at the Fae fighting Tristan. He looks at me, eyes wide with surprise, and gives me a nod. He'll let me do my own fighting if that's what I want.

Lightning strikes again, this time on the beach, and several Seafolk are thrown by the blast. The smell of smoke and blood fills the air.

"We need to find who's doing that," I yell to Tristan. My voice can barely be heard over the din, but he shakes his head.

"You stay right where you are. Trying to find him will only get you killed. He'll come to us."

Yeah, in the form of lightning.

I shift from foot to foot as I search through the fighters. He's out there somewhere, I just need to find him.

Clanging comes from the stairs, and I whip my attention to them, concern for my fellow humans making me grip my dagger tighter.

At the top of the stairs, Anneliese and Captain Wimark survey the battle. My stomach sinks. I'm not sure where I thought they would be, but I never factored them in for this fight. Maybe there was a part of me that hoped they would have died along the road, but that would be too much to ask for because then this battle never would have happened, at least not like this. These Fae wouldn't have had the gall to fight like conquerors if they didn't have someone intent on doing the conquering.

Anneliese finds my gaze and gives me a sly smile. She taps Captain Wimark on the arm and points to me, her lips upturned in a laugh.

They make their way down the stairs, Captain Wimark dispatching any lingering human who hadn't yet made it to the battle with the swipe of his sword.

I want to nudge Tristan and show him what's happening, but his focus is engaged in the fight in front of him and I don't want to take a chance at distracting him.

Lightning hits the ground to our right, sending up a spray of sand that knocks us off our feet. I just manage not to land on my own weapons as Tristan is already getting back on his feet and taking care of the Fae that fell with us.

I try to find the Fae responsible for the blast, but there's too much movement on the beach. No one looks like they've taken the time to send deadly strikes besides the ones given with their sword.

Another lightning strike shakes me off my feet and I fall into a mess of mangled bodies. Screams bubble in my chest as I try to free myself even while their lukewarm blood seeps into my skin. Panic almost overtakes me and then I'm heaved out of the pile by a firm hand.

I expect to see Tristan, but it's Azalea that stands before me, her mouth twisted in a wry smile. "Try not to get yourself killed, okay? Zale would never forgive me if something happened to you."

It's so strange to hear those words when I've wondered if she's thought them so many times. So many times, I've thought his death made me irredeemable, and here she is telling me otherwise.

I swallow the building lump in my throat before it has time to take root. I clasp her arm, holding her there as I give her a watery nod. She mirrors the motion and I let go so she can get back into the battle.

If Tristan took any time to watch us it doesn't show as he moves through the press of Fae, his shoulders tight under his tunic. I wish he had taken some time to get himself some armor when he was grabbing my dagger, but the time for that is past now.

Blocking a sword that skitters off one of the Seafolk's tails, I glance back at the stairs, but they're empty now. I bite my lip and follow them all the way to the beach, but I can't see Anneliese anywhere. Moving farther from Tristan, I try to peer through the moving bodies around me, but she's nowhere to be found.

A fear greater than any I've felt before blooms in my chest. She's here somewhere. There's no way she would have turned around unless she really thought she would lose. Just because I've thought that doesn't mean that's the same conclusion she came to when she saw us. I don't think she'd leave. That doesn't seem like her. She should be up there right now readying herself to gloat about how well she's done.

"Tristan." I put my hand on his back as he shifts to take on the next Fae. "I need to find Anneliese."

He doesn't say anything, but I don't expect him to. Metal rings on metal as he defends his home. He's busy and he's where he should be. I don't want him to worry about me.

Holding up my dagger and my trident, I make my way carefully along the beach. I have a couple of close calls as the men around me fight. Only a split second of thought keeps me from being impaled. But my heartbeat remains even, the fear of Anneliese is far greater than anything else I'll find here. At least if a sword catches me on the beach, my death will be quick. If Anneliese finds me before I can find her, I doubt I'll be able to say the same about whatever she has planned for me.

The broader view of the fighting I get makes my hope grow greater. We're doing it. We're beating the Fae back. Several of the banished have joined the fight on the beach, but I don't look too closely at them. I don't want to know who's out here. I don't want to move with the memories of my childhood so tightly wound in my mind that I can't focus on my purpose: finding Anneliese.

I get to the other side of the grotto, my hand lightly resting on the cold rock. *Where is she?* The path I traveled to get here has already been swallowed up by the fighting so there's no easy way back. I can't even see Tristan anymore.

A Fae lunges at me and I strike without thinking, my dagger sinking into his neck. We both stare at the wound and he looks at me with shock in his already glazing eyes as he sinks to the ground.

Blood coats my hand and bile burns in my throat as I pull the dagger from his still-warm body. His sword clatters to the ground and I try not to be too grateful that there wasn't room enough for him to use it this close to the wall.

"You humans are all the same." Even his voice isn't enough to draw me out of my drowning shock. "Nothing but killers. First the earth and now us who have done nothing but try to save it from you."

I turn slowly, wrapping my hand tighter around the dagger as it threatens to slip from my wet grip.

Captain Wimark stands behind me, the promise of death in his eyes as he takes a step forward. I hold up my trident and he just laughs.

"You really think that little trinket could do anything to me? I've been here since the beginning, and I will be here at the end. I will live long enough to see your bones turn to dust as the ocean finally takes you home." He knocks the trident away with his sword and grabs me by the neck with his other hand.

I hit at him with my dagger, but it glances off the armor he's worn for the battle. My efforts grow weaker as it gets harder to see and breathe as he lifts me off my feet.

"I've been wanting to do this since we met." His eyes gleam as he walks us farther up the beach.

I wait for the slice of the sword I know must be coming,

but his footsteps stay even as the sounds of battle become farther away.

"I see you have brought back my favorite little human."

Trying to turn my head only makes the darkness take over my vision faster, but I'd know that voice anywhere.

"I believe she was looking for you too," Captain Wimark says.

He thrusts me forward and my body hits the rocks with a solid thump. Looking up with bleary eyes, I can see the hem of Anneliese's dress where she sits above me.

"Foolish human. You have no idea who you're messing with," she hisses.

"I don't know who *you* think you are, outside of a woman who will *never* be Queen." I laugh and she gestures at Captain Wimark with a frown. He delivers a solid kick to my stomach that wipes the smile from my face. I curl into a ball, wheezing around the blow.

"What would you have me do with her?" he asks, his voice bored as though killing defenseless humans was a regular occurrence for him.

Anneliese nudges me with her toe, digging into the tender flesh of my face. "I think someone might be missing her. Someone we can convince to end this once and for all."

The blood drains from my face as Captain Wimark grins so wide I can see all his teeth. He grabs me by the shoulder and hoists me to my feet. "Where do you think we should put her? We would not want him to miss her for long."

"I know just the place."

TWENTY-SEVEN

Captain Wimark ties my hands behind my back, thrusting the trident far out of reach. I'm quick to slip Tristan's dagger into my skirt pocket, the weight a solid reassurance as he tightens the rope around my wrists. His body reeks of the days of travel and he hisses at me when I rear away from him.

"Do not bother with her," Anneliese says from her rocky throne. "This will all be over soon enough."

I can't help but hope for the same thing. One way or another this will be the end, for me at least. I just hope that whatever they do, Tristan doesn't listen to them. I want him to survive this. I want him to finish this. And I especially want him to finish *her*.

Anneliese pats my face with a cold hand. "You and I have been in this together. Such a shame it has come to this."

"What a shame no one else could see you for the snake you are," I spit at her.

She nods at Captain Wimark and he delivers another hard blow. I cough, feeling wetness growing up my throat.

She sighs. "I just hate when the humans look at me that way, like they think they are better than us."

She stands and the two of them start across the beach, making their way to the stairs. Captain Wimark holds me by the shoulder, forcing me to follow even as my body begs for him to stop.

Around us, the sounds of battle grow quieter, and I don't dare look to see why. Captain Wimark's grip on me tightens to a painful pressure as we reach the bottom of the stairs. The coppery smell of blood has overtaken the saltiness that permeated the air just hours ago. It must be close to over now. I work the dagger back out of my pocket, careful to keep my motions unnoticed by Anneliese or Captain Wimark. I work the blade against the rope, my hands twisted at an unnatural angle while I pray I don't accidentally slice into myself.

"Where are you, my little false king?" Anneliese calls, her voice traveling unnaturally over the dwindling chaos. "I have something for you."

Captain Wimark turns me around just in time to see Tristan find us. His face falls and he glances behind him to where I was only minutes before.

"Would you like to trade?" she asks.

Tristan's sword loosens in his hand, and he takes a step forward. "What will you ask of me?"

"Give up this charade. You were never supposed to be King, and you know it." There's a bite to her voice as the frustration of the last few years creeps over her. "Your father was a delusional man who never understood true power when he saw it. No longer will I be shoved to the side in favor of weak men."

"There must be something we can do to work this out." Tristan moves to the stairs and Captain Wimark's hand grows dangerously tight.

Annelise comes up beside me, "You will relinquish the throne to me. You will no longer pretend that you are anything more than the circumstances of your birth. You are nothing to me, just like your brother." Her spit hits the side of my face as she sneers at me. My stomach drops. The Prince. Did she kill the prince? "Relinquish the throne or we will find out if you scream like him too."

"Okay." Tristan holds his hands up, the sword held so loose that it points towards the ground, completely useless even as his jaw clenches tighter. His face grows red as he glances between her and me. "Let Mariel go. She has no part in your fight."

"She made herself a part of this!" The battle comes to a complete stop now as everyone looks up at Anneliese. There are so few Fae left that the beach looks littered with fish scales, but the gentle gleaming is their armor. I scan the crowd for Ry, but I can't find him. I just hope he managed to get away.

"She made herself a part when she decided to ally with those who stood in my way."

Tristan takes another step forward, and Captain Wimark presses a blade against my throat. I feel the snap of the rope holding my wrists come undone and move the dagger into a ready position behind my back.

"Not another move," Captain Wimark grunts.

"She's just a human," Tristan says. I have to close my eyes before he can see the pain that flashes through them. "She cannot hurt you. Let her go."

I grind my teeth together and work my knife closer to her, ready to strike.

"She might not be able to hurt me." The side of her mouth perks up in a smile. "But she is more than capable of hurting you."

Tristan's sword clatters to the ground. "You don't need to do this, Anneliese."

"I am afraid I do."

She pulls out a dagger, the metal blade gleaming in the faint sun reflecting off the water. I look at Tristan, even as I see her arm move. No matter what, he's the one I want to see last. But he's not even looking at me. He glances to the side of us, eyes growing wide as he steps forward.

I bring my knife up, ready to block her. She barely spares it a glance as a maniacal smile takes over her face.

"No!"

The one shout echoes off every rock in the grotto until it's grown loud enough to shake loose rocks lodged in the ceiling. Anneliese hesitates for just a moment, but it's enough. I'm knocked to the side by Ry's heavy body, my knife barely missing my side as we shift.

He lands hard against my chest and Captain Wimark loses his grip on me with the weight of both of us. We fall to the ground, Ry pinning me against the rocks as his body knocks the breath from my lungs.

Warm blood sinks into my chest as he gasps weakly on top of me. Time comes to a halt and all I can see is the light leaving Ry's eyes. Anneliese's blade sticks out from his chest with a crimson halo surrounding it.

"Ry," I cry when I'm finally able to breathe again. "Why?"

He smiles and blood trickles from his lips, his gaze warm as he looks into my eyes. His hand cups my face and I lean into it. "I would do anything for you, Mariel. Now you need to live for both of us."

"Ry." Tears trickle down my cheeks as I lift my hand and caress his hair.

He gives me one last smile and then he's gone, his body limp on top of mine.

A scream builds in my throat. All the pain and all the anger of the last year burning its way out as I hold Ry in my lap.

I collapse over his body as my lungs give out, my fingers digging into his tunic.

"Well, that was... unexpected." Anneliese moves her dress away from us as blood seeps closer to her. "And thoroughly unnecessary. I was never interested in *that* one."

Anger fuels my body, forcing me to get up and move Ry aside as my chest feels hot and heavy. Tears burn in my eyes as my hands clench into fists. "Don't you *ever* talk about him like that."

"I can talk about humans any way I want," she says with a sneer.

I grab for her throat and Captain Wimark resumes his hold on me, pulling back before I can touch her. But my lunge leaves a few blood splatters across her pale-yellow dress, earning a look from her that can only be described as pure hatred.

"This has become too much. You should put the human out of her misery," Anneliese says to the Captain. "And no blades this time. The look of blood is so unbecoming."

His hand comes around my throat, fitting into the bruises forming from the last time. "As you wish, my Lady."

"No." She holds her hand out and the pressure around my neck abates for a moment. "Your Queen."

He chuckles and squeezes tighter. "As you wish, my Queen."

I kick at him and dig my nails into his hands. I won't go down like this. He jerks me around as he avoids my blows, but blood still hits Anneliese's skirts, and her shrieks feel just as good as hitting him.

"Let her go!" Tristan shouts as my vision grows dark. I

can barely see him as he stumbles up the beach. "Release her!"

"Make your promise and I might let her go," Anneliese says, but even my fading hearing can pick up on her lies.

Tristan is completely covered in black that flows up the beach like a river.

"Do not make me do it." There's a tinge of fear in her voice.

He doesn't listen and the blackness touches the soldiers spread out around us in a half circle. The first of them begins to scream, but the sound is quickly swallowed up like it was never there as the blackness creeps closer.

"Stop this!" Anneliese shrieks. "You will never have your throne if you kill me like this. No one will ever respect you if you kill a lady for a human."

"I am not killing a lady," Tristan's voice booms out of the darkness he's created. "I am killing the false Queen."

Captain Wimark's grip on me loosens as he stumbles backward to get away from the blackness that is eerily silent. I fall to the ground, dagger still clenched in my hand. Anneliese moves to sprint up the stairs, but it won't end like this. I refuse to let her get away. She doesn't get to escape her fate after what she's done to Ry. I won't let her. Heart in my throat, I grab her by the ankle. She looks down at me with a sneer and moves to slap me away as Tristan's shadows come closer to us.

"You will never hurt anyone I love *ever* again," I scream.

I stab into the back of her knee with my dagger. Hot blood sprays across my face as I dig the blade in and wrench it out through the side. Her face goes white as she looks between the darkness, me, and her useless leg. Crimson stains her skirts as I let go of her and she hobbles up the stairs, still trying to get away from Tristan's darkness.

Captain Wimark grabs me again, forcing me behind him as he takes the stairs. Anneliese has barely left us behind, smearing her life blood across the stairs as she goes. Captain Wimark trips and I land hard against the stairs, the pain traveling up my body as everything wars for attention.

Tristan's shadows are fast, but somehow Anneliese still moves faster. Shadows nip at my heels. I stay where I landed, watching Anneliese as her face grows pale and her movements more sluggish.

Beside me Captain Wimark goes stiff. I keep my gaze pinned on Anneliese where she runs up the stairs and then the darkness swallows us whole before I can even make a sound.

TWENTY-EIGHT

My body grows tight as the nothingness overtakes me. I feel like I'm in deep water in the middle of the night as I try to move, but my body doesn't want to and I can't see anything. When the darkness took us, Captain Wimark let me go. So now I'm lost in this black sea alone. It's strange how I miss the contact of his hand on me just so I could know I wasn't alone in here.

After a few seconds of struggle, I stop trying to move. If it were possible to escape, then the men I saw swallowed up by it before would have made it out. At least one of them would have been able to get free, but none of them did. I just hope that my dagger did enough damage. Whatever happens to me, I just want Anneliese taken care of.

It's only when I stop that I notice the shadows feel different. They settle on my body like a blanket, tucking me in and holding me close.

I don't understand Tristan's magic, but I don't think this is how death would feel. I've trusted him countless times not to hurt me, I just have to keep trusting him now.

I feel his magic as it travels over my body, slipping off

me like water off a duck's back. It leaves my feet first and I'm able to wiggle my toes. Then my legs, my stomach, my arms, and finally my face.

I'm staring at the ceiling of the grotto and brown stone has never looked more beautiful. I take a deep breath, filling my lungs to keep panic at bay. Only now that I've made it do I let my body respond to how close it came to death.

"Mariel!" Tristan's shout carries across the sand.

I can hear the rocks shift as he runs to me. He lands heavily on his knees and takes me in his arms, my body still limp from the shadows.

"I just... I really thought..." He clutches me to his chest, his heart pounding fast next to my ear. "I thought I lost you. I thought you were dead, and I was the one that killed you."

Shaking my head, I pull myself free from his grip just enough to take in the beach. I expect to see it littered with the bodies taken in by his magic, but instead, there's a fine layer of colorful dust that coats the ground.

Bile churns in my stomach as I let Tristan pull me closer to him. He said his magic was dangerous. I guess I'm not sure what I expected that to mean, but not this...

"When he took you away, I just could not help myself. It happened before I could stop it. I am so sorry, Mariel. Forgive me, I beg you." His voice breaks and he tucks his head into mine.

Strength slowly returns to my limbs, and I reach around his waist and tug him closer to me. He chokes on a sob, tightening his fingers in my hair.

"I'm all right." The longer we sit here together the more I feel all right. I made it through. "You didn't hurt me."

Pulling myself from his arms, I glance at the stairs reaching up to the castle. Did I do it? Is it finally over? Tristan took care of everyone else; I just hope that I've done my part.

Tristan grabs my hand as I stumble closer to the stairs. Yellow fabric trails over the side of the railing. Bright red blood splatters Anneliese's dress with morbid polka dots and drips onto the rocks below.

She didn't get away; I did it.

"My Lord." A deep voice breaks our concentration and Tristan lets me go enough to handle the Fae man speaking as he approaches us. "We just came from upstairs. There was a massacre. Your brother... he is dead."

Another Fae comes up behind him and falls on one knee. "Long live the King!"

The shout is taken up by the others and the room echoes with the cheer. "Long live the King."

DAD MEETS us on the beach, his hand shaking as he grabs me and pulls me closer to him. I breathe in his scent and try to hold strong. He releases me and nods for me to go with Tristan as he kneels beside Ry.

I join Tristan as he climbs the stairs, passing by Anneliese's body where my dagger sticks out of her back and her eyes stare unseeing at the steps. I wait for the pressure in my chest to finally release, but even seeing her body doesn't bring me enough relief. Even with Anneliese dead, it doesn't bring back Ry; it doesn't bring back Zale.

Reaching the main castle, we're able to see what the men were talking about. Fae bodies litter the corridors. With how quickly the army was able to reach us, these men couldn't have put up much of a fight, despite how well-trained they were.

"Anneliese," Tristan curses under his breath.

"Could she really have affected all these people?" I've

never seen her able to manage more than one, and she always had to touch them first.

He shakes his head as he picks up a discarded helmet from the floor. "I saw her do it once when we were children, but never again. I thought it was a fluke. Obviously, I was wrong." He looks at me with sorrow in his eyes. "I underestimated her. I should have listened to you when you said she was dangerous."

I want to reassure him, but the words die in my throat. Even though I suspected with at Anneliese was up to, I never would have thought it would come to this. I reach out for his hand, letting my grip carry my emotions to him.

A Fae man marches up to us and gives Tristan a crisp bow. "We have the remaining army confined in the Great Hall. What would you have us do with them, my King?"

The words still feel weird to hear. It really happened. Tristan has exactly what his father wanted for him., even if he had to fight tooth and claw for it. The Prince should have been willing to work with Tristan. Why he thought he could trust her, I'll never know. None of that matters now anyway. Anneliese got to the Prince in the end anyway.

She made sure to punish him for rejecting her. He wasn't left like trash on the floor. It took over an hour for someone to be able to climb high enough to cut him down.

"I'll handle it." Tristan turns to me, reaching for my hand. "Will you wait for me in your room?"

I give him a small smile and nod, even as my heart starts to crumble. "Of course."

Their footsteps are solid on the stone as they march away to deal with business. I follow the hallways until I'm back before my bedroom door.

Entering the room, I know what I must do. I grab a bag from the wardrobe and look around for my things to shove in it, but it's then I realize that nothing here is even mine.

The few things I had have been systematically destroyed. There's nothing here for me. Nothing but Tristan.

And I can't have him.

My heart a solid lump in my chest, I put the bag down and head back through the door. I told Tristan I wouldn't stay here and hold him back. There must be a part of him that realizes that's what will happen and that's why he asked me to wait for him. I'm just doing what's best for us.

He'll understand... someday.

THE LOOK on my father's face when I ask to board his boat would be comical if not for the sorrow I see written in the lines of his face.

He nods. "Of course, you can come home. This ship will always be ready for you."

Behind him, Alon gives a nod.

Some of the tightness in my chest eases to see them both here alive. Not everyone made it, but I needed them to. After what happened to Ry... I don't think I could have withstood any more loss.

My father must see the pain written on my face because he wraps me deep in his arms. I breathe in his familiar scent of salt and sweat and sea and resist the urge to fall apart altogether. I can't do that now. I need to get far away from here and I need to be safe in my own room, alone.

Already the beach looks different than it did only a few hours ago. The rocks have been cleared of our losses and the Seafolk have already returned to the sea. My father says they made sure their expectations of what will happen to the sea were made clear before they left. I can't say I blame them. Their troubles are far from over if we continue on the path Zale led us down.

The water still laps against the shore with red tinges as puddles of blood left behind continue to leach their way down the beach. It feels like an outward representation of what's happened to me. So much is the same, but I have my own torments that have sunk deep, like blood in the sand.

I climb aboard the ship and feel the familiar wood under my hands. It does its best to bring me peace, but too much has changed for me to let it in. None of this will ever be the same again. My family will never look the same. How can we continue without Zale *and* Ry. It feels impossible.

"Leaving so soon?" Azalea leans against the rail, balancing a knife between her fingers as she surveys the boat. "I thought you'd stay on land forever after the fight you put up."

I shake my head. "There's no place for me here."

"You really think that?" She laughs and stabs the railing. "You don't think you have a place here with that fancy bastard turned king of yours? If you're having second thoughts on that, which I highly recommend you do, you know the rebellion will always take you."

I give her a wry smile. "I'm not sure I want to be sent on any more death missions."

"I think you've proven yourself well enough." She reaches out and clasps my shoulder. "You will always have a place with us if you want it. You are my sister. I won't forget you."

I nod and look away, keeping my gaze on the beach so she can't see the tears that well up in my eyes. I don't think I could ever take her up on that offer, but it means a lot to have her offer it all the same.

"Until next time then," she says. She pats my shoulder and climbs down the rope ladder.

"Until next time."

THE OTHER SHIPS have already made their way to sea, ours being one of the last ones in line to go. My father and brother move around me like any sudden noise will spook me away, but I'm much stronger than that. I've survived far worse than my brother dropping a pile of rope.

I need to get out of here. Every second that we're still in the grotto makes my chest grow tighter and my spirit feels like it wants to jump loose from my skin. I need to get away from this place and the memories before anything can happen that will change my mind.

This is the right thing to do. I know that. I have to stand firm.

When our boat finally starts moving, I glance across the beach one last time, lingering on the last places I was with Ry, with Tristan.

And then there he is.

Standing at the top of the stairs, he stands frozen as he watches our ship move slowly toward the opening that will take us back to the sea.

"Mariel." I can see his mouth move even if I can't hear him say the words.

I know I should have been brave enough to say good-bye, but the aching that starts deep in my core reminds me why I didn't.

"Should we stop?" my father asks as he comes to stand beside me, the boat making slow progress through the water.

"It's better this way."

He watches me, eyebrows furrowing but leaves me to my sorrow.

"Mariel!"

This time I do hear it. Tristan has run down the stairs and is already making his way across the beach.

"Mariel, come back!"

I shake my head, staring at the ceiling so the tears can't fall.

"There is no King!"

His shout startles me into looking at him.

"What do you mean?"

I'm not sure he can hear me, but he answers my confused thoughts anyway.

"I have dissolved the kingship. Come down and talk to me!"

He can't do that. I should have known he'd come up with some way to keep me here. Some lie to get me to stay until my father's ship is too far away to benefit me.

Tristan plunges into the water, sinking low as his clothes become waterlogged. My nails dig into the wood of the railing as he swims after us. The ship picks up speed and he falls farther behind, but that doesn't stop him. His face is red as he tries harder to catch up.

My father comes to stand next to me, watching him. "That boy really loves you, doesn't he?"

It's so funny to hear him described as a boy. I'm sure to my father he is, but all I can see is the man he's going to be, the years he's lived that I haven't yet. But I can't say anything or the fragile strength I've been holding onto will fall to pieces.

He grunts and throws a line of rope into the water. It trails back until it reaches Tristan. He grabs it and my father starts pulling him onto the ship.

"What are you doing?" Of all the things I expected him to do, this was the very last thing I could have imagined.

"A boy that cares about you this much isn't going to get

left behind on the beach. Face your problems, Mariel. Break his heart if you must, but you must do something."

My heart beats a mile a minute as I wait for him to reach the deck. Alon joins my father in helping pull him up. Tristan collapses on the deck in a splash of water and my father claps me on the shoulder before he and Alon disappear into their work.

"What are you doing here?" I cry. "I'm trying to do what's right."

Tristan coughs out some water and smooths his hair from his face. "Mariel, you are so busy trying to save everyone that you have never once asked if we actually want to be saved."

I gape at him, and he presses a wet finger to my lips to keep me from speaking.

"You think you have all the answers, but you didn't once ask what I wanted." He grabs my hand, staring into my eyes. "I want you, Mariel. Always and forever, I want you by my side."

"But they'll never let you be king if—"

"Didn't you hear me? There's no King, not anymore." He squeezes my hand as I stare at him in disbelief. "It wasn't right. I could see that once I started working with the banished and the Seafolk. You deserve your own say. That is why we will have a council."

"A council?"

None of what he's saying is getting through.

He grins, his smile wider than I've ever seen. "Yes. A council. Representatives from the Fae, the Seafolk, and the humans will be there. We will finally find peace and balance with each other. You're free, Mariel."

"You would do this, for me?" He shouldn't. He really shouldn't. How do I tell him that he's making a horrible decision when my heart is already leaping for joy?

"I would give up the world if it meant I could have you."
He gets down on one knee, holding my hand tightly in his.
"Please, Mariel, say you will be mine."

I glance over at my father and brother. Alon scowls at us, but my father gives me the tiniest of nods. He'll do this for me.

And I can finally do this for myself.

"I will."

Tristan scoops me into his arms, pressing his lips against mine so I can't change my mind. I melt into him, letting the fear and sadness of the last few months drift away, at least for now.

Against all odds, we did it. We survived and we deserve every happiness.

FROM THE PUBLISHER

Thank you so much for reading *Fight of the Fallen*.

We hope you enjoyed the journey and characters as much as we loved bringing them to you! We'd love for you to leave a review on Amazon and Goodreads while the story is fresh in your mind. Reviews are writing fuel for authors and help their books get into the hands of other hungry readers!

If you're a big fan of speculative young adult fiction, we invite you to join our street team. Get copies of our books in advance, early access to covers, and other freebies!

Stag Beetle Books
www.stagbeetlebooks.com

ACKNOWLEDGMENTS

I can't believe we've made it! It still doesn't seem possible that we've made it through four books! So much blood, sweat, and tears have gone into each of them; from my family, myself, and my fearless publisher, Laura.

Danny, David, Erik, and James: You are everything to me. I'm so grateful for all of the love and reassurance you gave me as I tried to find my way through this book. Thank you, Danny, for the nights of box mac and cheese when I had to get to meet deadlines. You keep us all going.

Kristina, Megan, Jake, and Nate: You'll never know how much your support has meant to me. From helping with plot holes, being my first readers for every book, and showing up tirelessly for all my events (and Megan for making so many events happen!), thank you.

Mom and Dad: Thank you for keeping me on track with my goals and for being my number one supporters as you've told everyone you've ever met about my books. It means so much.

Alan: I know you'll never read this (you've read my books far too many times already), but thank you for making this one happen. Without all your plotting help, this one really wouldn't have happened. Tight goals combined with nights of plotting and character discussion made this happen. Your insight into my books has been like gold.

Laura: Thank you for being a tireless cheerleader and for keeping me on track to reach my potential when I'm ready to give up. You always keep it real with me and have since we were kids. You've inspired my path more than you'll ever know.

Steve: Without your demonstrations (that left us all sore for days), I never would have been able to figure out my battle scene. You changed my perception of daggers forever and in every fight I will go for the armpit, just for you.

Heavenly Father: Thank you for my talents and for comforting me when the road has seemed too hard. I owe everything to you.

My wonderful, incredible readers: None of this could have happened without your support. Thank you for following me on this journey. Thank you for enjoying my characters as much as I do. I will continue every day to try and create the stories you deserve.

ALSO BY
ELIZABETH A. DRYSDALE

Out of Time

Curse of the Forgotten

Burden of the Banished Book One: The Exile's Promise